Sequoyah

Also by Robert J. Conley

THE REAL PEOPLE

The Way of the Priests
The Dark Way
The White Path
The Way South
The Long Way Home
Dark Island
War Trail North
The Peace Chief
War Woman
Cherokee Dragon
Spanish Jack
Sequoyah

The Rattlesnake Band and Other Poems
Back to Malachi
The Actor
The Witch of Goingsnake and Other Stories
Wilder and Wilder
Killing Time
Colfax
Quitting Time
The Saga of Henry Starr
Go-Ahead Rider
Ned Christie's War
Strange Company
Border Line
The Long Trail North
Nickajack
Mountain Windsong

Sequoyah

ROBERT J. CONLEY

ST. MARTIN'S PRESS ✠ NEW YORK

www.stmartins.com

Library of Congress Cataloging-in-Publication Data

Conley, Robert J.
    Sequoyah / Robert J. Conley.—1st ed.
        p. cm.
    ISBN 0-312-28134-X
        1. Sequoyah, 1770?–1843—Fiction.   2. Kings and rulers—Fiction.
    3. Cherokee Indians—Fiction.   I. Title.

PS3553.O494 S47 2002
813'.54—dc21

                                                                        2001057891

First Edition: June 2002

10   9   8   7   6   5   4   3   2   1

Sequoyah

I

Taskigi,
the old Cherokee country
in what is now the state of Tennessee,
1786

He was trembling. He wanted to scream and cry, but he was afraid to. His mother had told him to be quiet. She said if the white men found them, they would kill them both. White men were like that. They killed mothers and children. It did not matter to them. They only wanted to kill Indians. They didn't think beyond that. He was trembling from fear, and his mother was holding him close and tight. At eight years old, he was already a veteran of these wars. He remembered vividly, from when he was only two years old, the time that the white man named Christian had swept through their town of Taskigi at the head of a rabble force of loud and ugly white men on horses, shooting, shrieking, swinging their long, sharp knives, killing anyone or anything that moved. It had terrified him, and even at that early age, its horrors had been indelibly stamped on his memory.

Now, six years later, it was all happening again. This time the white man's name was Sevier. The town was the same, for the people who lived there had rebuilt Taskigi. He was older now, but everything else was the same. Someone had come running into town to shout the warning that the white men were coming. Mothers had grabbed their children. Everyone had run for the tree-covered mountainsides. They had crashed into the thick brush, ignoring the tangled brambles and the thorns of wild roses, to climb as fast and as far as they could.

They knew that the white men would not follow them up there.

When they had reached a certain height at which they felt safe enough, they stopped, and they settled down to watch in fascinated dread the frenzied activities of the white men down below in their town. The eight-year-old boy watched with wide eyes as the soldiers in his town hacked down an old man who had chosen not to run. Even from his height, he could see the blood fly from the slash of the long glittering knife blade. He saw the old body flinch, then go limp and drop lifeless to the ground.

He watched as the brutal white savages lit torches and rode from house to house setting the people's homes on fire. He saw them as they set the brand to his own home. Tears welled up in his eyes. He trembled uncontrollably, almost convulsively, and his mother squeezed him the more tightly. He wanted to look up into his mother's face to see if he could find any comfort there, but he could not pull his frozen gaze away from the horrors below.

The attackers had lost all semblance of order. The mounted men were riding back and forth and around in any and all directions, shouting and laughing, setting fire to everything, looking in vain for something else to kill. When there was nothing left for them to do to the town, some of them turned to the fields. They dashed madly for the beautiful tall corn, rode into it slashing at it with their long blades and dipped their torches to set it all ablaze. Some rode into the peach orchards where they chopped at trees and flashed their torches. Others rode into the fields of beans and squash trampling the plants and their fruit into pulp, mashing them into the earth.

He thought he was two years old again. He thought that it was the same as the other time. It was the same time. Nothing had changed. The six years in between had been but a dream. This was the reality. This was all that he knew. He wondered if the white men would catch him one time, if his mother would miss him when she ran and he would be left standing there alone in the middle of town waiting for the sharp death of the white men like the old man he had seen go down. He wondered what the sharp death would feel like. He wondered what would happen to him after he had been killed.

The noise and the frenetic activity in the town and in the fields abated. There was nothing left to do. Everything that had been alive had been killed. Everything else had been ignited. The flames roared and rose high, and the air was filled with thick smoke. He could smell it, and he could feel it in his nostrils even high up on the mountainside. The horsemen, some still waving their weapons, seemed lost. There was nothing left for them to do. Even so, they turned this way and that, looking for another victim, searching for something they had not yet touched. At last one of the men waved his weapon over his head and shouted something, words that sounded ugly, meaningless noises to the boy, and the horrible men rode on through the ruin toward the next Cherokee town on the road.

He felt sorry for the people in the next town. He knew some of them. He knew that same thing that had just happened in Taskigi would happen there. It had been that way the last time. There would be but few people killed there, he knew, for they also would have been warned and would have fled to their safety. But like the people of Taskigi, they would be left destitute, their homes, their belongings and their food supply all destroyed.

He tried to recall the last aftermath, the wandering and the hunger, the need to rely on the good nature in towns that had been spared. He did not recall all that so well as he recalled the attack, the killing and burning, the cold-blooded destruction. Suddenly the white men were gone, and he started to cry. He buried his face in his mother's bosom and sobbed and shook, and she held him tight, and she too wept.

The flames were almost gone. A few low fires burned. Mostly smoke rose from piles of black ash, as the people came back down from the mountain to look over what was left of their town. He walked beside his mother in a daze, feeling almost as if he had been killed. He hadn't been, of course. He was walking. He was looking at the ruin. The mass of black ash was ugly to his eyes, and the smell of smoke was terribly offensive to his nostrils. He wanted to turn and run away, but his mother held his hand.

They walked over to where their own house had been, and there was nothing recognizable to his eyes. It was all black ash. Smoke was still rising from the heap. There was nothing. Why were they looking? He had seen enough, too much. He wanted to leave. The bloody and twisted body of the old man lay not far away to his right. He did not want to look at it, but something made him do it. The sight was sickening, and it made him want to retch, but he did not. He realized that he was squeezing his mother's hand. He tried to relax his grip. He looked the other way, and he saw the smoldering body of a dog in a heap of ashes. He could smell the burning hair and the flesh that was beginning to cook.

Slowly they wandered back into the woods, back up the steep mountainside. The road would not be safe, not until the white men had worn themselves out with their killing and ruination and had turned around to ride back through on their way home. He walked beside his mother when he could, but in the thick woods, he usually walked behind her. They moved more slowly this time, for they were not running away from the attacking white men. They were simply wandering away from the desolate place that had once been their home. He knew what they would do, for he could recall it from that other time.

They would go into the woods and sleep on the ground throughout the night. Much of the night they would lie awake, unable to sleep because of their hunger and because of the images of horror which would dance in their heads throughout the night. With daylight, they would begin walking toward the nearest town they thought would have remained untouched by the white men. But the boy wondered if this time there would be any such town. Maybe, he thought, this time the white men would burn every Cherokee town. Maybe there would be no place for them to go. Maybe this time they would all die.

At last his mother sat down on the ground to rest beneath a large tree. She leaned back against the rough tree trunk to rest. He sat down beside her to do the same, and she put an arm around him and pulled him to her.

"Mother," he said, "why do they do that?"

"What?" she said, her voice sounding far away, sounding like she had not really heard his words.

"Why do the white men come here and do those things to us?"

"They're crazy," she said.

He looked at her, and her face was hard set and bitter. She would say no more. She offered no further explanation for the horrors they had just witnessed. He thought that there should be more to tell. There should be some reason for what was happening. His mind recalled stories he had heard old men tell about a time when there were no white men. He wished that he had lived in those times, or that no white men had ever found their way to this land. He tried to imagine a world without the white men, a world of peace and harmony, a world where children did not have to run for their lives, clinging to their mothers' hands or skirts, screaming in fear and terror.

But there was no such world, and it did not seem likely to him that there ever would be. He could not think of anything that would drive the white men back across the big water to the lands from which they had come.

"Mother," he said, "why did they come here?"

"They came to burn us out," she said.

"No," he said. "I mean, why did they come to this land in the first place?"

"They're crazy," she said.

And that was all.

At last his mother got up, and she started to walk through the woods. He followed along. Neither one spoke. Before long, she found some berries, and they stopped to pick them and eat them. They did that for a long while, but when she said that they should move along, he was still hungry. They walked until it was dark, and they stopped to sleep on the ground. The night air was cool, almost cold, and he did not sleep. He shivered. He was hungry. He kept seeing the mad white men on horseback with long glittering blades and torches. He kept hearing them yell and shout and laugh. He kept seeing the flames and smelling the smoke. And he kept wondering why they did the things they did.

When his mother woke him up at daylight, he realized that he must have dropped off to sleep at some time. He rubbed his eyes and sat up. He felt drowsy. The memories of the day before came rushing back on him, and he knew that they were without a home and food. He was terribly hungry. He wanted to cry, but he thought that he was too big for that. He knew that he had cried after watching the white men, and he was a little ashamed of that, but then, his mother had cried at that too. They got up and began walking.

They walked about half the day away before they came across some others from their town. They all walked together. No one talked much. Later they came across others, people from another town. They talked a little when they met. Then they all walked on together in silence. Late in the day some of the men who had managed to escape from their homes with weapons, bows and arrows or blowguns and darts, managed to kill some small game, squirrels, rabbits, and everyone ate a little meat. They ate berries and nuts with it, and they drank water. The boy felt a little better, but there really wasn't enough to go around, and he was still hungry. That night, they all slept together in the woods.

It was three days before they came to a town that had not been attacked, and they wandered in like beggars, ragged and hungry, homeless and wretched. The people took them in and fed them and found space for them to sleep. They didn't ask any questions of them until they had eaten their fill and rested. After dark, they all gathered around a fire and talked. The boy got as close to the men as he could and still remain inconspicuous. He listened as they talked. The Tennesseans led by Sevier, he heard them say, were gone.

"They think they've taught us our lesson," one man said, "and they're satisfied."

"For now," said another. "They'll be back another time."

"We should send someone to talk to them," someone said, "and tell them that they are attacking the wrong towns. It's the Chickamaugas they should be attacking. We here in the Overhills have done nothing to them."

"They don't care about that," another man said. "Some Cherokees have killed some white men, and they only want to kill some Cherokees. It doesn't matter which ones, and we here are easier targets for their revenge."

"What should we do?"

"Leave them alone. They're satisfied for a time now. They won't be back soon."

"But we don't want them to come back at all. They might burn this town the next time."

"They might burn all our towns."

"We should send someone to talk to them. We could make another treaty. If we all put our marks on their leaves, we'll have peace again."

"Only for a little while. We've put our marks on their leaves before."

"And every time we do that, we give them some more land."

A young man, his patience at an end, stood up. "We should join the Chickamaugas," he said. "We should follow Dragging Canoe and fight the white men."

"No," said an older man. "It's because of Dragging Canoe that Sevier and those other men burned our towns. If we do what Dragging Canoe is doing, we'll make them mad at us."

"What's the difference?" the young man said. "They burn our towns anyway. I don't know what anyone else will do, but I'm going to the Chickamauga towns. I'm going to join Dragging Canoe. I mean to fight and kill some white men."

"I don't think you should do that."

"And I don't think that you should just sit here and take it like cowards and crawl to them asking for a new treaty and give them more land and beg them to stop killing us and burning our towns. I don't care what you say. I don't care what anyone says. In the morning, I'm leaving here. I'm going to find Dragging Canoe and join with him to fight these white men. Does anyone else want to go along?"

The boy watched and listened, fascinated. He was hearing the things that his mother did not want to tell him. He watched with wide eyes as other young men jumped up and came forward. He listened as they spoke, declaring their agreement with the first young man and their intentions of going with him to join the Chickamauga Cherokees under the leadership of the war chief Dragging Canoe to fight the Americans, the white men who had declared and won their independence from England and who called themselves the United States of America.

He wanted to go with them, but he knew that his mother would not let him go. She would say that he was too young. He longed to be old enough to make his own decisions. He longed to be old enough to fight against the crazy white men who burned his home and his food. His thoughts were interrupted as the young men who had expressed their intentions of leaving turned and stalked away, and one of the old men stood up to speak.

"We can't stop these hot-headed young men," he said, "but I believe that we should send someone to talk to the white men for us. We should tell this man to say to the white men, we have not been making war on you. It's Dragging Canoe and his Chicka-maugas and some of our young men that we can't control. They're not part of us anymore. They're off by themselves. We want to sign another treaty with you and declare everlasting peace between us. Prepare the leaves, and we will make our marks."

The crowd broke up at last, late into the night, and he was walking along with his mother toward the place where a family had taken pity on them and made room for them to sleep in their home. They walked along in silence for a while before the boy spoke.

"Mother," he said, "what do they mean about making marks on leaves?"

"It's the way white men agree to something," she said. "It's the way they make promises."

"I don't understand."

"They have marks," she said, "and they have these large leaves. They have something they can draw with, and they draw their marks. Then they can all look at the marks and recall exactly what was said. We put our marks on the leaves, then at any time later, the white men can look at all the marks, and they can tell us, back on that day when we met, you said thus and such and we said thus and such, and we all agreed to it. He will say, you agreed to it as well, because your mark is here on the leaf. Understand?"

"No."

"Well, it doesn't matter. It's just the way white men do things, and white men are crazy."

"Do these marks on leaves have words that say we gave them our land?"

"Yes," she said. "And the marks say just where the land is. Like, on the other side of the river for three days' walk, and like that."

"But how do we know what the marks say?"

"The white men tell us what the marks say."

"You said the white men are crazy."

"They are."

"Do crazy men tell the truth?"

"I don't know."

"Then we really don't know what the marks on the leaves say. The crazy white men might tell us wrong."

"They might, but there's nothing we can do about it. They have the marks. We don't. That's enough talk now. We're here."

They had arrived at the home of their hosts, and he knew that his mother meant for him to be quiet. It would be time to go to bed. She did not want him disturbing the sleep of their hosts. They went inside and found their places, and soon he was stretched out and covered up, but he did not sleep right away. Now his head was really filled with strange new thoughts. He was still thinking of the frightening white men and the horrible things they were doing to the Cherokees, but now he had heard this new thing, and it was fascinating. He could not get it out of his mind. The white men made marks on leaves which they used later to say that the Cherokees had promised to give them some land. Supposedly these marks somehow saved the white man's words. The white men could read these marks, read their exact words at any time they wanted to, but the Cherokees could not. He wondered why they could not.

And now he thought that he would like to be with the young men who were leaving town in the morning to join the Chicka-maugas and fight the white men, and he too wanted to kill white men for the awful things they had done. But at the same time, he wanted to do something else. He wanted to learn more about the mysterious marks. He wanted to find out how they worked. He wanted to read and write.

2

Taskigi, rebuilt,
1788

H is knee was painfully swollen, and so his mother had told him to sit and rest. She was not too busy that day and would not need his help. He did not need to be told twice. He was not keen on working with the trade goods, the stacks of pelts brought in by the Cherokees in exchange for the things the white men brought from the east, many of which, they said, came from far across the waters: white man's cloth and ready-made clothing, guns, bullets, powder, axes, hoes, scissors, flints and beads. He did not care for those things, for they came from the white men, the men who called themselves Americans, the same men he had watched burn his town and destroy his crops, the men he had run from with his mother in order to save their lives.

He was ten years old, and he had experienced too much of war with the Americans already. There seemed to be no end to it. He had listened to the men talk, and he had begun to understand that these white men were called English, and they had come from a place far across the waters. They had a man back at their home they called king, and he had absolute rule over them, but after some time had passed, they no longer wanted to obey their king. They had stopped calling themselves English and begun to call themselves Americans, and they had fought a war to separate themselves from their king.

Dragging Canoe and his followers had fought the Americans. They had taken the side of the English during the war because the Americans wanted to move farther west, deeper into the Cherokee country. But the English had given up the fight and gone home, leaving Dragging Canoe and his followers, known as Chickamaugas to distinguish them from the other Cherokees who did not want to fight, to carry on alone.

His older cousin, Young Tassel, was fighting with the Chickamaugas, and he often wished that he was old enough to do so himself. His puffy and painful knee worried him though. He wondered if it would heal in time for him to join the war against the Americans. He was sometimes ashamed, secretly, of course, of his uncle, his mother's brother, Old Tassel, who had assumed the leadership of the Cherokees following the death of Agan'stat', the old warrior. Old Tassel only wanted peace with the Americans, and it seemed to the boy that often his uncle would accept that peace on almost any terms.

He thought about the way one careless moment had changed his life. He had been running, and he had slipped, falling forward and landing with all his weight on his left knee. His knee had come down on a flat rock. It had been a painful fall, and his knee had become swollen. Later, the swelling had gone down, and he had thought that it was all right, but now and then the pain and the swelling returned. He wondered if it would be that way for the rest of his life.

Lounging outside his mother's trading post, he tried to put those kinds of thoughts out of his head by drawing pictures in the notebook the white trader had given him. The white man's leaves were much better for drawing than were the other things he had used before: bark, skins, real leaves. He had even drawn pictures on rocks. But the white man had seen him drawing and had given him a bunch of leaves all stuck together at one end and a stick with which to mark on the leaves.

He sat on the ground outside the trading post, his leg with the swollen knee stuck straight out in front of him, leaning back against the trunk of a tree. He had drawn a deer leaping gracefully through the air. He folded back the leaf to reveal a fresh, clean one, and he was about to start to work on a buffalo, when he saw his cousin Young Tassel approaching. Young Tassel seemed to be in a hurry.

" '*Siyo*, cousin," he called out. He would have been happy to see Young Tassel's approach except for the look on his cousin's face. There was something wrong. He could tell. Young Tassel rode up close and jumped off his horse. He looked over at his cousin sitting there on the ground.

" 'Siyo," he said. "Is your mother inside?"

"Yes."

Convinced now that something was indeed wrong, the boy struggled to stand. Holding his paper and pencil in one hand, he followed his cousin inside. Young Tassel had already begun his tale.

"They've killed your brother," he was saying. "I'm sorry to have to tell you this. It was the men who follow Sevier. They met him under a white flag to talk. It was a trick. They meant to kill him all along. They blamed him for killing some white men, but he didn't do it. We all know who did it. It was Chickamaugas. I'm a Chickamauga, and I did not always agree with my uncle Old Tassel, but he tried to keep the peace, and he trusted them when they came with their white flag. He did not deserve to be killed in that way. Bob Benge is coming and some other Chickamaugas. We'll be revenged on those Americans."

"How did it happen?"

"They met inside the home of Old Abram," Young Tassel said. "Abram and Old Tassel and Hanging Maw and Abram's son. Sevier left, but he left his men in the house. Those men blocked the door and the windows, and they took out their hatchets and killed your brother and the others. They rode away and left them like that."

The boy wanted almost desperately to go off with his older cousin and kill the hated Americans. He wanted especially to kill Sevier. He felt devastated by the startling news of his uncle's brutal and treacherous murder. And it was not just his uncle. Old Tassel was the principal chief. He turned and walked back outside. He was trembling with rage. He knew, of course, that they would not let him ride with the Chickamaugas. He picked up a stick to use as a staff and headed for the woods alone.

1791

He was thirteen years old when he heard of the death of the great war chief Dragging Canoe. He had not been killed in battle with the Americans. He had simply died one night in his sleep. The news was both sad and demoralizing to the boy, but he knew that the Chickamaugas fought on under the combined leadership of Bloody Fellow, red-haired Bob Benge, Doublehead and his own cousin, Young Tassel, who was known to the whites as John Watts. Still, there was no one quite like the great Dragging Canoe. Even at his young age, he knew that the loss was a major blow to his people.

He hated the Americans, and he fervently wished that his cousin and the other Chickamaugas would drive them all into the big water or kill them all, but his mind was beginning to see the practical side of the issue as well. He listened to the men talk any time he had a chance, and he heard that there was just no end to the white men. He heard that there were too many of them to kill. He learned that the Cherokees were almost surrounded by them, and they were moving in closer to the Cherokee towns all the time. Every time, it was said, the Cherokees met with the Americans to talk about peace, they put their marks to another white man's leaf, and with that leaf, the white men stole more of their land. He thought more about those leaves.

He walked into the woods with his cousin Agili. His knee was not bothering him so much that day, and they went to the creek nearby. Sitting on a large flat rock, he asked his cousin, "What do you think of the white man's leaves?"

Agili shrugged. "I don't know," he said. "They say they put marks on them, and the marks talk to them. They can look at the marks much later and know what people said just before they put their own marks on the leaf. It's just something that white men can do, and we can't do."

"I can draw and you can tell me what it means." He picked up a stick and drew a quick sketch of a horse in the soft dirt and showed it to Agili. "Now. What is that?"

"It's a horse," Agili said. "Anyone can tell that, but can you make it say, 'I will give you twelve horses for all the land from here to the river'? Of course, you cannot. That's what the white men can do."

The boy sighed and looked at his drawing. "Maybe I can," he said. "I'll think about it some more."

1800

He was twenty-two years old. His mother had died, and he was running the trading post and working as a blacksmith and a gold-smith, trades he had picked up from the white men who came among the Cherokees. He was skillful at both trades and reliable, when he was sober. He had developed a taste for whiskey. His knee still troubled him from time to time. When people talked about him, they talked about his skill at drawing, at making beautiful things from silver and at blacksmithing, but they also laughed and made jokes about him. He was given to spells of laziness and drunkenness.

When he was sober, he had plenty of things to think about. Six years earlier, the Chickamaugas had at last given up the fight. They had signed a treaty with the Americans. Of course, they had given up more land. The Americans were closing in on them faster and faster. The U.S. government was trying to talk them all into moving west and giving up their ancestral lands.

Some Cherokees, many of them friends of his, all of them Chickamaugas, had moved west of their own choosing in 1794. They had killed some white men in a fight, and, fearful of retaliation from whites and other Cherokees alike, had gone west. He often wondered about them, where they had gone and what things were like for them there. Maybe, he thought, they had gone far enough west to be free of the pressures of the white Americans who were always wanting more land. Sometimes he thought that he would like to join them.

He also wondered if they had gone to find those other Cherokees who had gone west long ago, the ones who had followed Dangerous Man into the unknown west. He had no idea how long ago Dangerous Man and his followers had wandered away. He had only heard the stories. Once long ago, they had left, headed west, and that was all.

They called him Sequoyah. It was an old name, passed down in his family, given to him by an old aunt of his clan. They had called the opossum *sikwa* or *sequo* until the Spaniards had brought pigs into their country. Then they had begun calling the pig sikwa. To distinguish the new sikwa from the original, they began calling the opossum *sikwa-ujetsdi*, meaning the grinning sikwa, or *sikwa-ya*, or *sequo-ya*, meaning the original or real sikwa.

He sat outside in front of his store with his notebook, the batch of leaves he had acquired from the white trader, and his marking stick, the pencil. He had thought that he would draw a bear, but once he had gotten himself comfortable, he did not draw. He sat in thought. He considered that it was good that the Americans no longer attacked and burned the Cherokee towns, but it was not so good that they kept asking for more land. The old men were afraid of the possibility of more fighting, so they always gave in. White people were living already just across the Little Tennessee River from Taskigi. They were much too close for comfort. As he sat musing, Black Beaver came walking up.

"Sequoyah," he said, speaking Cherokee, "I need some balls for my rifle. I'll pay you when I bring back some skins."

Sequoyah got up and stretched. His knee was stiff. He walked with a slight limp into the store, followed by Black Beaver, and he got the lead balls and handed them to his customer. He often extended credit in this manner, and so he was afraid that he would forget that Black Beaver owed him a deerskin for the bullets. In his notebook, he drew a picture of a beaver and shaded it black. Beside the drawing, he made one mark. Black Beaver went on his way. Sequoyah was about to go back outside when Big Thighs and Wili came in.

"Sikwa," said Wili, "let's have some *wisgi*."

"I'm not a white man's pig," Sequoyah said. "Call me 'Se-quoyah.' "

"All right. All right, Sequoyah," Wili said. "Do you have some whiskey?"

"I have some."

"Good," said Big Thighs. "Let's all get drunk on it."

Sequoyah went behind his counter and brought out a jug and three tin cups.

"Let's go out back," he said, and he led the way out the front door and around behind the store. There were hand-hewn benches, chairs and a table there, and he put the tin cups on the table, uncorked the jug and poured three drinks. Each man took up a cup, and they all sat down to drink.

"So what's the news?" asked Big Thighs.

"I haven't heard any," Sequoyah said. He took a long sip of the whiskey and felt it burn its way down to his stomach. It was good, and it helped when he thought too much about what was happening around him, or when he recalled too vividly the things of the past.

"I heard something," said Wili. He was the only one of the three who could speak and understand English. "I heard a white man talking. He was talking with your cousin George Lowrey. They were talking English."

"What were they talking about?" Sequoyah asked, not bothering to remark on the fact that Wili had called his cousin Agili by his English name.

"They were talking about you." Wili laughed.

"Oh," Sequoyah said. "Did they say that I'm a worthless drunk?"

"The white man said that your father was a white man. He was the white man they call Nathaniel Gist." Wili pronounced the white man's name slowly and carefully. Some of the sounds of the name did not exist in the Cherokee language.

"Gess?" Sequoyah said.

"Yes. What do you think of that?"

Sequoyah shrugged and took another sip of whiskey. "It doesn't matter," he said. "I'm more interested in how you learned the white man's language."

"They sent me to the white man's school when I was a child," Wili said.

"Did they teach you about Jesus?" Big Thighs asked.

"Oh, yes. Of course. That was all they seemed to care about."

"And I suppose," Sequoyah said, "they told you that all our old stories are lies."

"Yes," said Wili. "They did. They said all the truth is in their book."

"Did you learn to read that book?" Big Thighs asked.

"I learned some," Wili said, "but it's hard. It's a gift of the white man: reading and writing."

"I don't think it's a gift," Sequoyah said. "It's just something they've figured out and learned how to do."

"Maybe you're right," Big Thighs said. "I once heard an old man say that a long time ago, our priests could read and write."

"You mean they knew the white man's talk?" Wili asked.

"No," said Big Thighs. "A long time ago, our priests could read and write our language."

"I don't believe that," Wili said. "If that were so, then why can't we read and write our language now?"

"You know," Big Thighs said, "they killed all the priests way back then. When they killed them all, there was no one left who knew how to do it. That's why."

"I don't believe it," said Wili. "Sikwa, do you believe it?"

"I don't answer to that name," Sequoyah said.

"All right," said Wili. "Sequoyah, do you believe that we once had priests who could read and write our own language?"

"I don't see why not," Sequoyah said. "It's not a gift, and it's not magic. It's just a matter of figuring out a system that works."

"I think you're crazy," Wili said.

"I'm inclined to agree with Wili," Big Thighs said. "Maybe our priests could do it, but they killed all the priests. If they could really do it, they probably did it with magic. I don't believe anyone can figure out how to write the Cherokee language. If you want to read and write, you'd better learn how to speak English first. Then you can learn how to read and write English."

"That's not easy to do," Wili said.

"I'm not going to try to do that," Sequoyah said. "I don't want to talk the white man's ugly language."

Wili set his cup on the table, and Sequoyah poured him another drink. Wili picked it up and started to walk around.

"I don't see why not," he said. "You have a white man father and a white man's name."

"What white man's name?" Sequoyah asked.

"White men take their father's second name," Wili said, "so your name is Gist."

"Oh. That Gess," Sequoyah said, pronouncing "Gist" as closely as he could. "Gess. Hmm."

He poured himself some more whiskey and looked at Big

Thighs. Big Thighs put his cup on the table, and Sequoyah poured it full. "This is the only thing I know of," he said, "that the white man brought us that is worthwhile."

"No," said Big Thighs. "There are other things."

"Name them," Sequoyah challenged.

"Guns and bullets and powder," Big Thighs said.

"Hard, sharp knives and axes," said Wili. "And hoes for farming."

"Cloth," Big Thighs said. "You're wearing a white man's shirt, and your turban and jacket are made from white man's cloth."

"But those are not necessities," said Sequoyah. "If we didn't have them, we could get along without them. Cherokees got along without them for a long time before there were any white men around."

"And you think whiskey is a necessity?" asked Big Thighs.

Sequoyah did not answer. He stared ahead, but he was not seeing the store or the trees or anything else that was right there in front of him. He was seeing Taskigi from the mountainside, from his mother's arms. He was seeing Taskigi in flames. There were bodies in the streets of the town, and there were white men on horseback firing guns and waving swords in the air, riding up and down, shouting, cursing, laughing. And he was a child, and he was trembling in his mother's arms.

"Yes," he said. "Whiskey is a necessity."

3

Hiwassee,
1807

The crowd gathered at Hiwassee was huge. Sequoyah thought that there must be people from every Cherokee town there. There were many people he knew, but there were many more that he did not know. And many of them looked like white people. He knew, though, that some of those were Cherokee people of mixed blood, offspring of Cherokee women and white men, mostly traders. That Wili had said that he was one of those, the son of his mother and a white man named Gess. It didn't matter. At least he didn't look like a white man. True, he was lighter than most, but no one had ever accused him of looking like a white man. So what did it matter about this Gess? He had grown up with his mother and with her brothers. Gess, or whoever else might have been his father, was of no concern to him. Had it been important, his mother would have told him.

He had traveled the distance to Hiwassee from Taskigi along with Big Thighs and his cousin Agili because of the big ball play that was taking place there. But the white whiskey peddlers had also come, and he was already drunk, he and Big Thighs. He had watched the game for awhile, and it was a good game, hotly contested. He had seen one swift-footed young man get hold of the ball, toss aside his sticks, put the ball in his mouth and run like a deer for the goal. He had been hit several times, but each time he bounced off his opponent, spun, and kept running until he had scored. He had seen one man hobble from the field, hurt so badly that he could not continue playing. Many of the players were bloody. But the more whiskey he drank, the less attention he paid to the game.

The sun had just gone down, and in the dusky twilight, Sequoyah saw a man staggering toward them. He elbowed Big Thighs and nodded toward the man.

"Oh," said Big Thighs. "It's my friend Bone-Polisher."

"Um," Sequoyah said.

Bone-Polisher came up close. "Big Thighs," he said, "how are you? You have some whiskey?"

"We have some," Big Thighs said, and Sequoyah held out a jug toward Bone-Polisher, who took it greedily and drank.

"It's a good game," Big Thighs said.

Bone-Polisher lowered the jug from his mouth and looked through narrowed eyes over the shoulders of Sequoyah at something. "What is it?" asked Big-Thighs.

"Look for yourself," Bone-Polisher said, and even though both Big Thighs and Sequoyah turned to look, Bone-Polisher answered the question. "It's Doublehead, that traitor."

Sequoyah stood on uneasy legs as he looked at Doublehead sitting on his horse, leaning back, looking out over the crowd and the ball field like one of those white plantation owners surveying his domain. And, indeed, Doublehead had become a plantation owner and a slave owner. He was becoming a rich man, like a white man. There was much talk about the man. He had signed some treaties with the Americans giving away Cherokee land, and it was said far and wide that he had been paid by the U.S. agents for his part.

Doublehead was a former Chickamaugan, but even then, he had been a controversial figure. Back in 1793, Guhna-geski, also known as John Watts, had led one thousand Chickamaugas, among them Whitekiller, Bob Benge, James Vann, Pumpkin Boy, the Ridge and Doublehead, toward Knoxville with the intention of attacking. Along the way, Doublehead had insisted on attacking Cavett's Station, a small blockhouse inhabited by one family of ten white men and boys and three women. Watts had tried to stop him, but Doublehead had persuaded enough others to join him that, to keep his force from being split, Watts had agreed.

The Cavetts had seen them coming and had taken refuge in the blockhouse, and through the chinks in the logs had fired at and killed three of their attackers. Bob Benge had gone to the house to talk, and he had convinced the Cavetts to surrender. He had told them they would be taken captive and almost surely traded for Chickamaugas held by the Americans. The Cavetts had surrendered and come out of the blockhouse unarmed, and Doublehead and some of his friends had swooped down on them and killed them all. Benge, Watts, Ridge and others had been horrified.

But that had all been some years earlier, and the war was over. Doublehead had more recently been elected speaker of the Cherokee Nation's newly formed government, and it was widely believed that he was using this position for his own personal gain.

"The Americans like to deal with him instead of with our chief," Bone-Polisher said, "because they know if they give him some money, he'll sign his name to anything."

Sequoyah had heard the rumors before, and he could not dispute them, but he did not want to get involved in a discussion about politics, particularly involving Doublehead, because Doublehead was his uncle, his mother's brother. He tipped up the jug and took another swig, thinking that he would walk away. He didn't know this Bone-Polisher, and he wanted no part of any trouble. But before he could move, Bone-Polisher walked away. Sequoyah relaxed, but only for a few seconds, for Bone-Polisher walked straight to where Doublehead was still sitting in his saddle. Sequoyah watched, his heart pounding, as Bone-Polisher reached up and took hold of the bridle of Doublehead's horse.

"You're a traitor," Bone-Polisher shouted.

"Let go," said Doublehead. "Go away or I'll kill you."

"You're a traitor. You're selling our land and getting rich."

Doublehead pulled a pistol, and Bone-Polisher jerked a tomahawk loose from his belt. Doublehead fired, just missing Bone-Polisher's head, and Bone-Polisher swung his ax, chopping a thumb off Doublehead's left hand. Doublehead roared in pain and anger and swung his pistol like a war club, bashing Bone-Polisher's head and crushing his skull. Bone-Polisher fell dead. Doublehead turned his horse and rode away furiously, slinging blood from his left hand as he rode.

"Let's get out of here," Sequoyah said. He felt sick.

"Come on," Big Thighs said. "There's a tavern in Hiwassee. We can get whiskey there."

They walked the three miles into Hiwassee and found the tavern. It wasn't crowded; most of the people were out at the ball field. It was dark inside the tavern, lit by only one candle. They got some whiskey and sat down, and only then did Sequoyah notice that Doublehead had arrived there ahead of them. He was seated at a table, his left hand wrapped in a bloody cloth. He was drinking. Then Sequoyah saw the Ridge come in with another man. They stopped inside the door and looked around. The other man walked across the room and took hold of the candle. Then he walked over to Doublehead and held the candle close to his face.

Ridge moved in quickly, pulled a pistol, pointed the barrel at the side of Doublehead's face, blew out the candle and fired. Sequoyah flinched at the sound. He smelled the pungent gunpowder smoke in the air. There were sounds of shuffling and running and muffled voices in the darkness. Sequoyah sat still. He heard the sound of the door slamming. He was glad that he would not have to go home and tell his mother what had just happened to her brother.

Finally, someone lit another candle. There was no sign of the Ridge or his companion. There was no sign of Doublehead. The tavernkeeper had also disappeared. Sequoyah looked at Big Thighs. Neither spoke, but they stood up together and left the tavern. Outside, Sequoyah noticed that Big Thighs was carrying a jug.

"Let's go someplace," he said, and they walked outside of town and sat on the ground beneath some trees to drink their whiskey. They did not talk about what they had just seen. Sequoyah did not know if Big Thighs knew that Doublehead was his uncle or not. He did not want to talk about it. He was thinking that the white men did not need to kill Cherokees anymore. They had gotten the Cherokees to start killing each other. Perhaps his uncle had been taking bribes from the Americans and selling Cherokee land to make himself rich. But it was the white men who had made him that way.

Sequoyah did not know how late in the morning it was when he woke up. He was still there on the ground where he had been sitting the night before with Big Thighs, drinking whiskey. He sat up and rubbed his eyes. He looked up into the sky to see how far the Sun had crawled along on her journey to her daughter's house directly above, and he saw that she was about halfway. He glanced over to see Big Thighs still lying there asleep, or still sleeping it off. He stood up, and he found that his knee was stiff. He moaned a little, and he started walking back toward the town. He walked with a limp.

Coming around the tavern toward the front, he heard the sound of voices, and soon he could see a crowd gathered at the town square. He walked toward them. Drawing closer, he saw Agili there. He moved to his cousin's side.

"Did you hear?" Agili asked him. "They killed Doublehead last night."

"I was there," Sequoyah said. "Big Thighs and I went to the tavern. We saw Doublehead in there. The Ridge and another man came in, and Ridge shot Doublehead."

"What else did you see?"

"That was all," Sequoyah said. "The light was out. When someone lit a fresh candle, everyone was gone. Big Thighs and I went out and got drunk."

"The other man with Ridge was Alexander Saunders," Agili said. "They said that the council condemned Doublehead, and they were appointed his executioners. They found him in the tavern, and Ridge shot him, and they thought that they had killed him, but later someone told them they had not. In the darkness, some men took Doublehead out a back window. The bullet smashed his jaw, but he was still alive. They took him to the loft of a house here to hide him."

"Then he's not dead?"

"Wait," Agili said. "Ridge found out. He went with Saunders and two men of Bone-Polisher's clan to the house, and they broke in. Doublehead pulled out a knife and reached for a pistol. Ridge and Saunders both snapped their pistols at him, but both misfired. Doublehead, hurt as he was, fought with Ridge until Saunders had reprimed his pistol. Saunders fired, but he only shot Doublehead through the hip. Then he pulled a tomahawk and drove it into Doublehead's skull. When Doublehead fell, one of the other men took up a spade and bashed his head in."

Back home in Taskigi, Sequoyah brooded more than ever. Doublehead was not his favorite uncle, but the violence of his life and death was troubling. What, he wondered, did the future hold for himself and for his people? Was there no way to escape the white men?

Later, Sequoyah busied himself with silver work. He made bracelets and gorgets, nose and ear ornaments. His cousin Agili purchased a fine set from him consisting of two large circular pendants to hang from his slit ears and a smaller one for his nose. Agili put them on and admired himself in a mirror there in Sequoyah's shop.

"You should have a way of putting your name on these beautiful pieces," Agili said.

"Put my name on my silver work?" Sequoyah asked.

"Yes," Agili said. "White men who do this kind of work stamp their names in the silver. Then anyone who sees the work will know who did it. They also put their names on paintings and drawings which they've made."

"I don't know how to draw my name," Sequoyah said. "A 'possum is not as easy to draw well as a deer or a horse."

"Go see Charles Hicks," Agili said. "He knows how to put down the white man's marks for reading. He can show you how to put down your name."

Sequoyah considered what Agili had suggested. He liked the idea of stamping his name on his work. The doing of it would be no problem, if only he knew how to make the marks. He picked up a silver cup he had been working on and studied it, trying to imagine what it would look like to have his name on there, but he had no idea what his name would look like. He wondered, if he knew, where he would put it. He turned it this way and that. He decided that he would go pay a visit to Charles Hicks.

———

"I could try to spell Sequoyah with English letters," Hicks said to Sequoyah, "but even if I could figure it out, no one would be able to read it. It's easy enough to write down English names, but I don't know about writing Cherokee. Even when white men try to write our Cherokee names, they make words that can't be read properly."

Sequoyah was disappointed. He started to thank Hicks and go on his way, but he hesitated. "Agili was sure that you could do it," he said.

Hicks shrugged. "If I wanted to write Agili's name," he said, "I'd use his English name, George Lowrey. I can write George Lowrey."

A quick thought came into Sequoyah's mind, and the momentary disappointment flew away. "I have an English name," he said. "It's Gess. Draw Gess for me."

"That's easy enough," said Hicks. "He sat down at his table with pen and paper and printed out "Guess." Sequoyah looked at the word.

"That says Gess?"

"Yes."

Sequoyah cocked his head and looked curiously at the word.

"How do you tell?" he asked. "It doesn't look like anything."

"These marks are called letters," said Hicks. "Each letter stands for a sound. To read the word, one only has to sound the letters out and put the sounds together. But listen. White men have two names, a first name and last name. Guess would only be a last name. Do you have a first name to go with this?"

"Uh, I don't understand."

"Like my English name," Hicks said. "Charles and Hicks. Charles Hicks. You know Agili's English name: George and Lowrey George Lowrey. You need a first name."

"The only English names I know are already someone's name."

"It doesn't matter," said Hicks. "The white men use the same names over and over. No one owns them. How do you like George? It's Agili's name, and it was the name of the Americans' great man George Washington. It was also the name of the great king across the water. King George."

"But it comes second with the king," Sequoyah said.

"It was still his first name. King is his title. His first name is

George, but the white men don't say his second name."

"Why not?"

"Because he's the king."

"Well," Sequoyah said, "Tsatsi is good. Call me Tsatsi Gess, and show me how to make all the marks."

Hicks leaned over the table again, and in front of "Guess," he printed, "George." He handed the paper to Sequoyah. "There you are," he said. "George Guess. Can you copy those marks out and make a stamp?"

Sequoyah studied the marks and nodded, a smug, satisfied look on his face. "Yes," he said. "I can make these marks and stamp my silver. I'll do it. Thank you, my friend."

Tahlonteskee, uncle of Sequoyah and brother of the slain Doublehead, stopped by Sequoyah's store. He found Sequoyah inside polishing a finished silver cup.

"Uncle," said Sequoyah, "look what I've done."

He held the cup out for Tahlonteskee to see. Tahlonteskee took it in his own hands and studied it. Sequoyah waited anxiously for some comment. Tahlonteskee handed it back.

"It's beautiful work," he said.

"Did you see my name drawn on there?"

Tahlonteskee took up the cup again and studied it.

"Turn it upside down," Sequoyah said.

Tahlonteskee turned it and saw the letters, but he could not read.

"Right here?" he said.

"Yes. It's Tsats Gess. That's my English name. It means Sequoyah."

"Well, where did you get that?"

"I got it from Charles Hicks. He drew it out for me. From now on, every time I make a piece, I'll stamp it with Tsats Gess. Then everyone who sees it will know that I made it."

"If they can read the white man's writing," Tahlonteskee said. "Sequoyah, I came here to tell you some news. You know they killed my brother."

The look on Sequoyah's face changed to somber.

"Yes," he said. "I was there at Hiwassee when they did it. I had gone with Big Thighs and Agili to watch the ball play."

"Do you know why they killed him?"

"They said he gave away our land."

"He put his mark on a treaty that sold some of our land," Tahlonteskee said. "And he got some money for it. I think there were other reasons too, but that was the last thing they had against him, and that's the reason most often mentioned."

Sequoyah nodded in silence. This was not a topic he felt like pursuing, but he could not cut off a conversation with his uncle.

"Do you know, nephew, that I too put my mark on that paper? That same treaty? They gave me money too. There may be some men thinking to kill me for my part in that sale."

"What will you do?"

"The American president has said that he'll give land to any of us who move west. He'll give us all the land we need, and he's promised that if we move out there, we'll never be bothered again. The land is much like this, they say, but there are no white people around, and the game is plenty. I'm going to move, and there are twelve towns that will move with me. Over a thousand of our people. Do you want to go?"

"I haven't thought about it," Sequoyah said.

"You have time," said Tahlonteskee. "We won't leave until the spring. Let me know if you decide to move with us. They call that place Arkansas, and when we get there, we'll have our own new government. We won't have to put up with all this fussing, and we won't have the white men pressing in all around us. Let me know what you decide."

When Tahlonteskee had left, Sequoyah sat alone and considered what his uncle had told him. It sounded good to be away from the white men. And there were already some Cherokees who had moved west. It had happened twice that he knew of. Dangerous Man had led some long ago, and more recently Bowl and his group of Chickamaugas had gone west. Sequoyah did not know if they had gone to Arkansas. It was a strange thing to think about, moving to a new and strange country, establishing a new government, leaving old friends and relatives behind.

But the other things: the plentiful game, the absence of white men, the end to interference by the United States, those things all sounded good. He would think more about it. He would talk with Agili and with other friends and relatives. He would see how they felt about this idea. Maybe it would be good.

4

Oostanaula,
in present Georgia,
1812

They gathered there to hear speeches made on important topics. Big things were happening. The Americans were fighting the English once more, but this time the Cherokees were not involved. The year before, Tecumseh, the Shawnee, had paid a visit to the Creeks at Tuckabatchee, a Creek town on the Tallapoosa River. The story had spread all through the Cherokee country. The Creeks and the Cherokees were old enemies, going back as far as anyone could remember, and recently they had been stealing horses from one another. The Ridge had gone to Tuckabatchee as ambassador to the Creeks to talk about this horse stealing problem and try to put an end to it, but really, everyone knew, he had gone to hear Tecumseh talk to the Creeks. He had known that Tecumseh was going to be there.

Ridge knew Tecumseh, for Ridge, as a young man, had fought with the Chickamaugas under the leadership of the great Dragging Canoe. Some Shawnees, young Tecumseh among them, had moved down to stay with and fight with the Chickamaugas. It was there that Tecumseh had learned of Dragging Canoe's plan to unite all Indian tribes against further westward movement of the whites. Now all these years later, Tecumseh was advocating the same plan.

Ridge had listened to him speak, and he had studied the reaction of the Creek audience. The Creeks, like the Cherokees, were sharply divided into two camps, one called conservative and the other progressive. Although there were striking exceptions to the rule among both Creeks and Cherokees, generally speaking, the conservatives were full-blood, the progressives mixed. One of the major Cherokee exceptions was Ridge himself. A full-blood, he was leaning more and more toward the progressive camp.

Ridge had noticed that the progressive Creeks spoke out against Tecumseh's plan and against any talk of war with the Americans, but the conservative Creeks were listening eagerly to the message. Tecumseh called for a return to old ways. He called for giving up things acquired from the white man. He told the Creeks to dance, but not to fight. Not just yet. He told them to wait for his word. He would let them know when the time was right, and they would be backed by the English. One of the leading Creek progressives, the Big Warrior, said that the Creeks were becoming civilized, and they would not go to war against the Americans. He said that he did not believe Tecumseh. Angry, Tecumseh declared that when he had made it back to his home up north, he would stamp his feet, and the earth would shake.

Before leaving Tuckabatchee, Ridge drew Tecumseh aside. "Don't come among the Cherokees with your speeches," he said, "or you'll be killed."

But on the sixteenth of December, just in time for Tecumseh to have gotten back home, the Cherokees and the Creeks felt the earth shake. The conservatives became excited. The progressives ran to the missionaries seeking an explanation. The missionaries had done their best to explain the earthquake scientifically, and the progressives had done their best to accept the explanation. But soon word had come from the west about just how bad the earthquake had been. Rivers had run backward. Lakes had risen above the ground. Lightning had flashed from the earth into the sky. Layers of earth had heaved up, and cracks had appeared in the earth.

Chief Bowles and the Chickamaugas who had left the Cherokee country back in 1794 to settle in Missouri had been in the middle of the worst of it, and when it was finally over, they had headed for Arkansas to join Tahlonteskee and the thousand or so who had moved there with him. It had taken a while for word of all this to reach the Cherokee homeland, but it had, and the Cherokee conservatives, like the Creek conservatives, were frightened.

Those were some of the reasons the Cherokees had gathered there at Oostanaula, and Sequoyah was among them. They talked about the things that had happened, and they talked about Tecumseh and his power. They said that the British were helping Tecumseh and that this time they would defeat the Americans. Sequoyah listened carefully. He remembered well the days of the wars with the Americans. He recalled vividly the attacks on his hometown of Taskigi. But he also knew that the Americans kept wanting more land. It was hard not to agree with Tecumseh. And really, the message was that of Dragging Canoe, and in Sequoyah's mind Dragging Canoe was the greatest Cherokee leader of his time, perhaps of all time.

Then a delegation from nearby Coosawatie came forward. They said they had brought their prophet, Tsali—Charlie to the English-speaking mixed-bloods—who had some things to say. The crowd grew quiet and attentive as the old man stepped forward. He was dressed in leggings, a breechcloth, and moccasins, and a wolf skin was draped over his shoulders. His head was shaved and wrapped in a red turban, and two large black wolves stood at his sides.

"They are spirit wolves," someone whispered.

Charlie stepped forward, the wolves moving and stopping with him. It was as if their movements were controlled by his thoughts. "I bring a message from the One Who Lives at the Seventh Height," he said. "He spoke to me in a vision. He is displeased with us because we have taken too many things from the white people. We are no longer living the way he told us to live. We have steel knives and iron pots. We have feather beds and books. We have hogs and cats. Guns. White man's clothes. We ride his horses. He told me to tell you to get rid of all these things. If you fail to heed this warning, we will all be driven west, clear to the Darkening Land, to the edge of the world. But if you do as I say, if you go back to the old ways, the game will return, and the whites will go away. If anyone dares to deny my message, the One Who Lives at the Seventh Height will strike him dead."

Sequoyah felt a cold chill run through his veins. People began calling out that Charlie's talk was good. In the face of all the cheering and all the excitement, Ridge stepped up before the crowd and called for quiet. Eventually, the crowd grew silent, allowing him to speak.

"My friends," he said, "what you've just heard is not good. If you listen to what this man told you, it will lead us into war with the Americans, and that will be disastrous for us. Charlie is not a prophet. His words did not come from on high. If they did, I stand here to challenge them. Let me be struck dead here in front of you."

Some of the crowd, conservatives who had been convinced by Charlie, apparently did not want to wait for vengeance from on high. They rushed upon Ridge, intent on beating him to death or tearing him apart. He fought them, and friends of his hurried to his side to help. Sequoyah saw that Ridge fell to the ground, but his friends fought the others back, and he got to his feet again. At last an old man stood up calling for order, and at last order was restored. Ridge and his friends left. Ridge had made his point. Other progressives left. The lingering crowd was almost all conservative, almost all convinced of the validity of the words of the old prophet.

Charlie came forward again, and the crowd was hushed. Sequoyah listened intently as the prophet predicted an ice storm that would destroy all. The only ones who would be saved from a terrible death by pounding hail stones would be those who would follow him to the peak of a high mountain. They would be safe there with him until the storm was over, he said. Then they could come down and resume their lives as in the past. Deer and buffalo would be abundant once again. "Come with me," he said. "Follow me." And Sequoyah and hundreds of others followed Charlie to the top of the mountain to wait it out. The storm never came.

Back at his store, Sequoyah pondered the mysteries of his confusing times. Ridge was a full-blood, a former Chickamaugan, and he spoke out loudly and strongly for the white man's ways. He berated the conservatives like old Charlie, and in the conflict with Charlie, Ridge had triumphed. According to Ridge, the way to survive was to adapt to the ways of the white men. Charlie's message was the opposite, but Charlie had been disgraced, and in the wake of his disgrace, Ridge's reputation had billowed. Charlie's predicted storm had not materialized. Sequoyah did not like the ways of the white men. He could not completely agree with Ridge and the progressives. He did not want to dress in white men's clothes and speak English. But what did he want? He was practicing the trade of a blacksmith and of a silversmith, both learned from white men, and he was operating a trading post. He was a good horseman, and he was earning money. He drew his pictures in a white man's notebook with a white man's pencil, and he had learned to sign his work with a white man's name, "George Guess."

"Tsatsi Gess," he said out loud. His knee had begun to hurt him again, and his thoughts were troubling. He took out a jug of whiskey and went out behind his store. He would just get drunk.

October, 1813

Agili burst into the store. "Sequoyah, the Creek Red Sticks have wiped out Fort Mims. The United States is at war with them. General Jackson is raising an army to fight them, and they want Cherokees to join them. Gideon Morgan has been made colonel, and my older brother a lieutenant colonel. John McLamore is a captain. I'm going to join them."

Sequoyah knew that the conservative Creeks were being called Red Sticks, and he knew, in spite of their English names, who the Cherokees were that Agili had listed. He wasn't at all sure about the English military ranks, but that did not matter to him anyway.

"I'll go with you," Sequoyah said.

"What about your leg?"

"It's all right," Sequoyah said. "It hasn't bothered me now for some time. Besides, I have a horse to ride."

Agili ran on to get himself ready, and Sequoyah sat wondering why he had so quickly agreed to fight against the conservative Creeks and alongside white Americans. Of course, the Creeks and Cherokees had always fought against one another, but somehow that did not seem to be enough explanation. Perhaps his life was just too boring. Perhaps, at thirty-five years of age, he just needed some excitement. He stood up. His knee really was hurting him, but he wouldn't say anything about that to anyone. He started gathering up the things he would need: rifle, shot, powder, knife, canteen.

They gathered at Hiwassee Garrison, up the Hiwassee River from the old Cherokee town of the same name: Ridge, John Walker, Agili or George Lowrey and his older brother John, Captain John McLamore, young John Ross, Gal'kalisk', Richard Brown, Whitepath, Goingsnake, Charles Hicks, Sequoyah and others. Sequoyah was called a private. Colonel Gideon Morgan arrived with Cherokee foot soldiers, and the Cherokees all waited for the arrival of the American general, James White. Jackson was somewhere else with his Tennessee volunteers.

Sequoyah watched as the messenger arrived and handed a paper to General White. The general read the paper, folded it and tucked it into his jacket. Then he said some things to Gideon Morgan, and Morgan spoke to McLamore. Soon the words had been translated to those, including Sequoyah, who spoke no English.

Agili told Sequoyah, "General White just got orders from General Jackson. The Creeks are threatening our chief, Pathkiller, there at Turkeytown. We're going there to protect him."

"General Jackson said all this?" Sequoyah asked.

"Yes."

"Where is he?"

"He's not here. He sent those orders on that paper the messenger brought."

"The paper said all that?" Sequoyah asked.

"Yes," said Agili. "Hurry up now. We have to get ready to go."

After a long ride, they reached Turkeytown, but the Creeks never came. Sequoyah wondered, if this was the way the white men made war, how they ever managed to win. They gathered together and waited around for days. Then they rode their horses or walked for days to another place where they sat around again for more days waiting for something to happen that did not come about.

Then a new paper came with new orders. There were Red Sticks at the Creek town of Tallaschatchee, and the Cherokees were ordered there to attack. Once more, they were on the move. Perhaps this time, Sequoyah thought, there will be a fight. His knee was bothering him, but he said nothing about it.

It was November 4 when they reached Tallaschatchee, and they found it already occupied by Tennessee militia. They had wiped out the Creeks in that town. The fight was over. Sequoyah heard the talk about the fight. Women and children had been killed as well as men. People had been burned alive inside houses. Scenes of the attacks on Taskigi in his childhood flashed through his mind. He tried to tell himself that these were Creeks, ancient enemies of the Cherokees, and that it should not matter to him. But it was hard to get it out of his head that Indians were being attacked in their homes by white men.

One of the white men there was a man called Davy Crockett. Sequoyah found Crockett amusing. The man seemed always to be the center of attention, standing in the middle of a small crowd, talking loudly and gesturing wildly. His listeners interrupted him frequently with laughter. Once Sequoyah saw Crockett sitting quietly and alone. He had a notebook resting on his thigh, and he was writing in it. Sequoyah suppressed an urge to walk over and look to see what kind of marks Crockett was making. He told himself that he should have brought his own notebook along. Then he could sit and draw marks on its leaves.

Another message came, this one with news as well as new orders. General Jackson, the message said, had defeated the Creeks at Talladega. The new orders were for General White to take his troops to the mouth of the Chatooga River and meet up with General Cocke there. Sequoyah expected that they would lay around there on the banks of the Chatooga for a few days, but this time he was wrong.

General Cocke had heard of Jackson's victory at Talladega, and he was jealous. He wanted a victory for himself. He knew that there were Creeks at a place called Hillaby. He ordered General White to take the Cherokees and some Tennessee militiamen to move against Hillaby and attack. They mounted up and rode quickly, moving as fast as they could. Toward the end of their first day, they came across a deserted Creek town. General White ordered them to burn the town. As Sequoyah helped put the torch to houses, he wondered if some small boy, held tight in his mother's arms, watched in terror from a secret hiding place.

They moved on. Along the way, they burned another deserted town, and at last, on the 18th of November, they arrived at Hillaby. White called a halt to the column and surveyed the town ahead. He took note of a possible route of escape for the Creeks, and he ordered Major John Walker to take some of the Cherokees to a spot of elevated ground over there to block off that avenue of retreat. Sequoyah rode with Walker. They rode around the Creek town to take up their position.

Sequoyah thought that something was strange about the behavior of the Creeks in the town. They did not seem to panic at the appearance of the troops. Some of the men were standing around calmly, looking at General White and the main body of the attacking force. They watched calmly, a little curiously perhaps, as Walker led his small contingent to the rise. No one was running. There was no sense of urgency among the town's residents. Had they been taken by surprise? Why had they not abandoned the town and fled to safety?

White's shrill call to action startled Sequoyah, even from his distant station. He watched with fascinated horror as the troops charged the small town. Only then did the Creeks seem to realize that they were in danger. Some of the men ran for houses, presumably to find weapons for defense. Women looked around frantically for their children. Children ran screaming or stood frozen in terror, crying as the soldiers, Cherokee and Tennessee whites, came rushing at them. He saw men and women fall from gunshots. He saw men hacked with swords. He did not want to watch, but he could not tear his eyes away from the bloody scene.

He and the others with Walker were useless to the general effort, for no Creeks attempted escape. There was no time for them to try. Those fighting men who might have tried to stand their ground were cut down where they stood, almost before they realized they were being attacked. Women and children huddled together, and at last it was all over with, almost as suddenly as it had begun. No Creeks were alive except the women and children. Sequoyah was glad that he had been sent with Walker. He was glad that he had not taken part in the slaughter.

They withdrew to a spot on the Coosa River and took several days to construct a stockade. The more than two hundred Creek prisoners, almost all women and children and some Black slaves, were taken by the Cherokee soldiers and sent to their homes back in Cherokee country. When the slaughter at Hillaby was over, one of the Creek women had informed General White, through a translator, that the reason they had not resisted was that they had already surrendered. They sent a man to General Jackson, and the general had accepted their offer. When they had seen General White and his troops approaching, they had assumed that it was to take them prisoner.

Lounging around the new stockade, Sequoyah felt depressed. He contemplated the horrors of war. He was not at all sure that he had made the proper decision when he had gotten himself involved in this bloody business. He also considered the irony of the Cherokee position in this present war against the Redsticks. Had old Charlie the prophet managed to somehow overcome the arguments of the Ridge, the Cherokees could very well have been the allies of the Creeks in this war. Instead, they were allied with the white Americans. But the situation was even more complex than that, for both the Creeks and the Cherokees were divided into conservative and progressive camps, and there were progressive Creeks as well as Cherokees allied with General Jackson in this effort to crush the Red Sticks, the conservative Creeks.

He thought of Ridge and of the peculiar twists of these changing times. In his youth, Ridge had been a follower of Dragging Canoe. Tecumseh was a disciple of Dragging Canoe. These Red Sticks were followers of Tecumseh, perhaps indirectly, but still they were his followers. Yet Ridge was on the other side. And now, so was Sequoyah. Sequoyah wondered where he might be had not Charlie called the people to the mountaintop to await the great storm, the storm that had never come.

Most of the full-bloods had believed Charlie, and had Charlie not made that one costly mistake, they would likely have continued to believe him. And Sequoyah was one of them. He would still be following Charlie had it not been for the prediction that never came true. He would be at home killing cats instead of riding with white men to kill Creeks. Or he might be with the Creeks, waiting for the white men to attack. He wondered if there was anything left in which he could still believe.

5

Gideon Morgan called all of the Cherokees together, and when they were gathered, he stood up in front of them and read aloud in English from a paper. Everyone remained silent and attentive throughout the reading, even those, including Sequoyah, who could not understand a word of the strange-sounding message. Sequoyah thought that the sounds of the English language were ugly, but he wondered again at the fascinating process of reading actual words from the peculiar marks on the paper. He recalled that Big Thighs had claimed to have heard that there was a time in the long ago past when Cherokee priests could read and write in the Cherokee language, and he thought that must have been a wonderful thing. He wondered if such a thing could be done again. If it had been done before, then why not? If one man could figure out how to do it, then could not another?

Morgan at last finished reading the paper talk. He folded the paper and tucked it inside his jacket. He said something else, turned brusquely, and walked away, and the formation of Cherokees began to disperse. Sequoyah turned to his cousin Agili and stopped him with a touch on the shoulder.

"What did he say?" he asked in Cherokee.

"Oh. He said that we're not needed here anymore," Agili said, "and we should go home, but we should stay ready for when they call us back. We're not finished. We're waiting for reinforcements and supplies. He said, 'Fifty nights shall not pass ere your swords, your lances and your knives shall drink the blood of your enemy. Your valor shall show them,' he said, 'the imbecility of their prophets and instill fresh fear in their hearts.' Then he said again that we should keep ourselves ready for when they call us again."

Sequoyah thought about that phrase, "the imbecility of their prophets," and he recalled waiting on the mountaintop with Charlie for the great hailstorm that did not come. Had Charlie shown his imbecility? Had Sequoyah been an imbecile for following Charlie?

"Are you going home then?" he asked.

"Yes. Let's travel together."

Back in Taskigi, Sequoyah got himself drunk in an attempt to numb the ugly memories of his recent military experience and the complex questions that were troubling his mind. The next day, sober again by midday, those memories and those questions returned. He went into his store and looked things over, thinking to occupy his mind in that way. He could not be sure, but he thought that there were some things missing. Well, he had been gone for some time. It wasn't surprising.

He looked at a pile of blankets on a shelf, and he tried to remember how many of them had been there when he had left. He was almost certain that there should have been three or four more. He wondered who had come in to help themselves in his absence. If I could write, he thought, I could write down twelve blankets, or however many there might be. Then if I should sell one, I could write that down, and that way, I would always know just how many blankets I should have at any given time. He glanced over to the table where he sat to do his work in silver, and there was the stamp he had made to put his name on his finished pieces. He stepped over and picked it up. "Tsatsi Gess," he said out loud. He tried to see Tsatsi Gess in the marks, but he could not. He had memorized their appearance, but they meant nothing to him, not really.

He thought to sit down with his notepad and draw some pictures, but he did not see it when he looked around. The store was in utter disarray. He could not blame that on anyone who might have come in during his long absence, though. He admitted to himself that he had left it in that condition. He started moving things aside, tossing some things out of his way, and eventually he found his pad and pencil.

"Ah, yes," he said, and he sat down at the table with it and flipped some leaves. He came to his drawing of a horse, and he said to himself, "*sogwili.*" He turned another leaf to a sketch of a deer, and he said, "*awi.*"

Of course I can write and read, he then said out loud, but almost immediately after, he contradicted his own words, telling himself, "I cannot make marks that will say, 'I rode on a horse to war.' " He pushed the notepad aside and rested his head on his hand. How did the white men write their words? How had the old Cherokee priests made theirs? If they could do it, he asked himself, why cannot I? In another moment, Agili walked in. Sequoyah handed him the pad.

"What do you see there?" he asked.

"I see a buffalo," Agili said.

"And that is all it says to you, isn't it?" Sequoyah asked. "*Yansa.*"

Agili looked at the drawing and shrugged. "It's a good drawing of a buffalo," he said. "One of the best I've ever seen."

"But it doesn't say anything more than just 'buffalo.' "

"No," said Agili. "It doesn't."

February 8, 1814

Ridge, now Major Ridge, had gathered the Cherokee soldiers together again, and to their numbers he had added new recruits. They were going to Fort Armstrong on the Coosa River to join forces with General Jackson; but the rains came, hard rains with no relief for a week. Again, Sequoyah thought, they had been called together to sit and wait. When at last they began to move, the going was slow because of the soft mud through which they slogged and the swollen streams they had to cross. Upon their arrival at Fort Armstrong, they found that Jackson and his troops had moved to Fort Strother. They marched again, this time south along the Coosa toward Strother. The ground was still wet and the stream beds still full.

At Fort Strother, Sequoyah got his first look at General Andrew Jackson, a lanky, haggard looking man with sickly, reddish skin and wild red hair, turning gray. Jackson looked older than his forty-seven years, perhaps, Agili said, because he was suffering from dysentery. Sequoyah also noticed that the general's left arm seemed to be useless. That made him conscious again of his own leg. The knee was once again swollen and sore. He did his best to walk straight, and he said nothing about it to anyone, not even Agili.

Again, they waited. This time, Agili told him, they were waiting for more troops to arrive. For the next three or four weeks, they came in until there were nearly five thousand in all: Cherokees, regular U.S. infantry, Tennessee militia, progressive Creeks. Gideon Morgan told the Cherokees and Creeks to adorn themselves with white feathers and deer tails to make them easy to distinguish from the Red Stick Creeks.

Sequoyah looked at the other soldiers, and among the Cherokees, he recognized many he knew. Besides Agili and Morgan, John Lowrey, John Ross, Richard Brown, Charles Hicks, John Walker, Goingsnake, Whitepath and Gal'kalisk' were back. In addition, Charles Reese and the Whale were there. Among the progressive Creeks, Sequoyah saw William McIntosh. He did not know any other Creeks, and Davy Crockett was there with the Tennesseans again. He was a little surprised to see young Sam Houston, the white boy that his uncle Ooloodega, known to the whites as John Jolly, had adopted a few years before.

One day, Gideon Morgan read another of the paper talks, and it was translated for the Cherokees who did not understand English. When the troops were dismissed, Sequoyah said to Agili, "I'd like to have one of those papers to look at." About mid-morning of the next day, Agili found Sequoyah.

"Look what I have for you," he said, and he handed Sequoyah a paper covered with writing. Sequoyah took it eagerly and looked at it.

"*Wado*," he said, thanking his cousin. He tucked it into his hunting jacket as if he were afraid that someone might see him with it.

"Do you want me to read it to you?" Agili asked.

"It doesn't matter," Sequoyah said. "I don't understand the white man's words anyway. I just want to look at the marks."

He waited until he found himself alone and felt relatively secure from prying eyes, and then he removed the paper and studied it. It was covered in squiggly lines with occasional breaks in them. He could make no sense of any of it. He wondered how the white men could look at these wavering lines and make words out of them, and if Hicks and the others who could read the white man's marks were to be believed, any white man, and some Cherokees who had been to school, could read out the same words that any other man would read. A white man who had mastered these scribbles could write down his words and send the paper to some other white man who had mastered them, and the man who received the paper could read the other's exact words. He thought of his drawings again. He could draw horse and read horse, but that was not enough. There was something else. Something he did not understand.

March 13

They marched out of Fort Strother, the mounted whites and Cherokees in the front, the foot soldiers coming up behind. For a week they moved through marshes and forests, fording rivers and streams. At last they stopped, and they built a hasty fortification at the mouth of Cedar Creek. Jackson sent out Major Ridge and some of the Cherokees to search for Creeks. Sequoyah rode with them, and they found and burned two abandoned towns. Sequoyah was weary of this war, and his knee was hurting.

March 22

They moved out with provisions for eight days, four hundred cavalry, including the Cherokees, Sequoyah among them, followed by two thousand foot soldiers. Through more marshes and thick woods they advanced for four long and weary days. At last, they camped. As Sequoyah dropped off to sleep that night, he wondered how many more days they would travel. He wondered where they were going.

March 27

"We're going to attack, Sequoyah," Agili said, interpreting the white general's words for his cousin. "We are close to the stronghold of the Red Sticks. Just ahead, the Tallapoosa River makes two sharp turns creating a peninsula of land or a horseshoe shape. The Creeks call it Tohopeka. The last six of the Red Sticks' towns have moved onto that peninsula. They know that we're coming, and they have built a breastworks across the peninsula's neck. Get your horse. We're going now."

"How do we know about the Creeks?" Sequoyah asked.

"Jackson had spies," Agili said. "Hurry now."

The horsemen were in line ready to attack, but they found themselves facing the breastworks across the neck of the peninsula. There was no way into the six towns except over the breastworks or across the river. Jackson called forward two small cannons and ordered them fired at the wall. With the cannons barking and spewing flame and grapeshot, Jackson, fiery-eyed, shouted out orders. Gideon Morgan repeated them, and Agili called out to Sequoyah and other non–English-speaking Cherokees, "Follow Colonel Coffee."

Coffee led the mounted Cherokees to the east. They splashed into the river and rode across, then turned south and made their way along the east bank of the river to a place near the tip of the peninsula. From there, they could look across the river and see the houses of the Creeks. They could also see a line of canoes over there on the other side. They sat on their horses awaiting further orders. They could hear the cannons continuing to fire. Rifle shots cracked. Men shouted. The battle was raging elsewhere, and the Cherokees just sat on their horses waiting.

"Why are we here?" Sequoyah asked.

"In case the Creeks try to swim across the river here to escape the attack," Agili said. He waited a moment, and then he said, "Are you ready, in case they come this way?"

"I'm ready," Sequoyah said.

"How's your leg?"

"It's all right." His leg was hurting him. He was glad to be sitting in a saddle. The smell of burnt powder was beginning to reach his nostrils, and the sounds of the battle which he could not see grew louder to his ears.

"What are we waiting for?" he heard Ridge shout in Cherokee. Coffee must have lost his patience about the same time, for he said something in English, and a man turned his horse north and rode off. In a few minutes he returned and spoke to Coffee. Coffee answered. Agili looked at Sequoyah.

"He says that the battle is not going well back there. Their shots aren't doing any good, and they can't get over the wall."

"We've waited two hours," Ridge shouted. "That's long enough. Some of you follow me."

Ridge jumped off his horse and plunged into the river, swimming with powerful strokes toward the canoes on the other side. Charles Reese followed him, and so did the Whale. As they reached the canoes, a Creek appeared from between two houses and fired a shot that caught the Whale in the shoulder. Agili raised his own rifle to his shoulder and shot the Creek from across the river. Ridge and Reese helped the Whale into a canoe. Then Reese paddled the canoe containing the whale, and Ridge got into another. Soon both canoes were on the Cherokee side of the river. Cherokees dismounted and climbed into the canoes to row back to the Creek side.

Once across, each man got another canoe to take to the waiting Cherokees. Soon all of the Creek canoes were filled with Cherokees, and as they returned to the Creek side, the Cherokees disembarked and ran into the towns, shooting at anything that moved. The Cherokee attack was so ferocious that the Creeks in the towns were driven north into their own breastworks. Sequoyah, because of his painful leg, was bringing up the rear. He had not yet fired a shot when he saw the young Creek man level a rifle at him. Quickly, he brought his own rifle to his shoulder. The Creek rifle misfired, but Sequoyah's did not. The Creek fell dead, a huge hole in his chest. Sequoyah stared wide-eyed for a moment, then moved on.

The fight was carried to the wall, where the Red Sticks were backed up. They turned to face their attackers and fought back ferociously. Suddenly, from the other side of the wall, soldiers came swarming. Jackson, apparently having seen what was happening inside, ordered an attack. The Red Sticks were caught from both sides, but the wall was holding back the troops with Jackson. Bayonets and swords were poked through holes in the breastwork at Creeks, and occasionally men tried to climb the wall but were repulsed.

Ridge, seeing the problem, called out to the Cherokees to attack, and the Cherokees came out from behind and between the Creek houses, rushing in a mass on the Creeks who were there with their backs to the wall. With all their attention suddenly on the Cherokees, the Creeks were no longer able to defend the wall. Sam Houston climbed it first, but he was immediately followed by a swarm of soldiers and militiamen. Sequoyah was hesitant to join in the struggle until he saw that Agili was about to be overpowered. Limping, he ran to his cousin's aid, and coming up behind the Creek with whom Agili struggled, he bashed the man in the head with the butt of his rifle.

Turning, looking around in confusion, he saw the gaunt figure of General Jackson on the ground. A Creek had raised a war club and was about to strike. Jackson covered his face with an arm, but just before the blow would have fallen, Gal'kalisk' stepped in behind the Creek and jabbed him in the back with his knife. As the Creek fell dead, Gal'kalisk' helped Jackson to his feet.

At last, with many Creeks lying dead all around, the remaining ones fled to the river and jumped in. As they swam toward the opposite shore, the Cherokees who were still waiting over there with Coffee began firing at them, shooting them like fish. Ridge, and other Cherokees who had been seized by a killing frenzy, jumped into the water after the Creeks, and Sequoyah saw Ridge kill a man in the water with his knife. The waters of the Tallapoosa were soon stained red.

Some few Red Sticks had managed to escape and hide behind piles of brush and timber. The fight was over. Jackson turned to McIntosh, the progressive Creek. "Do you have a man who can speak to them?" he asked.

"Yes," McIntosh answered.

"Have him tell them that if they surrender and come out, they won't be harmed."

McIntosh called a man forward and passed on the general's instructions. The man walked toward the brush piles and called out in the Creek language. Some of the Creeks fired, and he dropped dead in his tracks. A soldier picked up a torch and flung it at the brush piles, igniting them. Soon they were blazing. As Creeks ran out from the flames, soldiers shot them down. As night fell, the firing stopped.

Any Red Sticks who had survived the slaughter had managed to slip away. There were no prisoners. Bodies were lying all around. Sequoyah was sickened by the sight and the smells. He marveled at the images which still filled his head of the way in which men he knew, the Ridge, his own cousin Agili, and others, hacked and chopped and stabbed at other human beings. He wondered at the glee with which some men flung themselves into bloody battle.

Jackson called for a count of American dead and wounded, and it was announced that they had lost thirty-two killed, ninety-nine wounded. Of the dead, eighteen were Cherokee. Of the wounded, thirty-six. A count of the Creek dead would wait until morning. The officers, on Jackson's orders, called the men off the battle field into a makeshift camp for the night. Sequoyah thought at first that he would not sleep, but soon he did. He slept, but it was not an easy or quiet sleep. Rather, it was a sleep filled with horrors, with killing and screaming, with smoke and fire and blood. It was a long night bothered by demons, and those demons were in human shape and form.

6

The way home was long and weary with lots of time for thinking, for remembering what he had just been through, what he had seen and what he had done. He could not stop thinking that he had just helped do to the Red Stick Creeks what had been done to his own town twice during his childhood, a thing that he still had bad dreams about. He had stopped excusing his participation in the war by reminding himself that the Cherokees and Creeks were ancient enemies. That was—well, ancient.

He did not like the white men, the Americans, and to further complicate the matter, they were again fighting the English, the men who had been the allies of Dragging Canoe only a short time ago. These Americans were always wanting more land from the Cherokees and from other Indians. Why, he asked himself, had he helped them? And he found that he was unable to answer that question. Part of the answer was that Agili had come to him excited about going to fight. He had answered quickly, too quickly perhaps, that he would go along.

He had seen war in his childhood, but in his adulthood, he had not. Perhaps another part of the answer to his question was simply that he had not had his chance to fight. Maybe the need to fight had been in him since he watched, a helpless child, on the mountainside in his mother's arms. Maybe he just had a need deep inside to do some fighting and some killing, and this had been his first chance. Well, he decided, if that had been the reason, then this one experience was enough. So he had been a soldier, a warrior, once, and once was enough. He would go back to being a storekeeper, a blacksmith and a silversmith. He could make plenty of money that way. He could keep himself busy enough, too.

He imagined what he would do when he arrived back home. He would straighten up his store first. He recalled how he had left it in some disarray. It was a shortcoming of his. He knew it. He resolved to try to do better. Once his store was tidied up, he would have time to devote to his silver work, and drawing. He again asked himself why he had not brought along his notepad and pencil. He thought about all the different pictures he could draw, and he considered again that if he drew a picture of a horse, any man could look at it and say, "horse."

That made him recall the messages the American generals had sent back and forth to one another, and he furrowed his brow at the thought. He could not figure out how to draw, "We will be moving south," or any other of the kinds of messages the Americans had sent around during the war. He wondered if there was a picture for "horse," could there be one for "moving," or for "south"? Perhaps, when he had some time, he would see if he could draw pictures for those words and others. It shouldn't be difficult. If everyone simply agreed on the meaning of the picture for each different word, then everyone would be able to read.

He expected disarray from his own neglect and perhaps a little pilfering from his neighbors, but he did not expect what he discovered upon entering his trading post. It had been thoroughly ransacked. He could see it at a glance. The only things remaining were those items that could not be carried by a man on foot or horseback. He had not gotten over the astonishment of the sight before Agili came in.

"You too?" Agili said.

"What do you mean?"

"The white soldiers came through on their way home," Agili said. "They stole everything they could carry or drive. My horses, my cattle—all gone. I talked to my neighbors, and they told me what happened. They robbed everyone."

"After we went to help them in their war?" Sequoyah said.

Agili shrugged. "They have no respect, no gratitude."

"What kind of creatures are these Americans?" Sequoyah asked. "They don't even act like human beings. Do they love their mothers? Do they steal from each other or just from us?"

"I've heard they even steal from each other," Agili said. "That's why they lock their houses and their stores. Ah, well, we have to learn how to deal with them. That's all."

"Diwali and Tahlonteskee and others don't think so," Sequoyah said. "They moved west, away from the white men."

"Yes, they did. So what will you do, Sequoyah?"

Sequoyah walked over to his work table. His notepad was lying there, and so was his pencil. Casually he sat down and opened it up to a clean page. He sketched a deer and held it up for Agili to look at.

"What do you see?" he asked.

"A deer."

Sequoyah turned a page and made another quick sketch, some abstract lines. He held that up for his cousin. "Now what?" he asked.

Agili looked at the drawing, raised his hands to his sides and said, "I don't know. It doesn't look like anything to me. Scribbles."

"What if I told you that this drawing is 'west' and that any time you see it, you should say, 'west'?" Sequoyah asked.

"You think you can draw west?"

"Of course I can," Sequoyah said. "If we agree that this is west, then I can draw it, and you can read it, or you can draw it, and I can read it. Then we can tell others, and they too will be able to read it and draw it."

"I think you're wasting your time," Agili said. "Especially now with so much work to do."

Sequoyah looked around at the mess left by the American spoilers. "They didn't leave me much to clean up," he said. "Why should I bother?"

Her name was Utiyu, but she had another. Like Sequoyah, Agili and other Cherokees, she had an English name. It was Sally Waters, and that was the name she used: Sally. He had been to Toquo before. It was the next town south from Taskigi along the river. When she came with her mother and her uncle into his store, he was surprised to hear that she had lived in Toquo all her life. How, he wondered, had he managed to live all his life so close by without having seen her?

They came into his store about a year after he had returned from the war with the Red Stick Creeks. They looked around, but they found nothing they wanted. He was not surprised. He had not bothered building up much of an inventory after the Americans had stolen so much from him. He worked in silver, and he did occasional blacksmithing. Sally's uncle inquired about shoes for his mule, and Sequoyah took care of the job. But Sally admired his silver work. He showed her all of the pieces he had on hand, and she told him how lovely they were. Then she caught sight of his notepad lying on the table, opened to a page with a drawing of a buffalo.

"I've never seen a better one," she said.

Sequoyah shrugged. "I just do it to keep my hands busy when I'm—well, they're not important. It's just to pass the time."

Sally turned a page to reveal a horse, then a deer. "They're all very good," she said. The next page she turned showed the abstract marks he had made to try to convince Agili that he could make a mark for any Cherokee word. She looked at it, puzzled. "What's this?" she asked.

He smiled and cocked his head to one side. "It's nothing," he said. "Scribbling. That's all."

After that, he made excuses to travel to Toquo at least once a week, and on each visit, he paid a visit to Sally and her mother and uncle. It didn't take long. Everything was arranged, and they were married. In the old days, Sequoyah would have moved to Toquo to live with his wife and her family. In the old days, when they had children, the children would belong to their mother and trace their descent only through her. But times had changed. Sally became Mrs. George Guess and moved to Taskigi where her husband had his business. He was thirty-seven years old. She was twenty-six.

Sequoyah began to pay more attention to his store. He restocked, and his sales increased. His blacksmithing business was good, and he was selling silver pieces regularly. Things were looking good. Sequoyah felt himself to be a very fortunate man. He had a good business and a lovely wife. He would be starting a family late in life, but that was all right. He believed that he would appreciate it more than had he done the typical thing and begun earlier. And his children would not see their town burned down around them. Times had changed.

Times had changed, but the Americans had not. Or if they had changed, they had become more greedy than ever for land. In 1816, only two years after the Cherokees had helped General Andrew Jackson win the war against the Red Sticks, on March 22, in Washington City, representatives of the United States government had pressured the Cherokees into signing two treaties. In the first one, the Cherokees gave up all their land "beginning on the east bank of the Chattuga river, where the boundary line of the Cherokee nation crosses the same, running thence, with the said boundary line, to a rock on the Blue Ridge, where the boundary line crosses the same, and which rock has been lately established as a corner to the states of North and South Carolina; running thence, south, sixty-eight and a quarter degrees west, twenty miles and thirty-two chains, to a rock on the Chattuga river at the thirty-fifth degree of north latitude, another corner of the boundaries agreed upon by the State of North and South Carolina; thence, down and with the Chattuga, to the beginning." For all this, they were to be paid five thousand dollars.

In the second, the boundary line between the Cherokee and Creek Nations was agreed on, the Cherokee Nation allowed the United States to build roads through its country, and the United States agreed to compensate Cherokees, like Sequoyah, who had lost property to the U.S. troops returning home after the Red Stick war. Both treaties were signed by John Lowrey, John Walker, Major Ridge, Richard Taylor, John Ross and "Cheucunsene," the latter being a scrivener's attempt at spelling Tsiyu Gan'sini, or Dragging Canoe, Young Dragging Canoe having dropped "Young" from the front of his name following the death of his late and great father. The land ceded amounted to 148 square miles, or 94,720 acres.

Word was around before long, though, that General Jackson was furious and was raising hell in Washington. It seemed that Jackson believed the treaty had given Creek land to the Cherokees, and what was worse, it was land that Jackson believed he had won from the Creeks in the war. He was demanding a new treaty, and he had managed to get himself appointed by President Madison to a commission to treat with the Cherokees.

They met on the 20th of August, at Willstown, one of the old Chickamauga towns in the Creek country claimed by the state of Alabama. The Cherokees gathered there selected delegates to attend the meeting scheduled by Jackson at the Chickasaw Council House for the next month. Sequoyah was one of those selected, and he and the other delegates were told to sell no land. After the meeting, Sequoyah talked with Agili.

"Why did they choose me?" he said. "I'm not important."

"You're as important as any Cherokee man," Agili said. "You're married, and you're a successful businessman. You're a veteran of the last war."

"I didn't do much. Why does Jackson want us to meet at the Chickasaw Council House?"

"He wants to get treaties with us, the Chickasaws and the Choctaws, all on the same day. He thinks he doesn't have time to waste with us."

"Do you think he wants more land?"

"Of course, he wants more land," Agili said, "but you can't let him have it."

"I know. We have our instructions." Sequoyah recalled the gory execution of Doublehead. "I don't need to be reminded of that."

"Well, you'll do all right. I have confidence in you, and in the rest of our delegates."

"They told us not to give up any land," Sequoyah said.

"But Jackson means to have it," said Springfrog. "He says that it's not ours anyway. It belongs to the Creeks."

"He's wrong," Bawldridge said.

"But he won't listen," said Springfrog. "And what do you think he'll do if we continue to refuse to sell it to him?"

"He'll do to us what he did to the Red Sticks," Sequoyah said. "It will be like the old days, when Sevier came, and Christian."

"That's right," said Springfrog.

"He's willing to pay our government five thousand dollars when we sign," Springfrog said, "and six thousand a year for ten years."

"It won't do any of us any good," Sequoyah said. "Remember what happened to Doublehead."

"I have an idea," Bawldridge said. "Let's tell Jackson that we don't have the authority to sign the treaty. If he forces us to sign, let's say that it's no good until it's ratified by the whole council."

"Unless it has those words in there," said Springfrog, "we won't sign."

And so they met again, this time at Turkeytown with the "whole Cherokee nation in council assembled." Sequoyah had put his X on the document beside the words "George Guess," but he was not there at Turkeytown for the ratification meeting. He'd had enough. He had not liked seeing Jackson again, and he had not liked being subjected to the kind of pressure which Jackson was so fond of using. Instead of going to Turkeytown, Sequoyah stayed home with Sally. They were in front of their house in Taskigi looking at the stars in the night sky when Bawldridge and Springfrog came by. Sally gave them coffee.

"We're safe, Sequoyah," Springfrog said. "The council ratified the treaty just the way we signed it, but because they signed it for the ratification, they sold the land, not us."

"We played our part," Sequoyah said.

"There are nine new names on the treaty," said Bawldridge. "None of them are the same as when we signed. There was nothing else we could do. Since the council agreed and put their names on there too, that proves it. They couldn't hold out against Jackson any more than we could."

"Jackson's a devil," Springfrog said.

"He's a chicken snake," said Sally Guess.

Bawldridge and Springfrog left shortly after, and Sequoyah sat silent. Sally waited a few minutes before speaking. "Sequoyah," she said, "is something wrong?"

"I'm all right," he said.

"You don't seem to be. You should be pleased that the council did what they did. Now you can't be blamed for selling the land. No one will come after you to punish you."

"The problem is that we've lost more land to the greedy white men," Sequoyah said. "They'll be living on top of us before long."

"Well, we don't need all that hunting land anymore anyway," Sally said. "You don't hunt now. You keep a store. All we need is this space right here."

"How long will they let us keep that?"

"They won't take it all, will they?"

He shrugged. "I don't believe the white men will be happy until they have all our land."

"If they took it all, where would we go?"

"They'd say, that's not their concern. They'd tell us to go west with the others. They're already trying to talk us into moving out there."

They both grew silent then, and Sequoyah thought about his name on the treaty. He thought about the way one of the white men had written his name, George Guess, and then he had put a mark beside it. He had not understood any of the English talk, and when it had all been put on paper, he could make no sense of the marks. Of course, he and the other Cherokees had their interpreters there, Wilson and McCoy, and Sequoyah had no reason to distrust either of them. Still, it would be good, he thought, to have the document marked down in his own language so he could go back to it and look it over and recall in that way just what all the words were. Already, he had forgotten much of what they said was written down on the paper he had signed.

"Sally," he said, "do you think that someone could figure out a way to write Cherokee words?"

"Ha!" she said. "Writing is for the white man's words. Not for Cherokee."

"Why not?"

"My uncle told me a story one time," she said. "He told me that when God made the Cherokees, he gave them a book. Then he made the white men, and he gave them a bow and arrows. The Cherokees looked at the book and couldn't make any sense of it, so they threw it down and walked away. They white men looked at the bow and the arrows and thought they were useless. They threw them down. When they walked away, they saw the book where the Cherokees had tossed it, and they picked it up. The Cherokees saw the bow and the arrows and picked them up. That's the way it's been ever since, and that's why we can't write our language."

"I've heard that tale too," Sequoyah said, "but I don't believe it. I heard another story once. Someone told me that he heard an old man say that one time a long time ago, we had priests who could read and write."

"You believe that?"

"I don't know. It seems to me that if white men could figure out how to put their words down to keep on paper, then Cherokees can figure it out too. White men aren't any smarter than Cherokees."

"They're getting all our land," said Sally.

"That's because there are so many of them," Sequoyah said, "and because they're so mean, and because they can write down their words to read back later on." He reached down and picked up a stick, and then he traced some lines in the dirt. "Look at this," he said. "Look at it."

Sally moved over to take a quick look at the abstract lines her husband had drawn. She shrugged and went back to sit down again looking very disinterested.

"What if I told you," Sequoyah said, "that this picture means your name, and every time you see this mark, you should say your name?"

"I'd say you're crazy," she said.

"What's crazy?" he said. "If I remember the mark, and you remember the mark, and we agree that it says 'Sally,' then we can read your name. That's all there is to it. What more could there be? It's not magic, and it's not a gift."

"It's late," she said. "I'm going to bed."

Sequoyah tossed down the stick and heaved an exasperated sigh. This woman is dull, he told himself. She's not interested in anything. What could I have been thinking about when I asked her to marry me?

7

He spent the rest of the next day making marks on paper, and he gave each mark he made a word to stand for. Each time he drew a new mark, he recited the whole list of words, assigning each to its mark. He was feeling pleased with himself. All he had to do, he thought, was keep varying his marks so that there would be no two alike. His paper supply was limited, so from the beginning, he made several symbols on each page, and when he came to the last page of his precious notebook, he began marking on the back sides of the sheets.

He stopped to look over his work, and he began to worry that he would run out of paper before he had gotten a good start on the job. Oh, well, he told himself, he would just have to make do. He would use bark, or skins, rocks even, until one of the white traders came around again with another notebook. He was anxious for the trader's visit all of a sudden. He decided that he would buy several notebooks and several pencils. There were many, many words to record.

He flipped back to the first page. Looking at the first mark, he said a word out loud. Then he looked at the second mark, and he could not remember the word he had drawn it for. He studied all the marks on the first page, only to discover that he had forgotten all the words to go with the marks. Frustrated, he slapped the notebook down on his tabletop. This was not the way. He could see that. There were just too many words, too much to remember. What had he heard about the white man's system? The marks stood for sounds. So, should he then try to isolate all the sounds

of the Cherokee language and make a mark for each sound?
Maybe.

Just then, Sally walked in. She looked angry. She looked around
the room. It was a mess. The tabletop on which he worked was
piled up with his tools, pieces of silver, papers. The blankets and
skins on the shelves around the room were piled up in no partic-
ular order. Many of them were not folded. Instead, they were
tossed in wads and heaps.

"Look at this mess," she said.

Sequoyah looked up calmly. "What?"

"This place is a mess. What do you do in here all day?"

He lifted his notebook. "I've been working on this," he said.

"On those silly marks of yours?" she said. "Why don't you give
that up and get back to work the way you used to? People are
talking about the way you ignore your business. They say you're
lazy, and they're taking pity on me because of you."

"Let them talk," he said.

"I don't like them talking about my husband. I don't want their
pity. I want you to be the way you used to be. You used to take
good care of this business, and your other businesses too. How
long has it been since you made something in silver? How long—"

He held up his hands for silence, and she stopped talking. "I'll
try to do better," he said. He stood up. "Look. I'll clean the store
up right now."

A tear ran down Sally's cheek. "I don't mean to nag," she said.
"I just want us to have a good life. It's not just for us, you know.
There's a little one coming now."

Sequoyah's eyes opened wide, and he looked at his wife in
amazement. He crossed the room to her, and he put his hands on
her shoulders.

"You?" he said. "You're going to have a little one?"

She smiled and nodded.

"That's good," he said. "That's very good. Now, you sit down.
You sit down, and I'll go to work. I'll work hard. You'll see. First,
I'll clean up this place. In the morning, I'll go see Springfrog. He
needs a wagon wheel mended. I told him before, I was too busy,
but now I'll tell him I have time. I'll work."

And he did, and he prospered, and when the time came, Sally

bore a son. He was named Tseeseletah, and they called him Tee-see. He was a joy to his proud parents. Sequoyah sat dandling him on his knee while Sally cooked. Agili came by for a visit.

"You'll stay and eat with us," Sally said.

"Thank you. That's a fine-looking boy you have there."

"Yes," Sequoyah said with a broad smile on his face. "We're both very happy with him."

"And you're doing well here again."

"Yes. I have to work hard now. I have a wife and a child."

"It's good for you," Agili said. "You're looking good."

"Yes. I feel good."

"Have you heard the news?"

"You mean that Jackson came for another treaty?"

"Yes," said Agili. "That news."

"That chicken snake," Sally said.

"That same Jackson," Agili agreed. "Did you hear about the terms?"

"No one has come around who was there," Sequoyah said. "Were you there?"

"Yes, I was," said Agili.

"And how much land did we give up this time?"

"A great deal," Agili said. "But there was something new this time."

Sequoyah waited for Agili to continue. When his cousin remained silent, he said, "So what was new?"

"They didn't offer us any money for the land. They offered us land in Arkansas where our relatives are already living. They said, anyone who wants to go west can go. They really want all of us to go out there."

"I knew it was coming," Sequoyah said, "but I didn't think it would be so soon." He held up little Teesee and looked at his fat face. "I was hoping I'd be ready for it."

"Sequoyah," Agili said. Sequoyah looked at him.

"Yes?"

"Your uncle is going." Sequoyah's only answer was an inquisitive look. "Ooloodega," Agili continued. "His son the Raven came back, and the Raven is working for Jackson. He's trying to talk us into moving west. So his father said that he would go."

"The white men are getting closer to us on all sides," Sequoyah said. He looked over his shoulder at Sally. "It might be smart to move now before they're on top of us."

"Our relatives out west are at war with the Osages out there," Agili said.

"Better the Osages than the chicken snake," Sequoyah said. "Maybe we'll go out there too."

Sequoyah rode into Willstown. He had heard that his uncle Ooloodega and his adopted brother the Raven would be there signing people up for the move west. He had talked it over with Sally, and they had agreed. It was a good time to make a move. Out west they would have friends and relatives. Sequoyah's uncle Tahlonteskee was there already. From what Sequoyah had heard, Tahlonteskee was the chief out there. They called themselves the Western Cherokee Nation. And going west with Tahlonteskee's brother, Ooloodega, he would have two uncles there. He and Sally would build themselves a new home away from the pesky Americans, and Teesee would have a good place in which to grow up.

Willstown was bustling with activity. As he rode in, he could hear people arguing about the idea of removing themselves from their homes and going to some place unknown out west. They talked about Jackson, and they talked about his minion, Sam Houston, Sequoyah's adopted cousin, or brother, the Raven. They talked about how John Jolly, Sequoyah's uncle Ooloodega, was at that very moment signing people up to move west. Some of the talk was hot. People were angry with Ooloodega and the Raven. The more Cherokees that moved west, they said, the fewer would be left at home to resist the white men.

Sequoyah rode on. He saw some people standing in a long line, and when he rode closer, he could see that they were waiting to get up to a table. Then he saw that a man was sitting on the other side of the table making marks on a paper. Ooloodega was standing beside the man. Sequoyah rode over to the back side of the table and dismounted.

"Uncle," he said.

Ooloodega turned to see his nephew Sequoyah standing there and smiling. He clapped his hands on Sequoyah's shoulders. "I'm glad to see you, nephew," he said. "What brings you to Willstown? Are you going to sign up? Will you be going with us?"

"I came here to talk with you about that," Sequoyah said.

"Sam," said Ooloodega, "look who's here."

Sam Houston turned his head and looked up to see Sequoyah. He smiled and stood up, pushing back his chair, and he threw his arms around his adopted cousin.

"Brother," he said. "It's good to see you."

"It's good to see you," Sequoyah said. "But I've come at a busy time for you."

"We'll have some time soon," Houston said. "When we get through here, we'll go someplace where we can sit and visit, just the three of us. We have much to talk about."

They found a table in a corner of a local trading post where they could sit and visit in relative privacy. Sam Houston got a jug of whiskey and three cups. He poured them all full and passed them around.

"So what's new with you?" he asked Sequoyah.

"I have a wife now," Sequoyah said, "and we have a son. Just before I started over here, she told me another one is coming."

"That's wonderful," Houston said. "I'm anxious to meet your family. And they're all doing well, I hope."

"Everything is good," Sequoyah said. "Except that the whites are coming closer all the time. That's why I came looking for you two."

"Are you thinking of going west with us?" Houston asked.

Sequoyah sipped his whiskey and nodded his head. "I'm thinking about it. Out there, what will it be like? Will it be the way it is here?"

"It's like it used to be here," Houston said. "Game is plenty. Whites are few."

"There's a new country," Ooloodega said. "The Western Cherokee Nation, and my brother is the chief."

"I heard there's a war," Sequoyah said.

"Yes," said Houston. "With the Osages. But the Cherokees are whipping them easily, and the United States is trying to negotiate a peace between the two tribes. The Osage war is nothing for you to worry about. They don't get into our towns. The Cherokees are led by Dutch and Degadoga. They've carried the war to the Osages. The Cherokee towns in Arkansas are safe."

"And there are no whites?"

"There are soldiers at Fort Smith and at Fort Gibson," Houston said.

"And there are missionaries," added Ooloodega.

"I don't like soldiers and missionaries," Sequoyah said.

"There aren't very many," said Houston, "and they won't bother you."

"To make my living," Sequoyah said, "I'm a blacksmith. I'm a silversmith. And I have a store. How will I make a living if I move west?"

"The same way," Houston said. "We need blacksmiths and we need trading posts. You'll have plenty of work."

"Well," Sequoyah said. He took another drink. "Will you put my name on your list?"

"Gladly," Houston said. "With a family of three?"

Sequoyah thought about some relatives and friends in Taskigi. "Put down twelve," he said. He drank again. His cup was empty. When he put it on the table, Houston refilled it.

"Twelve," Houston said. "That's good. I'm glad you came today, Sequoyah. I haven't seen you since the Horseshoe. That was a great fight, wasn't it?"

"Yes," Sequoyah said, but he thought, *it was a slaughter, and I wish I had not been there.* He took another drink to try to drive the war images out of his head.

Houston reached into his coat for a rolled-up paper. "I might as well get your name on this while I'm thinking about it," he said. He rolled the paper out onto the table and took out a pencil from his pocket. Sequoyah watched closely as Houston made some small marks on the bottom of the paper. "There," he said. "You're signed up." He rolled the paper again and tucked it back inside his coat.

"Sam," Sequoyah said, "what did you draw?"

"I wrote 'George Guess from Taskigi,'" Houston said, "and then I wrote, 'twelve.'"

"Tell me about when you wrote Tsatsi."

"In English," said Houston, "it sounds like George. George. I spelled it this way: G-E-O-R-G-E. George."

"I don't understand," Sequoyah said.

"Well, they're called letters," said Houston. "A letter stands for a sound."

"I heard someone else say that," Sequoyah said. "The marks—letters—stand for sounds. Show me."

Houston drew a big G on the tabletop.

"This one is called gee," he said. "And it makes that sound. Gee. Or rather, it makes the beginning of that sound. It takes other letters with it to make a word, or a syllable." He went on to spell the word out slowly and give a sound to each letter as he added it. Sequoyah listened, fascinated, but he thought that it all sounded a bit complicated. Besides, it wouldn't do him any good. It was white man's spelling for white man's words. He had only been interested in the principle, and he had gotten that. The marks, symbols, stood for sounds. He had heard it before, but he now had it confirmed by the Raven.

So that was what he needed: marks for sounds. Not pictures for words, but marks for sounds. He resolved that when he had time to get back to it, that would be his new approach. He would make marks for sounds. He wondered how many sounds there were in all the Cherokee words. He wondered how long it would take him to figure it all out. He took another drink, and he told himself that he would tell no one. He would work on it in secrecy. No one else need know what he was up to.

Then he thought about the coming move. It was a major move. One that would take weeks. Maybe months. He wouldn't have any time for his studies for a while. First, there was packing to do; everything had to be packed. And if he wanted to take all of his things, his and Sally's, then he would need a wagon and a team to pull it. There was much to do to get ready for the move.

Then there would be the actual move. And once they arrived in the new location, he would have to locate a home site and a place for his store, and then he would have to build them and then unpack everything. He sighed and took another drink. It would be a good long while before he would have the time to start sorting out the sounds in the Cherokee language.

"Brother," Houston said, "you got awfully quiet."

"I'm thinking about the big move," Sequoyah said, and it was at least partly true. "It's going to be a lot of work, and it will take much time."

"That's true enough," Houston said.

"But it will go quickly," Ooloodega said. "Soon we'll be in Arkansas, in the Western Cherokee Nation. It will be worth all the work and all the time. You'll see."

Sequoyah woke up the next morning on the floor of the trading post. He opened his eyes slowly and looked up to find that he was under the table. He rolled onto his side and then onto his stomach. With a moan, he got up to his knees, but he bumped his head on the tabletop. He moaned. He backed out from under the table. Then, with a hand on the tabletop, he managed to get himself to his feet. His knee hurt. He stretched and looked around. There was no sign of Ooloodega or of the Raven. That was all right. He knew when and where he was supposed to meet them again to start the trip west.

He was hungry, and he thought about finding something to eat, but then he decided that he wanted some more whiskey. If he could find him some more good whiskey, he wouldn't really need any food. Whiskey would do all right. That was all he needed. It didn't take him long to find it, and soon he was drinking again. He lost track of time, and when he at last started home, he had no idea how many days he had been gone. He was still woozy, and he still had some whiskey. He drank as he rode, and his body leaned first one way, then the other in the saddle.

Sally did not yell at him when he got home. She didn't ask questions. She looked hurt, but all she did was ask him if he was hungry. He said that he was, and she got him some food and put it on the table. He almost wished that she would call him names and chastise him. He didn't like this silence from her, this long-suffering look on her face.

She made him feel as if he had done something terrible to her, to her and to little Teesee, and to, well, to the other one that was coming. He was supposed to be responsible. He had a wife and a child and another child on the way. He had a business to take care of, and he was planning to take his family on a major trip to a country unknown to them. Suddenly he was conscious of his appearance. He was dirty, and his clothes were rumpled. He knew that he must smell bad, too. He was ashamed of himself.

He finished his meal, thanked his wife quietly, got up from the table and left. He got some clean clothes and headed for the river. He would clean himself up and then go back to the house. He had to tell Sally what he had done. They would have to talk in order to make all their plans and get all the packing done. There were a number of decisions to be made. They had to get ready for the big move.

He wondered what sort of mood she would be in when he got back to the house. Then he told himself that it did not matter. If she yelled and screamed at him, he just wouldn't listen. If she said that he was crazy and refused to make the move with him, well, so be it. He would make the move without her.

8

Sequoyah and Sally began preparing for their big move, but they did not pack up the things he needed for his work. It would be a while before they would start west, and in the meantime, they would need money. They would also need money to finance the journey, so he went back to work at all his trades. Sally gave birth to a healthy and beautiful baby girl, and they called her Ahyoka. Teesee was walking and beginning to talk. Things were looking good until the day the white trader came by the store.

"I don't want to buy anything," Sequoyah told the man. "I'm trying to get rid of what I have."

"Oh? Are you going out of business?" the man asked, in his passable Cherokee.

"I'm taking my family west with Ooloodega," Sequoyah said. "To the Western Cherokee Nation."

"Oh. To Arkansas. I see," the man said. "Well, I wish you luck and a good journey. But, say, I do have something here I think you might be interested in."

He smiled and his eyes glinted as he reached into his pack and pulled out several notepads and pencils. Then Sequoyah's eyes lit up. The man knew him, all right. "Yes," he said. "I'll take those."

As soon as the white man was gone, Sequoyah sat down at his table with a new pad of paper, and he thought for a moment about the sounds of his Cherokee language. He thought first of his name. Sequoyah. Then he thought of the opossum and the hog. Sikwa. He thought of the color, blue. *Sakonige*. The number one came into his mind. *Sagwu. Sasa*, the goose. *Sali*, persimmon. *Selu* and *sedi*, corn and walnut. Lots of words began with that same hissing sound. Several more came into his mind, and he was not even thinking hard about it. He made a mark on the paper. He told himself it represented the hissing sound, and he was pleased. He could start to write all those words and many more with that one mark. At last, he thought, he was on the right track.

But it was only a beginning. As he thought through the list of words that began with the hissing sound, he realized that most of them had different second sounds: sagwu, sikwa, selu. He would have to come up with many more marks to represent all those other sounds. He made more abstract drawings. Soon, though, he realized that he had forgotten what sounds he had assigned to some of the symbols. He heaved a sigh and started over again. Slowly, this work began to consume his days.

It was a few days later before Sally noticed what was happening. They were packing, and they were trying to eliminate all their inventory in the store, so the lack of business there caused her no immediate concern. But one day a man passing by saw her outside her home gathering sticks of wood and stopped to chat.

"What's your husband doing with his time?" he asked. "I have a mule that needs new shoes. I asked Sequoyah to do the work, but he said he didn't have the time. He was too busy with other work. I couldn't see that he was busy with anything except making funny marks on paper. They didn't even look like anything either. They weren't pictures of anything. Just funny marks. What's he up to anyway?"

The man left shortly after that. It was a cold day, too cold to stand outside and make small talk. But he left Sally puzzled and worried.

That same day some men stopped by the store to see Sequoyah. Charles Hicks was with them. They found Sequoyah at his table busy at his work on the symbols, but they did not ask him about the peculiar marks. Usually people were curious and asked him what he was up to. They were full of questions when they saw him at work. Hicks and these others did not seem to care about what he was doing. They had something else on their minds. That much was clear.

"Come in and warm yourselves at my fire," Sequoyah said.

The men gathered around the fireplace, and Charles Hicks

stepped forward. "Sequoyah," Hicks said, "we've come to see you because we heard that your name is on that list of Ooloodega of people who are planning to move west."

"Yes," Sequoyah said. "It's true. I put my mark on that paper. Ooloodega is my uncle, my mother's brother, and the Raven is his son by adoption. So the Raven is my brother. They told me about the move. They said it's good out there. My other uncle, Tahlonteskee, is the chief of the Cherokees in the west. So we're planning to move out there with them, me and my wife."

"We came to ask you to reconsider," said Hicks. "Many of the people are angry at Houston and John Jolly. They're angry at the others, those like you, who agreed to make the move with them."

"I don't understand," Sequoyah said. "Why should they care where I or Ooloodega or anyone else lives?"

"We care," said Hicks, "because the Americans want to kick us all out west. They want all of our land. When you agree to go, you're helping them. They get a few of us out of here at a time. Then they'll come back for more. And when they told you there was land out there for you, they took some of our land here in exchange. It's another way of getting our land. We want you to sign this paper." Hicks produced a paper from underneath his jacket and held it out toward Sequoyah. Sequoyah took it and looked at it. It was covered in the white man's marks, which, of course, meant nothing to him. "It says that those whose names are on there have changed their minds," Hicks said. "It says that even though you signed that other paper, you've decided to stay here."

Sequoyah pondered the thought. He had told Ooloodega and the Raven that he would move. It had seemed like a good idea. Sally was getting ready to move. He didn't like to go back on his word, and he did not know what Sally would say if he told her he had changed his mind.

"Umm, I don't know," he said. "I told everyone that I'd move."

"Sequoyah," said Hicks, "it's dangerous for you to have your name on Ooloodega's paper. Some people are very angry. They're even talking about killing those of you whose names are on that list."

"Killing?" Sequoyah said. "Just because I mean to move? Am I not a free man to live where I want to live?" He looked at Hicks, and then he looked at the other men, those who had remained silent all this time. The expressions on their faces were stern.

"These are dangerous times," said Hicks. "We're in a war with the Americans, only it's a war of paper. It's a war for our homeland and our way of life."

"The more the whites press on us here," Sequoyah said, "the more our way of life is changing. The Raven said that we can live the way we want to live out west."

"That may be true, but there are many others who don't see it that way. They say that this is our land. The Creator made this land for us. We've always been here. Our fathers and their fathers are buried in this land. We built our farms here and our homes. No one has a right to take that away from us. It says all that on this paper."

Sequoyah thought again. Hicks's case was a good one. He tried to recall all the reasons the Raven and Ooloodega had given for going west, and in the face of these new arguments, they suddenly seemed weak. The thought of someone coming to kill him for having his name on that paper was more than a bit unsettling, and besides all that, he was busy with this other important work.

"Sequoyah," Hicks said, "just because the Americans aren't shooting at us, don't think that this war is not serious. If you help them, some will call you a traitor."

"All right," Sequoyah said. "Put my name there on your paper, and I'll make my mark."

"You won't move west?"

"No. I'll stay here."

Hicks and the others left, pleased that they won Sequoyah over to their side, and Sequoyah went back to his work. He was frustrated. The business about the move did not matter all that much to him. He was beginning to get lost in his symbols. That was the source of his frustration. There were too many of them, and he could not remember the sound values he had placed on them. He was struggling with them, when Sally came in carrying Ahyoka and leading Teesee by his hand. She slammed the door behind her.

"What are you doing?" she demanded.

"I'm working," Sequoyah said.

"You're wasting your time with that foolishness again," she said.

"This is important work," Sequoyah said. "If I can just figure out—"

"If you would do some real work, we'd have some money," Sally snapped, interrupting him. "You don't hunt and you don't farm. So we have to have money."

"I'm minding the store," he said. "I can't make people come in."

"But you can run them off if they come bringing you work to do," she said.

"What do you mean?"

"I know you sent a man away who came looking for a blacksmith. He told me so. You said you were too busy. Too busy with what? With your silly marks? Your pictures that don't even look like anything? Would you care if I and the children starved to death? I don't think so. Our neighbors think you're lazy. They're talking about you again. Some of them think you're crazy—or worse. One old woman told me that she thought you were conjuring with those strange marks of yours. 'They're good for nothing else,' she said. 'He must be making magic with them.' "

"You know what I'm doing," Sequoyah said. "I've explained it to you. What difference does it make what our neighbors think?"

"I don't want them thinking I'm married to a crazy man. I'll be glad when we leave this place and get away from these neighbors."

"We're not going," Sequoyah said.

"What?"

"Charles Hicks and some others came by today. They said they don't want us to go. They said some people are thinking about killing anyone who put his name on that list. They had a new list of people who changed their minds, and they asked me to put my name on that list."

"And you did?"

"Yes."

"So now you can't even make a decision and stick to it. Well, if we're not going, then you should get back to work on this store."

Ahyoka started to cry.

"Now see what you've done by raising your voice," Sequoyah said. "You've upset the baby."

"You make *me* cry," Sally said. "Not going. After all the packing I've done."

"You don't want them to come and kill me because I made my mark on that paper, do you?"

"No," she said. "Instead they'll come and kill you for being a witch." She stalked over to the table and jerked his notepad up. "For making these stupid marks." She carried the notepad across the room with her and tossed it into the fire. "There," she said. "Now do something worthwhile with your time."

Sally grabbed Teesee by the hand and pulled him out of the corner where he had been lurking. The baby in her arms was still crying as she jerked open the door and stormed out. She didn't bother closing the door behind her this time. Sequoyah sat and stared after her. Finally, he got up and walked over to shut the door. He turned and looked at the notepad, its pages curling and blackening in the fire.

It doesn't really matter, he told himself. I had forgotten what all those marks meant. I was on the wrong track again. Perhaps Sally did me a favor by burning those leaves. Now I'll have to start over. He went back to his chair at the table and opened a new pad. He took up his pencil and stared at the fresh, blank page. Who was it had told him about that old story? Ah, yes. Big Thighs. Big Thighs had told him about the priests of long ago.

It was cold, and his knee was hurting, as he rode up to the front of Big Thighs's cabin. As he dismounted, the door of the cabin opened, and Big Thighs peeked out. When he saw who his visitor was he threw the door open wide.

"Sequoyah," he said, "come in."

Sequoyah went into the cabin and limped across the floor to stand by the fire. Big Thighs closed the door. "What brings you around?" he asked.

"I want to talk to you," Sequoyah said. "I want to ask you about something you told me once."

"All right," said Big Thighs, "but first, let me get us some whiskey. My wife has gone to visit her mother, so we're safe."

He laughed as he went for the jug, and Sequoyah laughed with him. In another minute, they were seated at the table and Big Thighs had poured their drinks. Sequoyah took a sip.

"Ah," he said, "that's good whiskey. I'm glad your wife is gone." Both men laughed again.

"So what did you want to talk about?" Big Thighs asked.

"You told me once, I think, that there was a time when the Cherokee priests could read and write our language."

"Oh. That. Well, I heard such a tale one time. You know, they say that we had priests a long time ago, and they ruled over us. They could do anything they wanted to do. You've heard that story."

"Yes," Sequoyah said. "They were called the Ani-Kutani, and when a hunter came home to find out they had taken his wife, he got his friends together. They killed all the priests. I know that much, but you said that the priests—"

"Could read and write. Yes. I know. But I didn't really tell you that the priests could read and write. I told you that I heard someone say that one time. A long time ago, he said, our priests could read and write. But what difference does it make? They killed all the priests. And it was a long time ago. So even if it's true, it's lost. It doesn't make any difference to us today."

Sequoyah took another drink. "It makes a difference to me," he said. "I want to know about it. Who told you that tale?"

"I think it was old Goingsnake," Big Thighs said. "Yes. It was Goingsnake. He told the story. He said, 'in those days, our priests could read and write.' But he also said that we came into this country from a place far north of here that was covered in ice where the nights were long. So how can we believe what he says? I heard that this place right here was given to us by the Creator, and that we've always been here."

"Yes," Sequoyah said. "I've heard that too. But what if Goingsnake is right?"

Big Thighs shrugged and took a drink. Then he poured more whiskey into his cup and into Sequoyah's. "What difference does it make?" he said. "The white men are trying to take all our land anyway. What difference does it make if we've always been here or if we came here from a cold place in the north, if we all have to move west anyway?"

"Charles Hicks said we don't all have to move west," Sequoyah said. "I took my name off of Ooloodega's list. I'm not moving."

"Maybe not this time, but the next. The Americans will come back, and they'll take more land. Maybe next time, they'll take the land your house is on. Maybe this land right here, where my house is. Then they'll make us move."

"Maybe you're right," Sequoyah said. "I don't know." But his mind was not on the future. He was thinking about the priests and whether or not they could read and write the Cherokee language. If they could, he wondered, how did they do it? What did their marks look like, and what did they stand for? Part of him wanted to make an excuse to Big Thighs and leave to go look for Goingsnake and hear more of the story. But Big Thighs's wife was gone, and Big Thighs had good whiskey. Part of him wanted to stay. He took another drink.

"You know," he said, "if those priests had written down the story of where we came from, and if they had kept it for us and taught us how to read, then we'd know the truth. But since they did not keep it for us, we have those different tales, and we don't know which one to believe."

"It doesn't matter," Big Thighs said.

"We need to be writing things down now," Sequoyah said. "Otherwise, our grandchildren will have the same problem about these times we're in right now. They won't know what really happened. All they'll know is what the white man has written down, and it will all be lies. We need to write down the truth for our grandchildren."

"But we can't write, Sequoyah. Even if the priests did write things down, they were all killed, and the men who killed them most likely burned all their writings. It's lost, if it ever existed. We can't write our language. Maybe some Cherokees who've gone to the white man's schools can write it down in English."

"That won't be any good," Sequoyah said. "If they've learned English and the white man's writing, then they've learned other things too from the white men. They've been taught lies about us. They no longer know the truth about their own people."

"Well, it's the best that can be done. Quit worrying about it. Here. Have some more whiskey."

He poured again, and Sequoyah took another drink. Big Thighs could not be right about this, he thought. There had to be a way to do it. If white men could make marks to represent the sounds of their ugly language, then marks could be made for the beautiful sounds of Cherokee. He was convinced of that. No white man was any smarter than a Cherokee. And if any Cherokee could figure out a way to make the signs work for the language, then he could do it, for he was also convinced that he was as smart as any other man. He took another drink, and his head was beginning to feel light.

"Well," he said, "I'm going to go see Goingsnake. Maybe in the morning. I'll get him to tell me the whole story."

He noticed that his speech was slurred, and he knew that he was drunk. Soon, nothing more would matter to him. Not the writing. Not the white man's hunger for Cherokee land. Not whether to move or not to move. Not Sally's anger at him for neglecting his work, or for changing his mind, or for wandering off to see Big Thighs without telling her where he was going. None of it would matter to him once he was drunk enough. And Big Thighs had good whiskey.

White man's whiskey. It was at least as wonderful an invention as was writing. It was fast and sure relief from boredom, from anxiety, from fear, from ugly white men and from nagging wives.

"Whiskey is the best thing," he said. "It will never let you down."

"At least, not until the bottle's empty," Big Thighs said. Then he laid back, belched, farted and passed out.

9

It was late when Sequoyah woke up the next morning. He was on the floor of Big Thighs's cabin. He sat up and looked around. Big Thighs was still out cold. Sequoyah stood up on unsteady legs. His knee hurt, and he staggered as he moved over to the table. He lifted the whiskey jug and found that it was empty. No wonder he had slept so late, and no wonder that Big Thighs was still asleep. Sequoyah checked his clothing. It was not too badly rumpled. He smoothed the white trade shirt he was wearing and looked around for his buckskin jacket. He found it, shook it out and put it on. His turban was unwound and in a rumpled pile on the floor. Leaning over with a groan, he picked it up. In a few minutes he had it wrapped neatly around his head. A pan of water sat on a sideboard against the wall, and he washed his face in it. Then, shaking the excess water off his hands, he left the cabin.

The late morning air was cold on his wet face and hands as he saddled and mounted his horse. It didn't bother him. It was invigorating. It would help to wake him up and to sober him up. He knew that Sally would be looking for him, but he had urgent business. He was sober, it was a new day and he had need to visit with Goingsnake.

It was late in the day when he at last arrived at the home of Goingsnake. He found the old man at home with two of his wives, sitting in front of a fire inside his cabin. When Goingsnake saw that he had a visitor, he had his wives prepare *kanohena*, the sour hominy drink traditionally served to visitors. It was a tradition, like many others, that was not often kept in these changing times, and

Sequoyah appreciated its unexpected presentation. After the ka-nohena, coffee was served. Then they made some small talk, and at last, the old man said, "What is it that brings you to see me, Sequoyah?"

Sequoyah suddenly became totally serious, almost somber. He leaned forward in his chair, his elbows on his knees.

"I heard a story," he said. "Or a part of a story. It was Big Thighs who told me, and he said that he heard it from you."

"I'm an old man," Goingsnake said. "I'm filled with stories."

"This one was about a migration long ago," Sequoyah said. "It said that our ancestors came from someplace in the far north, a place of cold and ice and long, dark nights."

"Yes. I remember that one," Goingsnake said. "My own grand-father told it to me. He said that the people traveled for many days without ever seeing the sun. They were looking for the sun and a place that was not covered by ice and snow. At long last, they came to this place, and they settled here. They thought to remain here forever, but they had never heard of the white man."

"Yes," Sequoyah said, "but there was something more."

"Oh?"

"Big Thighs said that you told him, 'in those days, our priests could read and write.' "

"Oh, that." The old man smiled and nodded his head slowly. "That's what my grandfather said. 'In those days, our priests could read and write.' "

"The Ani-Kutani?"

"I believe so."

"The ones who were all killed?"

"Well, almost all."

"You mean, some survived?"

"So I was told."

"And the writing?" Sequoyah asked, unable to conceal his ex-citement.

"You want to know about the writing?"

"Yes."

"Ah, well, I know very little. I'm afraid that it's lost."

"But it did exist?"

"Yes, I think so. I believe it did."

"Then it can be done. If it has been done before, it can be done again."

Goingsnake shook his head slowly. "I don't know," he said. "It would be a very difficult task."

"So the writing was lost when the priests were killed?"

"No. It seems that at least one of the priests who survived knew the writing. He had been away when all the killing was done. When he came home, the people were no longer in the mood to kill. He abandoned his role as priest and tried to live the rest of his days as an ordinary human being, but he did not want the writing to be lost. Secretly, he taught his nephew." Sequoyah's eyes opened wide. "It was passed along in that way for several generations, but at last, someone forgot to keep it going. It's lost, as far as I know."

Sequoyah leaned back in his chair, disappointed. "It would seem so," he said. "Most people think that I'm crazy for even believing that it can be done."

Goingsnake wrinkled his brow and studied Sequoyah. "Why are you asking these questions about the writing?" he asked.

Sequoyah gave a shrug. "I've been thinking," he said, "that we should be able to write our language. That's all. But my wife and all our neighbors think that I'm crazy. You've heard that story about the book and the bow?"

"Yes," said Goingsnake, nodding with amused understanding. "It's not a very old story."

"Others say it doesn't matter. They say that if I want to write, I should learn English and write in the white man's words. But if we could write, then we wouldn't wonder if we came from the cold country or if we were always here. It would be written down. We could send messages to each other in troublesome times, the way the white men do. We could have letters from our relatives in the west, and they could tell us what it really is like out there."

"You're quite serious about this, aren't you, Sequoyah?"

"Sometimes I think of nothing else for days at a time. I made pictures for some words, but then I found that I couldn't make pictures for all words. I could draw 'horse,' for example, but I could not draw, 'I want to buy a horse.' Then I tried to make marks for different sounds, but there are so many sounds that I forgot what some of my marks were supposed to sound like. I keep thinking that there ought to be a way to do it."

The old man asked one of his wives to bring more coffee. When she had poured it, he leaned back in his chair. "I'll tell you what I remember," he said. "It's not very much. We have two kinds of sounds, Sequoyah. The first kind has six different ones. Ah. Eh. Ee. Oh. Oo. Uh. But we can't make words out of just those sounds. So we use other sounds to put with those five. Like ga, ge, gee, go, goo, guh. Do you understand that?"

"Yes. I think so."

"With just the 'oh' sound, there is go, ko, lo, ho, mo, jo, do, so, and on and on like that."

"So for the writing—"

"You could make a picture or a mark for each of those different sounds, and if you could do that, you could write any word in our language."

"I can do that, Goingsnake. Do you recall any of the marks?"

Goingsnake shook his head a little sadly. "No," he said. "Not well. Maybe I can remember how to write down one word. But I don't have anything to write it on or to write it with."

"Old man," said the oldest of the two women. Goingsnake looked around sharply. "Use my dye and this stick and draw on the table."

She brought a bowl and a stick to the table, and Goingsnake stood up and made his way over there. He sat in a chair at the table, and he took up the stick and dipped it into the dye. Sequoyah hurried over to stand behind him and watch over his shoulder.

"I'll write Jalagi," Goingsnake said. He had already started his first stroke. Sequoyah watched with fascination as the first symbol began to take shape. It was an elaborate symbol with beautifully flowing, curving lines. When Goingsnake had finished it, he said, "That one is for 'Ja.'" He drew a second for "la," and a third for "gi." He leaned back with a sigh. "That's all I can remember," he said.

Sequoyah asked for the use of the stick, and he copied the symbols onto the white sleeve of his shirt. "It will be enough," he said. "I'll make the rest."

May, 1819

Sequoyah was busy at his notepad creating symbols to go with all the syllables in the Cherokee language. He worked hard to make his new symbols consistent with the design of the three he had gotten from Goingsnake, and so that he would not forget the sound values of the symbols, he tried to come up with pictures to go with each. For instance, he drew a picture of a horse, and underneath the horse, he wrote the new symbols for the three syllables, "so," "qui," and "li." The process was slow, but it was steady, and Sequoyah was happy with his progress. He had just finished a drawing of a bear so that he would have a picture to remember the symbols for "yo" and "na," when Agili came in. Sequoyah looked up from his work.

"Welcome, Agili," he said.

"I come with bad news," said Agili. "When you hear it, I may not be so welcome."

"What is it? Tell me."

"We've signed yet another treaty. This time your land is sold. This very place where we are right now. It's gone, Sequoyah. So is your house. You'll have to move."

"How could someone sell my home?"

"The Americans demanded this land for the land they say they have given us in Arkansas."

"I didn't take any of that land."

"They said your name was among those who signed up to go out there."

"Of course it was. I signed that paper with the Raven and Ooloodega, but then I signed another that said I changed my mind. And here I am. So I did not go, did I?"

"Still they said that they must have this land for that in the west. I'm sorry, cousin. You have to move."

So Sequoyah's great work was interrupted. He was forty-one years old, and he had lived all his life there in or just outside of Taskigi. Now he and Sally packed everything they could take with them on the backs of a few horses. They left behind everything that was too big or too clumsy for that mode of travel.

"They took our homes away from us for land in the west," Sequoyah said to Sally. "I guess maybe we should go on and move out there, but Willstown will be a good place to start from. We'll go to Willstown first. Maybe we can get a wagon there."

"Will we get me a new spinning wheel and cotton cards?" she said. "I don't care about the plow and the harness. You never used them anyway. But what about my table and chairs?"

"I'll get a new table and chairs for you," Sequoyah said. "And a new spinning wheel."

They found themselves a place to live in Willstown, but they needed money for their trip west. Sequoyah sold a few silver pieces, and he did a little work as a blacksmith, but soon he was back at work full-time on his writing. Anytime anyone said anything to him, he would run through the syllables of all the words that person had said to see if there were any he had overlooked. Every day, he was creating new characters for newly noted syllables. Then he would search for something which contained those new symbols for which he could make a drawing to be sure he would remember the sound value of the symbols. It was time-consuming work, and still, Sally did not understand the importance. Still she nagged at him for neglecting to do his part in feeding and clothing the family. She reminded him of her lost spinning wheel and cards and table and chairs.

He listened for a while to the nagging, to the children running and playing and sometimes crying, but at last it was too much for him. It was interfering with his work. One morning he got up from bed and walked off into the woods carrying an ax. He selected a spot for a small cabin, and he started cutting trees. He worked hard, and he worked fast, and in a few days he had built himself a cabin. In another few days, he had a rough table and chair. He brought his papers and his pencils to this cabin, and there he could work on the writing without disturbances. The work went well.

"They say that Sequoyah has gone crazy," one man said. "He's practically abandoned his wife and children."

"He spends all his time in that little cabin he made in the woods. All alone. And what does he do there? He makes strange marks on paper," said another.

"They must be conjuring marks," said a third. "He's a witch, and he'll be using those marks and other things against us."

"Are you sure they're conjuring marks?"

"Of course. What else could they be? They're not pictures of anything."

"Someone said that he thinks he can write our language."

"That's crazy."

"Well, whatever the truth may be, someone should make him stop all that craziness."

They crept through the woods carrying torches for light, but the torches were also for something else. The man in the lead stopped. He held up a hand to halt the ones coming along behind him. They waited for his signal. He studied the cabin ahead, a lone cabin in the woods. No light came from the cabin. It appeared to be empty. If the crazy man had been there, he would have a candle burning for light. Besides, they had checked at his house in Wills-town, and someone had said he had seen him come home. The man felt sure that the cabin was empty. He waved an arm and stepped forward. The others followed.

The leader stepped up to the door, and the others spread out to both his sides. They were nervous. The flames of their torches caused eerie shadows to dance around them in the woods. From somewhere in the darkness, a whippoorwill called out its lonesome song, and an owl hooted. The men looked around themselves in all directions, as their leader opened the door to the cabin and jumped back—just in case.

Nothing came out at him. There was no sound from inside. He stepped in with his torch and looked around. No one was there. On the table, papers were spread all around. He stepped over and held his torch high. He saw a drawing of a horse, and another of a pig. He saw sheets of paper covered with the strange marks, and he shuddered and felt a cold chill run over his skin.

A second man stuck his head and his torch inside the cabin.

"Well?" he said.

"He's not here," the leader said, "but his evil marks are here on the table. Let's burn it."

He dropped his torch on the tabletop, turned and ran for the door. The other man moved quickly out of his way, and then he stuck his own torch underneath the lowest log on the front wall. The other men planted their torches here and there around the outside of the cabin. They all backed off to wait and watch. Soon the inside of the cabin was lit up with the flames from the torches in there. Then, slowly, fire crept up the outside walls from three different locations. The men waited until they were sure the blaze would consume the entire cabin and everything in it. Then they turned and ran through the dark woods.

Sequoyah felt good that morning. He knew that he was almost done with his great work. He was still listening carefully to everything he heard spoken in his own language, just to make sure there were no syllables he had failed to account for. But he believed that he had drawn them all. And he had made pictures which included almost all of the sounds so that he would not forget which sound went with which mark.

He knew that Sally was angry and frustrated, and he really could not blame her. She was working hard, trying to take care of their family. There was no way she could understand the importance of what he was doing. But it wouldn't be long before he would be able to tell everyone. He would show everyone what he had done, and then they would all understand. They would understand, and they would make use of his work, and then all would be forgiven. Sally would at last know that he was not crazy, or lazy, but that he'd had great work to do for the good of all Cherokee people. He was proud, and he was anxious.

He walked through the woods towards his cabin, and as he drew close, he thought that he could smell smoke and burnt wood in the morning air. The closer he came to his cabin, the stronger the smell. At last, he stepped into the small clearing, and he saw it. He saw, not his cabin, but a pile of black ash where his cabin had been. He thought of the time and the labor he had spent cutting the trees, notching the logs, fitting it all together to build his cabin.

Then he thought of all his paper with all his work: the symbols, the pictures, the entire writing system for the Cherokee language. The fools, he thought. What do they think they know? They have no idea what they've destroyed. There is no way they can know the value of that work. They call me a madman, but one day they'll see. I'll show them the truth. He stood quietly, staring at the blackened mess. Then he thought, "sogwili," and in his mind, he saw the three symbols for the word. He thought, "yansa," and he saw those two symbols. He thought of longer words and phrases, and he found that he could recall all of the symbols.

Then he laughed out loud, and he thought with glee, they've not wasted my labor. Last night, when they came out here to do this, they wasted their own. They thought me a fool, but they are the fools for sneaking around in the middle of the night and burning down a house. They wasted their own foolish efforts because all of the work is done. I can write down anything that anyone can say in the Cherokee language, and I can read it back, word for word, ten days or a year from now. It's finished, and it is all in my head. Now it cannot be lost unless they kill me.

10

He was still sitting there alone in the woods staring at the blackened spot where his cabin had been, when Agili came up beside him. Sequoyah looked up at his cousin. Neither man spoke for another moment, until Agili sat down beside Sequoyah.

"I came to see how you are," Agili said.

"I'm all right."

"I heard some talk in town," said Agili. "They were saying that some men had come out here last night and burned your cabin. I went by your house, but Sally said you had left early this morning. She said you'd be out here. She hadn't heard about the burning yet."

"Did you tell her?"

"Yes."

"I suppose she was pleased about it."

"She did not seem particularly displeased," Agili said. "Sequoyah, I know who did this to you."

Sequoyah shrugged. "I doesn't matter," he said. "I know many who would approve of the action whether they were the ones or not. It doesn't matter which ones actually did it."

"But all your work—"

"It doesn't matter."

"What will you do now? Will you give it up? Because if you don't give it up, I'm afraid the next time will be worse on you. Some are saying that you've been involved out here in making bad medicine."

"I'm not a medicine man," Sequoyah said.

"But they won't believe that. They're saying that there is no explanation for what you've been doing other than witchcraft. Some are even saying—"

"What? That I should be killed?"

Agili looked at the ground between his feet. "Yes," he said.

"Don't worry, old friend. I'll be all right."

"The time has come for me to do something," Sequoyah told Sally back at their home in Willstown. "I'm going to make a long trip. I don't know how long it will take, but I'll be coming back."

"Where are you going?"

"I'm going to visit Arkansas and the Cherokees out there. I have something to do," he said, "and while I'm there, I'll look it over and see if we should move."

"What am I supposed to do while you're gone? How will I feed our children? Aren't you even worried about leaving me and the children alone?"

"Sally," he said, "if I stay here, Agili says, I might be killed. There are people here who think that I've been making bad medicine. They're afraid of me. That's why they burned my cabin. If I stay, and they kill me, then you and the children will be left without me anyway. If I go and do what I have in mind to do, when I return, everything will be all right."

"But what is this thing you mean to do?"

"You wouldn't understand it," he said. "When I've done it, you and everyone else will understand, and everything will be good. I'll leave you all the money I have. You have your garden, and your brothers will help. You'll be all right."

Sally was not happy with Sequoyah's decision, but no matter how she argued or fussed, he could not be dissuaded. He had made up his mind. He was going to make this trip no matter what she said. She helped him pack the things he would need. The next morning, early, he said good-bye to her and to the children. He mounted his horse, and leading a pack horse, he rode out of Willstown heading west.

Arkansas,
The Cherokee Nation West, *1821*

At Sequoyah's request, John Jolly, Ooloodega, had gathered some of the most important men together at Dwight Mission, the place built by Reverend Cephas Washburn to educate young Cherokees to the ways of the white man. Degadoga, the old war chief was there, and Captain Dutch, his second in command. Reverend Washburn was also in attendance. All were curious to know why Sequoyah had asked them to meet. When at last they were ready, Sequoyah stood in front of them. He had a notepad and a pencil in his hands.

"I've been working on something for a long time," he told them. "It's done now, and I've come here to show it to you. If I were to try to show it at home, I might be killed. The people there don't understand what I've been doing. They've called me lazy and crazy, and then they accused me of being a witch. I came out here to show it to you."

"What could you have that would make people call you all of those things?" Ooloodega asked. Reverend Washburn looked on with interest and curiosity. He could not understand the Cherokee they were speaking.

"I can write and read in the Cherokee language," Sequoyah said.

"No wonder they called you crazy," said old Degadoga. "No one can do that."

Everyone in the small gathering muttered and murmured, and Washburn pulled Ooloodega by the shoulder, until Ooloodega translated for him what had just been said. Washburn looked at Sequoyah with an astonished expression on his face. He turned back to Ooloodega and said, "Tell them to let him proceed."

Ooloodega called for quiet.

"I'll show you," Sequoyah said. He turned his back on the crowd and held up his pad so all could see. Then he drew three characters on the page. "I have written 'Tsalagi,' " he said. "This first symbol represents the sound of 'tsa.' The second represents 'la,' and the third is 'gi.' When they are read aloud altogether, the sound is 'Tsalagi.' "

"What has he written there?" Washburn asked Ooloodega.

"He says that he has written 'Tsalagi,' " Ooloodega said. "That's 'Cherokee' in English."

"With three signs only?" asked the reverend.

"He says the first sign is 'tsa,' the second is 'la,' and the third is 'gi.' "

Sequoyah went on to demonstrate the writing of his own name, Ooloodega's name and the name of Degadoga.

"You can make your strange marks and say that they mean anything," Degadoga said. "How do we know what they mean?"

"I can teach you," Sequoyah said. "All you have to do is learn the different marks and what sound each one stands for."

Again, Ooloodega translated for Washburn, and he added, "No one here believes him though."

"But wait," Washburn said. "If what he says is true, it is genuinely amazing. No man in the history of the world has invented a writing system for a people other than the legendary Cadmus. Let's test him further. Have him write out a long statement and then read it back."

"Degadoga," said Ooloodega, shifting back into the Cherokee language, "make a speech for Sequoyah to write."

"Here then," Degadoga said. "I think you're crazy. I think the people back in Willstown drove you out for good reason. I think it's a wonder that they didn't go ahead and kill you, not for being a witch, but for being such a liar. Write all that down, if you can, and then read me back my exact words."

Everyone sat still and quiet until Sequoyah had finished writing. Then he looked them over, and he held up his pad and started to read.

"I think you're crazy," he read. "I think the people back in Willstown drove you out for good reason. I think it's a wonder that they didn't go ahead and kill you, not for being a witch, but for being such a liar. Write all that down, if you can, and then read me back my exact words."

Washburn whispered in Ooloodega's ear. "Well?"

"He read back Degadoga's exact words."

"Amazing," said Washburn.

"It was not a long speech," Degadoga said, in Cherokee. "He just remembered it. That's all."

"Then give me a longer speech," Sequoyah challenged. "I tell you, I can write down anything you say in our language. If you have something to tell your relatives back home, I can write it down for you and take it back to them. Then I can read to them your exact words. But even better than that, I can teach you these symbols, and you can write to your friends and relatives. I can carry your letters back to them, and I can teach them to read and write, and they can read your words for themselves."

"How can you teach them these things if they want to kill you?" asked Degadoga, still stubborn and skeptical.

"If I bring them letters from you," Sequoyah said, "I think they'll at least listen to me before they kill me. If they listen, I can convince them."

Now and then, Ooloodega translated for Washburn the gist of the discussion, and Washburn listened intently. At last he said, "I have a test in mind that will prove it one way or the other. Please tell the others, and ask Sequoyah if he's willing to submit to my test."

Ooloodega put the reverend's request into Cherokee, waited for a response from the crowd and from Sequoyah, then turned back to Washburn. "All agree," he said. Washburn then opened up his Bible and turned some pages.

"When I read to you," he said to Ooloodega, "you translate what I've read into your tongue for Sequoyah to write down."

And then he began to read, pausing frequently for Ooloodega to translate and for Sequoyah to write. He read on and on, and the Cherokees gathered there all waited patiently. Degadoga sat with arms crossed over his chest and a stern frown on his old face. Sequoyah covered a page of his pad and turned to a fresh page. Washburn read on and on. At last he stopped. He looked at Ooloodega, and he said, "Ask him to read it back."

As Sequoyah read the Cherokee he had written, and Ooloodega turned it back into English, Washburn followed the text in his hands, nodding with approval and rubbing his chin. When at last Sequoyah was done, the reverend announced, "He has done it."

Ooloodega stood up and turned to the others. "He's done it," he said in Cherokee. "He wrote down all of those words. As he read it back in Cherokee, I remembered what I had said, and it was exact. When I put it back into English for the preacher, he agreed." Ooloodega walked over to Sequoyah and shook his hand vigorously. "Sequoyah, I was skeptical like all the others, but now I see that you have done what you said you would do. I congratulate you on your great work."

There were exclamations of surprise, astonishment and admiration all around, and Sequoyah was feeling great relief. The first step had been taken. The first crucial test had been passed. He did his best not to look puffed up with pride, but inside, he felt a tremendous, smug satisfaction. At last the talking became a low murmur, and then even that subsided. Old Degadoga stood up, and everyone grew still again. They watched as the old man walked up to Sequoyah. Sequoyah waited anxiously for what the war chief would say or do.

"Sequoyah," said Degadoga, "teach me to write and read."

The process was remarkably fast. Degadoga and the others who asked to be taught learned the symbols in a matter of a few days. Then they taught others. The writing spread throughout the Cherokee Nation West like wildfire. Sequoyah became a major celebrity and a highly respected man among them. People came to him as if they were approaching a great wise man and respectfully asked if he would teach them to write, and, of course, he never refused to do so. And no one failed to learn. It was easy. Sequoyah was pleased. He had always maintained that it would be an easy thing to do. He had only to hit on the right approach. With his system spreading so quickly and easily, he often asked himself why it had taken him so long and such hard work to achieve such an easy thing.

As he watched Cherokee people, young and old, male and female, studying his writing, learning it, using it, he thought that it had all been more than worthwhile: all the nagging of his wife, the ridicule, scorn and persecution of his neighbors. They had called him lazy and pitied poor Sally. They had called him crazy and laughed at him. Finally, they had called him a witch and burned down his cabin and threatened his very life. But he had survived, and he had overcome all the misunderstanding, at least in the West. He still had those back in the old country to deal with, but he knew just what his approach would be. He had a plan.

And, true to his word to his wife, Sequoyah did take advantage of his visit to Arkansas to look over the country of the Western Cherokee Nation. He found that the things he had been told were true. The country was hilly and heavily wooded. Clear streams and rivers flowed through. Game was abundant. But the best thing about it, to Sequoyah's thinking, was that there was no pressure from the Americans to get out, and there was no bickering among the Cherokees about who was a traitor for talking about going west and who was a patriot for resisting. There was no fighting among the Cherokees in the west. Sequoyah found it to be restful and peaceful. When he had a chance, he talked to Ooloodega about the possibilities for him there.

"I keep a store at home," he said.

"You could do that here, Sequoyah."

"I sometimes work as a blacksmith."

"We have need of more blacksmiths in this country. There is plenty of work to be done. In fact, I can get you some work out here right now if you like."

Sequoyah thought for a moment about that. "I might," he said, "if the right tools can be found."

The more he saw and heard, the more Sequoyah believed that the Cherokee Nation West was the place to be. He knew, of course, that he would have to be careful about saying that when he got back home. The only possible disadvantage he could see was the war with the Osages, but during his visit, he had seen none of that. Degadoga and Captain Dutch had rounded up some men to go over into the Osage country and attack an Osage town. They were doing that because some Cherokee hunters had been killed by Osages. But in Sequoyah's mind, that was nothing compared to the turmoil in the old country. The Osage war was not happening in the Cherokee towns.

Ooloodega found all the right tools for Sequoyah to use, and he brought in some customers for Sequoyah. For several days, Sequoyah worked as a blacksmith. He still took time to help people with the writing when they came to him, but there wasn't much teaching to do. Once it had gotten started, the writing seemed to spread by itself. There was no stopping it now. One day, to Sequoyah's great pleasure, a boy brought a wagon and team and handed Sequoyah a note written in his signs. The note said, "Sequoyah, here is what I want you to do. I want you to fix the right wheel on the front. I want you to look at the left rear shoe of one of the horses and there is a kettle in the back of the wagon that needs mending. This boy has some money. He will pay you for the work."

In just another few days, Sequoyah packed up to leave. He rode first to the home of Ooloodega. Inside the house, Ooloodega's wife poured coffee for her husband and Sequoyah.

"So how soon will you leave?" Ooloodega asked.

"I'm on the way right now," Sequoyah said. "I just stopped by here to tell you."

"I wish you'd stay here with us."

"I have a family back in Willstown," Sequoyah said. "But I think that I'll bring them all here. I think I will move here and stay with you. First, though, I have some other things to do back there in the old country."

"Well, at least, I'm glad to hear you say you'll be coming back. Did you hear about the fight with the Osages yesterday?"

"I knew that Degadoga and Dutch and the others went out," Sequoyah said, "but I haven't heard anything more."

"They came back last night with many scalps. Only a few Cherokees were hurt, but they killed lots of Osages, and those that were not killed ran away like scared rabbits."

"Good, but I think it would be even better if this war could be stopped," Sequoyah said.

"Degadoga says the only way to bring an end to the war is to kill all the Osages," said Ooloodega. "He says that it does no good to negotiate a peace with them. They'll just break it, and it's true enough that's what has happened in the past. Because of that, Degadoga says that it's useless to talk peace. He says the Osages are a nation of liars."

"Well, it's just too bad that someone can't find a way to make them stop," said Sequoyah. "Degadoga and the Osages need to realize that the white man is the real enemy of us all. Indians should not be killing other Indians."

Ooloodega shrugged.

"I want you to do something for me," Sequoyah said.

"What is it?"

"I want you to write a letter to Agili. On my way out of this country, I'll stop to visit with others. I'll take letters from anyone who wants to send them back to friends or relatives in the old country. But I especially want you to write one to Agili. Agili is well known and highly respected. I want to show him his letter first of all."

Ooloodega looked at Sequoyah and smiled. "I see your plan," he said. "All right. I'd like to say some things to Agili anyway. This is a good time and a good way for me to do that."

When Sequoyah at last rode out of the Cherokee settlements in the Arkansas country, he took with him a bundle of letters. He was not yet exactly sure how he would make his writing known to the people back in the East, but it was a long ride back, and he would have plenty of time to figure out a plan along the way. The only thing he was sure of as he headed home was that Agili would be the first one he would approach. Agili was his cousin, clan brother, and a life-long friend. Agili knew him better than anyone, and Agili trusted him. Agili knew that he would not lie. Sequoyah knew that he could show Agili the letter, and Agili at least would not respond by killing him. And once he had won over Agili, why, the rest would be easy. Agili would back him up, and they could show one more, or a few, maybe even many at the same time. He would think all of that over on his long trip back home, and by the time the trip was over, he would have figured out the plan.

II

Willstown

I t had been a long journey and a tiring one, all the way to
Arkansas and back. It had been a lonely trip, and it had given
him all the time he needed to think about what he would do
next, and to plan just how he would go about it. He was well
pleased, yet it had taken much out of him. Sequoyah felt as if the
journey had taken several years from his life. His bad knee was
bothering him more than usual, so when he at last dismounted
there in front of his home in Willstown, and Sally and the two
children came out to greet him, he hugged them each, and then
announced his intention of going straight to bed.

"We'll unpack for you," Sally said.

Sequoyah went into the house, and Sally unsaddled the riding
horse. Then she began unburdening the pack animal. After carrying an armload into the house, she came across a large bundle of
letters. She did not know what they were. All she knew was that
they were bundles of papers with Sequoyah's strange marks all over
them. She hesitated, wondering what she should do. The bad talk
about Sequoyah in the neighborhood had died down during his
long absence, and she was suddenly afraid that it would all start
up again. She had hoped that the long trip had gotten all of that
craziness out of his head. Obviously it had not. She looked over
at the fireplace, hesitated, then put the bundle down on the tabletop and went on about her work with a heavy sigh.

Sequoyah was up early the next morning feeling much refreshed
and anxious to get about his work, but his knee was still bothering

him. He decided that he did not want his handicap to hinder him more than he could help it, so he took a small hand ax and a knife and went out into the woods. He found just the right stick, and, with a little cutting and shaving, made himself a nice walking stick. He tested it, and then he went back into the house. Sally looked at the stick. She didn't say anything. She knew that his knee had troubled him off and on for years.

"Sally," he said, "I'm going to visit Agili."

"But you just got home last night," Sally said. "The children haven't yet seen much of you. I haven't either. You were gone a long time from us. Can't you wait a little before you go visiting?"

"This is important, Sally," he said. "Soon it will all be taken care of, and then we'll have plenty of time, you and me and Teesee and Ahyoka."

She didn't like it, but she didn't argue as he walked out the door. She went on about her work in the cabin. Outside, Sequoyah saddled his horse, tucked the bundle of papers into the saddlebag, mounted up and rode away. He carried his walking stick. Along the way, he saw several old friends and exchanged greetings. He had to pause and make small talk with a couple of them. He noticed a few giving him hard looks, and he knew that the old feelings were still around. At last he reached Agili's house and found his cousin at home. Agili invited him in and poured coffee.

"So how was your trip?"

"It was long," Sequoyah said. "It made me tired, and it made me feel old, but it was good."

"Tell me," said Agili, "how are all of the people out there? How is my friend and uncle, Ooloodega?"

"I'll let Ooloodega himself tell you," Sequoyah said. He reached inside his jacket and withdrew a letter. He unfolded it and laid it out on the table. Agili looked at it sternly.

"Sequoyah," he said, "are you still—"

"Wait," Sequoyah said. He started to read. " 'To my friend Agili. I send you greetings from Arkansas by our kinsman Sequoyah. Things are good here. I hear that there's trouble back in the old country because the whites want to get you out of there, and I wish that you and all my friends and relatives would move on out here with us where you will be out of their reach.' " Sequoyah continued reading for a time, and at last finished with Ooloodega's closing and signature. He picked up the letter and handed it to Agili. Agili held it tenderly, as if he were afraid that he might break it, and he stared at it almost in awe.

"Did you really read all that on here?" he asked, astonished.

"Of course I did," Sequoyah said. "I've been telling you and the others all this time that I could do it and that I meant to do it. That's the reason I went out West. I finished my work here, and I wanted to show it to someone and teach it to others. I would have started here, but people were already angry at me. They burned my cabin. Even you said they might kill me, so I thought it would be best to go out there and do it. Ooloodega learned to write and read. He wrote this letter to you himself. Many others have learned it as well. Even Degadoga. I brought back a great many letters from our people in Arkansas."

"Sequoyah, this is amazing. Even I never truly believed you could do this. It's really real?"

"Yes. It is. Will you let me teach it to you?"

"Do you think I could learn it?"

"Of course you can. It's really very simple."

Sequoyah spent much of the rest of the day with Agili, showing him the different characters and teaching him their sound values. Before they were done, Agili was reading, a bit slowly, through his own letter from Ooloodega. At last Sequoyah stood up to leave. He stretched, and he yawned. His knee was hurting.

"I have to go home now," he said. "Don't tell anyone about this. Not yet. In a few more days, I'll ask you to call a meeting where we will tell everyone, but for now, keep it to yourself."

Agili shrugged. "If that's the way you want it," he said, "then that's the way it will be. But Sequoyah, what you've done is truly wonderful. I'm very proud of you, and before long, all Cherokees will be as proud of you as I am right now."

Sequoyah sat at the table in his own home and gathered his family around him. Sally and both children sat waiting patiently for what he wanted to tell them. He took out his notepad and pencil and turned to a clean page.

"I have something to show you," he said, and he looked at his wife. "Don't interrupt me until I've finished. This is what I've been working on all this time. It's what made you and others angry at me. It's the reason I've been called names and laughed at. But it's all done now. The trouble is all behind us. I can read and write our own language. While I was gone, I taught many of our people in Arkansas how to read and write, and they wrote letters to people back here. I brought the letters, and soon I'll take them around to the people they belong to. But now, I want you to know about this. I want you to learn it."

He began writing symbols and telling them what sound each symbol stood for, and after he had made a few symbols, he put them together into words. Then he wrote complete sentences. Ahyoka, especially, was fascinated, and Sequoyah soon realized that his young daughter was learning faster than her older brother or her mother. He was pleased with that. He could also see that Sally was at last convinced that he had done what he had set about to do, but she was not yet convinced that it had been worthwhile. She still frowned and looked skeptical. At last, he let them get up from the table. Ahyoka stayed.

"I want to draw the signs," she said.

Sequoyah smiled and handed her the pencil. She took it in her stubby little fingers and began to carefully draw the symbols she had learned.

"Look," she said, "I made my name."

"Yes, you did," Sequoyah said, and he was beaming with pride. "Write some more."

Four days later, at Sequoyah's request, Agili began gathering people at Sequoyah's house. He had invited some of the most influential of the Cherokees from all around. Sequoyah had a makeshift table set up in front of the house, with benches made of split logs on each side. As the people began to show up, John Ross and Elias Boudinot came riding by.

"Whose place is this?" Boudinot asked.

"Oh," said Ross, "that's the home of George Guess."

"It's certainly in bad shape," Boudinot said. "The house needs repairs, and weeds are grown up all around. Is he unable to work?"

"He's just foolish," Ross said. "He thinks he can come up with a way to write the Cherokee language, and for a long time now, he's neglected all his other work. I pity his poor wife."

"He seems to have lots of friends," said Boudinot.

"Hmm, I don't know what's going on there," said Ross. The two men rode on.

Over in front of Sequoyah's neglected cabin, most of the people Agili had asked to show up had arrived. Big Thighs was there, and so were Springfrog and Bawldridge. Sally served coffee to them all. At last, Sequoyah was ready. This was the moment he had waited for. His heart pounded with excitement and anxiety. Some of these were the very people who had wanted to kill him for conjuring. He asked Agili to get their attention.

"My friends," Agili said, and they all grew quiet, wondering what Agili wanted with them at the home of the crazy man. "I asked you here at the request of my friend and kinsman, Sequoyah. He has something truly wonderful to show you. Some of you will be impatient. You won't want to listen. Old fears, resentments and anger will resurface. But if you'll hear him out, you'll understand. I know what he's done. I know he's telling the truth. Trust me, and listen to Sequoyah."

Sequoyah stepped out in front of the small crowd. He was holding his notepad in one hand. He leaned his walking stick against a nearby tree and held up the pad for all to see. The symbols on the top sheet were clearly visible to all.

"Big Thighs," he said, "do you recall what you told me about the priests?"

Suddenly self-conscious, Big Thighs looked at the tabletop. "I told you only what I had heard," he said.

"And what was that?"

"I heard that a long time ago, our priests could read and write."

"They could read and write our own language," Sequoyah said.

"Yes," said Big Thighs. "That's what I heard."

There were murmurs all around, and one man shouted out, "I don't believe that."

"Is that what we came here for?" said another. "To listen to more of this crazy talk?"

Agili stepped out front again and held up his hands for quiet. "Show respect and listen," he said, "at least until he's finished."

"I can write in Cherokee," Sequoyah said. "And I can read. I have taught others to do so, out in Arkansas, and I have brought letters back to each one of you here from your friends and relatives in the West. I took Agili's letter from Ooloodega to him first, because I knew that he'd listen to me. I showed it to him, and I read it to him, and I taught him to read it."

All eyes turned on Agili. Some of the people there were astonished, some unbelieving, others accusing.

"It's true," Agili said. "I have learned to read and write our language with the system that Sequoyah has devised. And I tell you, any of you can do the same."

"It's magic," said one.

"It's witchcraft," another said.

"It's neither one of those things," Sequoyah said. "It's something you have to learn. That's all."

"And it's easy to learn," Agili said.

"Let me show you how easy it is," said Sequoyah. "Ahyoka, come over here."

The tiny four-year-old girl walked over to stand beside her father. Shy in front of the crowd, she half hid behind his leg.

"Ahyoka can read and write," Sequoyah said. "I'm going to walk over there and wait." He pointed to a tree off at some distance. "When I get over there, I want one of you to tell her what to write. When she's done with it, call me back, and I'll read it to you."

He retrieved his walking stick and limped to the tree to wait. After some chattering and arguing, Agili managed to get the crowd quiet again. He selected one of the most belligerent of the crowd, and then he knelt beside Ahyoka. She held the pad and pencil. Agili put an arm around her and spoke quietly into her ear.

"Just write down what the man says," he told her.

The man selected stood up and puffed out his chest. He looked over the crowd with a smirk on his face. "All right," he said. "Mark down this. I believe Sequoyah is crazy. I believe he should be beaten and chased away from this place. If he should ever dare to return, he should be beaten to death."

Ahyoka looked at Agili, terrified. He hugged her tight.

"It's all right," he said. "Just write it down."

Ahyoka wrote, and when she was done, she handed the paper

to Agili. He looked at it and smiled. "Good," he said. He stood up. "I can read this," he said. "Of course, I was right here and heard what was said. You might not believe me." He waved an arm at Sequoyah, and Sequoyah walked back over to the crowd. Agili handed him the pad. Sequoyah looked at it for a moment. He looked up at the crowd and read aloud the exact words the man had said.

"I don't believe it," the man said. "It's a trick."

"It's no trick," Sequoyah said. "I can read and write, and so can my little daughter, and so can Agili. We'll separate ourselves any way you want us to. You can give a message to me or to Ahyoka or to Agili. You can ask any one of us to read it back."

For the next hour, notes were sent back and forth until even the most skeptical was convinced. With no more arguments or threats, Sequoyah decided that it was time to move on. He began showing the people there one symbol at a time. He spelled out short words. He had them read. He let them write. They were still going when the sun was gone from the sky.

"Come back in the morning," Sequoyah said. "We'll do some more."

Most of them went home, but a few who lived too far, stayed the night. They slept on the ground outside Sequoyah's cabin. Sally had been watching off and on from a safe distance, and at last she realized that her husband had indeed done something great. The most skeptical of the people were convinced. The angriest were softened. All of them were suddenly enthusiastic over the new writing. She felt a little ashamed that she had doubted him. She recalled the hard times, and she was sorry that she had not given him her support. Instead, she had added her own scornful voice to those around who were calling him names and making threats. Lying beside him in bed, she said, "Sequoyah, I didn't believe you. I'm not very smart. I should have been a better wife. Now, I'm proud that you're my husband."

He stretched out an arm and pulled her to him so that her head was resting on his chest, and he held her close. "Sally," he said, "those days are all behind us. And we're still together. That's all that matters now."

They came back in the morning, and many of them brought others along. Sequoyah resumed his role as teacher, and Agili even worked with a small group. When some began to feel confident with the symbols, they turned to help their neighbors. Soon Sequoyah was out of paper. They were writing in the dirt. They worked at it all day long. Some stayed all night again, and they worked the next day. As the days went on, the people who learned the quickest left to go out and help spread the new knowledge around that much faster. Other people heard about it, and came to Sequoyah's house to see for themselves and to learn. Word spread to the white traders, and soon there were white men all around with paper and pencils to sell.

Everywhere people sat together in small groups reading and writing. The people who had received letters from the West wrote letters in response and brought them to Sequoyah to take back to Arkansas. Even the white missionaries came to Sequoyah to learn this remarkable new system of writing in the Cherokee language, and when they had seen how it worked, they called it a syllabary. It did not matter to Sequoyah what they called it. He had created it, and the people were using it.

One day Agili came to see Sequoyah. "You know what the people are saying?" he asked. "They're saying that you're a great man. Your fame has spread even among the white people. They're calling you a philosopher and a genius. They're saying that what you've done is miraculous."

It made Sequoyah feel good to hear those things said, but he tried not to let himself get puffed up with pride. "I'm none of those things," he said. "As you know, the writing is simple. It's a matter of learning it. That's all."

"Yes, my friend. That's true, now that you've devised the system for us. But it took you to devise it, and it took you to convince the rest of us that it could be done, and that it was worthwhile. Why, the missionaries already are talking about translating their Bible into Cherokee and writing it down so that everyone can read it."

Sequoyah frowned. "I didn't figure out the writing for the white preachers," he said. "If I could stop them from using it, I would."

"Sequoyah," Agili said, "your system has a life of its own now. You couldn't stop it if you wanted to. No one can stop it now. It's grown way beyond you. You set it in motion. Now all you can do is watch it spread. Watch it grow."

It was a sobering thought, what Agili had said. He had not really considered that once the people had learned to read and write the system would no longer be his. He would have no control over the way in which it was used or by whom it would be used. It had never occurred to him that white men would learn it. He should have known. He knew some white men who could speak the Cherokee language. He should have realized that they would learn his writing. But the missionaries . . . it was indeed a sobering thought, and he did not want to be sober. He wanted some whiskey.

12

S itting beside Wills Creek, Sequoyah contemplated his changed situation. The very people who had called him lazy and crazy and accused him of witchcraft were now hailing him as a "chief." He had become a prominent citizen of the Cherokee Nation, almost overnight. It seemed as if, all of a sudden, everyone wanted to be known as his good friend. It was almost enough to make him dizzy. Sometimes he enjoyed his new status, other times it annoyed him. Where were these same ones, he would ask himself, when I was working alone and suffering so much abuse? Was he less crazy or less lazy just because his writing worked?

And he was not at all sure that he liked his new surroundings, the changing Cherokee Nation around him, especially there in Willstown. He had become a celebrity in a land that was becoming more strange to him every day. Willstown was looking more like a white man's town all the time. Agili was operating a grist mill. And Sequoyah recalled the day Agili had brought the white preacher to his house, not all that long ago. Agili had actually invited the white man to build a mission right there in Willstown: Willstown, the former home of John Watts, Bloody Fellow, Bob Benge and even the great Dragging Canoe. Agili had taken to referring to himself by his English name, George Lowrey. Then one day to Sequoyah's surprise, Agili had made the astounding announcement that he himself had become a Christian, and he had invited Sequoyah to join him and the others at the mission.

"I will never do that," Sequoyah had said.

To make matters even worse, a young Cherokee man called David Brown was working with the missionary, whose name was Chamberlain, to put the white man's holy book into the Cherokee language, and they were using the very system that Sequoyah had devised. Agili had been right about one thing. The writing had grown on its own. It was no longer Sequoyah's. It had grown beyond him, and it now belonged to the Cherokee people. That much was all right. But Sequoyah had never considered that the white preachers would use it to their advantage, and that they would be assisted in this endeavor by Cherokees.

Then Agili had invited Sequoyah to a meeting with Chamberlain and Brown and a few others. They gathered at Agili's house, where Agili's wife fed them and served coffee all around, and they talked in English for the sake of Chamberlain. When Sequoyah needed to know what had been said, either Brown or Agili repeated it for him in Cherokee. At last they got around to the reason the meeting had been called. They were all seated around a long table. David Brown spread out some papers. One was covered over with Sequoyah's symbols. Brown and Chamberlain talked for a while in English, and at last Agili translated the conversation for Sequoyah.

"Your symbols are too difficult," he said. "Many of them look almost alike, and there are too many curves and curls in the lines. They're confusing. Chamberlain and Brown want you to help them redesign the symbols we are using to give them straighter lines and to make them look more like the English letters. The reverend is thinking that one of these days, we might want to have the symbols cast in type so that our language can be printed the way the English language is printed, in newspapers and books. It would be very difficult to cast type for the symbols the way you've drawn them."

Sequoyah sat listening in silence. He did not like the idea of changing his signs. He particularly did not like the thought of making them look like the English signs. People were already using them. They would have to learn the signs all over again. But he reminded himself that the signs were no longer his.

"We want you to help design the new symbols," Agili said, "and then to write out a chart showing the old and the new. Then the people who already use the writing will know that you helped to make the change. We can make many copies of the chart you write out and distribute them so that people can learn the new signs easily."

Sequoyah thought about arguing, but he knew that would be useless. It was no longer his system, as Agili had said. They would do this thing with or without his help. He could tell that about them. They were determined to make the change. And maybe they were right about the type. He knew nothing of type and of printing. His response was a shrug. He would sit there and let them do it. Then, of course, they would tell the people that he had helped. Ah, well, it was all beyond his control now. He supposed that he should be pleased that they had even bothered to invite him to participate in this process.

David Brown began picking symbols out of a book and talking about them and writing them down. Again, Agili translated.

"We can use this one here in place of this old," he would say. "Look how much simpler it is."

Sequoyah wanted to say, *If this is so simple, why did you not do it in the first place instead of telling me that I was crazy*, but he did not say that. He did not resist, and when they had finished, he wrote down the entire list of signs again, and beside each old symbol, he drew the new one. When the job was done, he made an extra copy of the chart and took it with him when he left Agili's house. He too would have to memorize the new signs.

Sitting there beside Wills Creek, he considered all these radical changes in his life and in his surroundings. He was no longer content to live his life there in Willstown. He realized that he could never again be content there. Nothing had been the same since they had forced him away from Taskigi. It was no longer his old home, the old Cherokee Nation. He thought about Ooloodega and the others who had gone out West. Perhaps it was time for him to go. He had considered it before, had even signed up to go once, but he had allowed others to frighten him out of making the move. Then he had visited the Cherokee Nation West, in Arkansas, and he had liked it out there.

There were not nearly so many whites. There was no pressure on the people there to sell their land and move. There was plenty of room and abundant game for hunting. True, there was a white man's mission school, and some of the western Cherokees were becoming Christians, but not so many, and the preacher was not nearly so likely to show up at one's home out there as was this one in Willstown. He made up his mind. It was time to make the move. He decided to walk home and tell Sally.

He was limping, leaning heavily on his walking stick as he made his way through Willstown, and along the way, he was passing by the home of Big Thighs. His old friend saw him going by and called out to him. Sequoyah hobbled over to meet Big Thighs in front of his small log cabin.

"Sequoyah," said Big Thighs. "What are you doing?"

"Nothing much," Sequoyah said. "I was just on my way home."

"Let's get drunk," Big Thighs said. "I have some whiskey."

They walked around the cabin, Big Thighs leading the way. "Be quiet," he said. "My wife's inside." Behind the cabin, he retrieved a hidden whiskey jug, and he led the way into the woods. At last he stopped to uncork the jug. He smiled a broad smile. "She won't find me here," he said. He handed the jug to Sequoyah, and Sequoyah took a long drink. The whiskey felt good burning its way down his throat. It warmed him from deep inside. He gave the jug back to Big Thighs and looked around for a place to sit. Big Thighs drank as Sequoyah sat on a large, flat rock. Then he too sat down.

"I'm going West," Sequoyah said.

"For another visit?"

"No. This time, I'm moving out there to stay. I don't like the way things are going around here."

"I don't either," Big Thighs said. "There are too many whites around close."

"They're getting closer all the time."

"And they're always wanting new treaties and more land."

"They want to kick us all out of here," Sequoyah said. "They won't be satisfied until we're all gone."

"They have their preachers in here among us," Big Thighs said, handing the jug back to Sequoyah. "They want us all to pray to Jesus."

Sequoyah took another drink. "Agili has joined them," he said. "He's a Christian now. He prays to Jesus."

"Agili?"

"That's right."

"I wish I'd been old enough when Dragging Canoe was fighting," said Big Thighs. "I'd have been out with him killing the whites."

Sequoyah shook his head. "It wouldn't have done any good," he said. "Look around us. All the fighting that Dragging Canoe and the others did to defend our land and our way of life has come to this. It did no good. Besides, if you'd been there fighting, you might be the one that got killed. You wouldn't even be here drinking this whiskey."

Big Thighs took the jug and drank again. "I guess I didn't mean what I said. I'd rather be here drinking whiskey than be dead."

Sequoyah laughed and took the jug for another drink. "Yes," he said. "Me too."

"When will you leave, Sequoyah? I'll go too, and I know some others who will go with us. I'll talk to them. We'll all go to Arkansas. We'll get away from the teachers and the preachers and the white men with their treaties."

"They're fighting Osages out there," Sequoyah said.

"Ha. Then we'll fight Osages."

"And maybe get killed."

"Maybe," Big Thighs said. "But right now, we'll get drunk."

It was the next day before Sequoyah got home to tell Sally his plans. She did not argue with him. She could tell that he had made up his mind. She recalled the other time he had said they were going to Arkansas, and he had changed his mind, but this time, she believed him. After all, he had gone out there by himself. He knew the way, and he had seen the country and the way the people were living out there. She started packing and making preparations for a long trip.

Sequoyah and Big Thighs got some people together who felt the same way they did, and they visited and talked about their plans. Finally, they decided that they should write a letter offering to trade their land for land out West. They composed the letter in the Cherokee language, Sequoyah writing in the new characters, and then one among them who could speak and write English, translated and re-wrote it. They addressed the letter to the governor of the state of Tennessee.

1824

They took pack horses and a few riding horses, but they had no wagons, so much was left behind. Sequoyah, Sally and their two children, and four other families headed west together. They took what food they could, but they would hunt along the way. They had some money. They left Willstown and moved along the south bank of the Tennessee River, camping at night along the way. The going was slow. They left the riverbank where the river turned north and rode northwest across Tennessee to Nashville. There they had their horses reshod, shopped for coffee and flour, lead and powder. They were careful, though, with their money; there was still a long way to go. From Nashville, the party went to Memphis and paid a ferryman there to take them across the wide Mississippi River. Alternately riding and walking, they headed west across Arkansas until they came to the Arkansas River, and they traveled along its northern bank until they at last came to the Cherokee settlements.

Arkansas,
The Western Cherokee Nation, 1825

Ooloodega and Sequoyah rode side by side on a narrow lane, going north from the Arkansas River along the east bank of Illinois Bayou. They had ridden about fifteen miles from the Cherokee settlement of Dardanelle, on the south bank of the Arkansas, when Ooloodega spoke. "I thought at one time of making my own home up here," he said, "but when I became chief, I decided that I had to stay closer to the people in the towns. You'll like it though. It's far enough from the river. Most of the white people we see are traveling the river. You'll be away from them up here."

"That's good," Sequoyah said.

"Your nearest neighbors will be those we passed already. The widow of the agent, Lovely, the missionaries and our children at their school called Dwight."

"I haven't seen any homes since we passed the school," Sequoyah said.

"There aren't any."

"Will my wife and children be in danger from the Osages way out here alone?"

"If the Osages dare come this far into our country," Ooloodega said, "they'll come along the river to attack our towns. They wouldn't think of looking for your family up here. You'll be safer here than if you were to settle in Dardanelle."

They rode a little farther, and Ooloodega stopped and gestured ahead. Sequoyah looked at the mountains in the distance. He studied the tree-lined banks of the bayou and the flat clearing there in front of him, and smiled.

"It's good," he said.

"It's better than that," said Ooloodega. "Come with me. I'll show you your livelihood, if you want it."

It was a saline spring, a source of the valuable commodity salt. Sequoyah looked at Ooloodega with wide and bright eyes. This would be better than farming. Crops could fail. Bad weather could destroy crops. But one could always sell salt. He nodded his head. "Yes," he said. "This is good."

And there he built his home. It was a small cabin, but it was enough for Sequoyah, Sally and the two children. Teesee was now seven years old, Ahyoka was six and Sequoyah was forty-six. He acquired the necessary kettles in which to boil the water away and leave the salt, and he fashioned his salt works right away, as soon as the work on his cabin was done. He spent days at a time at his work. Sometimes Ooloodega came by to visit, and one day the chief brought with him the old war chief, Degadoga. They sat in front of Sequoyah's cabin visiting, smoking and drinking coffee.

"Sequoyah," said Degadoga, "we need a blacksmith. I heard that you are a good blacksmith. Why don't you start doing that work for us out here?"

Sequoyah shrugged. "When I moved, I had no wagon. I couldn't bring the tools with me, so I don't have any tools."

Degadoga looked at Ooloodega. "Can we get some blacksmith tools for Sequoyah?"

"We should be able to collect the money," Ooloodega said. "You and me and some of the others."

"I have some money," Sequoyah said.

"Good," said Degadoga. "It's decided. Now there's something else I want to talk to you about. The white man Washburn has a school down there near the Arkansas River."

"Yes," Sequoyah said. "I've seen it. And I've met Washburn."

Degadoga nodded and puffed his pipe. "He's teaching our young men to wear britches like white men," he said, "and he's teaching them to talk and to write in English. I don't like that."

"He's also teaching them the white man's religion," said Ooloodega, "and I don't believe that's bad."

"I don't think it's so good," Sequoyah said. "If the white man's religion was good, then there wouldn't be so many bad white people. All they want to do is steal from us. I've never seen an Indian as bad as a white man."

"Aha," said Degadoga. "That's just what I'm talking about. Washburn is all right himself. I visit with him sometimes, and he tries to make me believe his religion, but I won't. I believe he's misguided. I'm only one voice, and I can't make him stop teaching our young people, but I believe that if we learn to keep our own stories and our own information in our own language, we'll be equal to the white men. I want everyone to learn to write your writing, Sequoyah. I have a village with young people who are not going to Washburn's school. I want you to come there and teach the young people."

Sequoyah thought for a moment. He had already spent several days at the salt works, and he could afford to take some time off. He already knew from experience that it took only a few days for people to learn his system. Besides, it would be his first chance to show the new symbols that Agili and Brown and the white preacher had devised to substitute for his originals. He needed to spread them around, so that when the people back in the old country sent letters, those in the West could read them.

"I'll do it," he said.

Sequoyah thought that he was going to like this new home. He was away from the pressures of the whites back East. He had a home in a quiet and peaceful location. He had a new business that was surely going to prove profitable, and now he was about to start up his old work as a blacksmith again. He didn't really like farming anyway, and with the salt works and the blacksmithing, Sally would be satisfied. He would make them a better living that way anyhow. He might even get back to his silver work some. And now he was to teach. Better than anything, he liked teaching his writing system to other Cherokees. He was grateful to Degadoga, and he looked forward to meeting the young people in the old chief's village.

But Sally was thinking of something else they had talked about, something which had not seemed to be of any great importance to Sequoyah. The Western Cherokees had just reorganized their government. And in the process, they had elected Ooloodega president and Degadoga vice president. When their two visitors had left, Sally heaved a satisfied sigh and looked at her husband fondly and with pride.

"You've become an important man, Sequoyah," she said.

"The writing is important," he said. "Not me. Agili told me that it is growing by itself now. It's not mine anymore."

"But your uncle, John Jolly, is the most important man in the nation. He's the president. And Degadoga is second, and they came to see you. They came all the way out here to visit with you."

"They're friends of mine," he said.

"They came to see you," she said. "They're important men, and when they come to see you, that means you're an important man."

Sequoyah made no response. Instead he took out his pipe and tobacco. He filled the pipe bowl and put the tobacco pouch away. Sally brought him a punk from the fire, and he lit his tobacco. Leaning back in his chair, his brow wrinkled, he puffed thoughtfully. He wondered if she could be right. That would certainly be different, he thought, to be an important man.

13

Things went well for Sequoyah and his family in Arkansas. The salt works proved to be profitable, and Sequoyah abandoned almost all of his other work. He did occasionally work as a blacksmith, if someone happened to catch him at home at just the right time. He almost never worked in silver, and he had even quit teaching the writing. Degadoga had gone on a long trip, and the young people of his village had all learned the writing quickly. There was really nothing more to be done there. Then word had come back to the Western Cherokee Nation that the old war chief had died in Kaskaskia, Illinois. His loss was greatly felt. Sequoyah recalled the last time he had seen Degadoga.

"They tell me that the white man has a plan," he had said. "He wants to kick all Indians out west, to places west of the Mississippi River."

"Yes," Sequoyah had said. "I've heard that. But Ross and Boudinot and Ridge and others are resisting those efforts."

"They're making a mistake," Degadoga had said. "I think we should help them. I mean to visit all Indians who still live in the east and tell them to move west. I'm going to help the white men accomplish their purpose."

"Why would you do that?"

"Because when we get all the Indians out here," the old man had said, "then we'll kick all the white people back on the east side of the big river and keep them there. The river will become our permanent dividing line."

Well, Sequoyah had thought, that did not sound like a bad idea. He had wished Degadoga a good journey and much success, but then the word had come back about Degadoga's death. Sequoyah wondered if anyone would follow in his footsteps. Dragging Canoe had envisioned an alliance of all Indian tribes, and later, so had the Shawnee, Tecumseh. Degadoga wanted the same thing, but he wanted it west of the Mississippi River. Sequoyah hoped that his death did not signal the end of the pursuit of that grand plan.

"Oh, well," he said to Ooloodega one afternoon, "at least now perhaps we can actually bring an end to the war with the Osages."

"I don't know," Ooloodega said. "There's still Dutch. He's just as bad. You know, they say that after the last peace was concluded, Dutch killed and scalped an Osage right across the river from the main gate of Fort Gibson and waved the scalp at the soldiers, shouting out his own name. It was as if he was telling them that no one could tell Dutch that he can no longer kill Osages."

"I heard that he'd moved to Texas," Sequoyah said.

"That's true, but he still rides all the way up to the Osage country for raids. The council has told the U.S. Army and the Osages that Dutch is no longer one of us. He's moved away beyond our control. He's an outlaw. We've kept the peace, but they don't believe us. They keep blaming us for Dutch. We'll see."

Sequoyah did not often lose his temper, so Sally was surprised when he came storming into the house one afternoon. She could tell right away that he'd been drinking again. He stumbled over to the table, sat down heavily, dropping his cane to the floor and slammed his fist down on the tabletop.

"What's wrong with you?" she asked him.

"That David Brown," Sequoyah said.

"The young man who worked with Reverend Washburn?"

"Yes. That one."

"I thought he had gone back to the old country."

"He only went back for a visit, but now he's back here. There's a new white preacher back in the old country. They called him Woostah or something like that. David Brown is working with him now. He has already translated much of the white preacher's book into our language by using my symbols. And they're going to order type and a printing press. They mean to put the whole book into my symbols. I wish I had never made them."

"You shouldn't say that, Sequoyah," Sally said. "You spent years working on the writing. You put up with much abuse for it, even from me. But now our people can read and write in our own language. Almost everyone. You should be proud of what you've done."

"The preachers tell everyone that everything we believe in is wrong. Then they tell them that what it says in their book is right. Now it seems, I've given them a new weapon in this fight. I wish I had never done it."

Suddenly straightening up out of his chair, he attempted to stamp around the room, but in his condition and without his cane, he staggered, stumbled and fell happily onto his bed. He mumbled something and then was silent. Sally looked down on him as if he were a misbehaving child. She thought about undressing him, but she heard the sound of someone approaching her house. She hurried to the door and opened it just as John Jolly, Ooloodega, was stepping up.

" 'Siyo, Sally," he said.

As she returned his greeting, she stepped aside, and he came into the house. "Is Se—" He stopped, having seen Sequoyah on the bed. "I heard that he was—in that condition in town," he said. "I also heard that he was headed home and that he was upset about something. I just came out to make sure he made it home in one piece and everything is all right."

"Let me pour you some coffee," Sally said, and as she poured, Ooloodega sat down at the table. He noticed Sequoyah's cane on the floor and bent to pick it up.

"Did he—did he say anything before he—went to bed?"

"He's mad at David Brown and those preachers," Sally said, putting the cup of steaming coffee on the table in front of Ooloodega. "He said he wished that he had never made the signs for writing."

"Why would he say that?"

"The preachers have a weapon now, and he gave it to them. That's what he said."

"I see. Well, when he comes around again," Ooloodega said, "tell him that the new printing press will be used for other things as well. Back home, the Cherokee Nation intends to print its laws.

It is planning to start its own newspaper. A Cherokee newspaper, printed in Cherokee. Tell him that. There are some wonderful things happening, all because of his work."

"A newspaper," Sally mused.

"Yes. They're going to call it the *Cherokee Phoenix and Indian Advocate*. That's what I heard."

Sally wrinkled her nose. "What's that mean? That fee—"

"Phoenix," Ooloodega said. He shrugged. "Elias Boudinot came up with that, they say. He's to be the editor of the paper. He says that it's a Greek bird that died and got burned up and came back alive out of its own ashes. And he says that the Cherokees are like that."

"I never heard of it," Sally said. "I never heard of Greeks either."

Ooloodega sipped some coffee and lowered the cup. "Well," he said, "you tell him what all is going on. Maybe he'll feel better about it. Oh, yes. I was so worried about him, I almost forgot."

"What?"

"Maybe the most important news," he said. "The Council of the Cherokee Nation voted and made his 'syllabary,' they call it, official for the Cherokee Nation, and they voted to give him a medal. It's to be made of silver, and it will say, 'Presented to George Gist, by the General Council of the Cherokee Nation, for his ingenuity in the Invention of the Cherokee alphabet, 1825.'"

"They did that back home?"

"That's part of the news that David Brown brought back with him," said Ooloodega.

"Well," said Sally, smiling, "maybe all that will make him feel better. I hope. Thank you for coming out here to tell me."

December, 1827

Sequoyah was fascinated by the large paddle. He stood at the rail on the steamboat for hours at a time, watching it churn tremendous quantities of river water and shove the huge boat along its way. It was by far the best part of the trip. Overall, the long journey was tedious and tiring, and if anything, it confirmed his already held conviction that moving west had been the right thing for him to do, for all along the way, he took note of the swarming population of white people.

He was on his way to Washington City, along with Black Fox, James Rogers, Thomas Graves, Thomas Maw, George Marvis and John and James Looney. They were a delegation sent by the council of the Western Cherokee Nation to complain about the intrusion of white settlers onto land just west of their Arkansas lands, known as Lovely's Purchase, and to arrange for a survey of their western lands. And there was money due them for the lands they had abandoned back in the east, money they had never been paid. Because of the past experience of Cherokees in dealing with the U.S. government, the council had admonished them to sell no land.

The land west of Arkansas was land that had been claimed by the Osages as hunting grounds, and it was that land more than anything else that had been the cause of the long-standing war between the Osages and the Western Cherokees. No Osage lived there, and no Cherokee had settled there. Both hunted there, and they had fought many battles there. Then Agent Lovely had purchased the land from the Osages for the use of the Western Cherokees, and then whites had begun to move in. Sequoyah saw it as the old pattern repeating itself. He had not thought to see it so soon in the West.

But traveling the Mississippi River and the Ohio River, viewing Memphis, Louisville, Cincinnati and numerous other towns along the way, traveling the National Road from Pittsburgh to Washington City, watching the heavy traffic, viewing the rows of houses, Sequoyah saw where they were coming from, these unwelcome whites. By the time the delegation reached Washington, he was convinced that there would be no end to their westward flood onto Indian lands. He had not escaped them by moving west. He had merely delayed the moment when they would catch up to him again.

February, 1828

They had been taken to rooms in a large building called the Williamson Hotel. Along the way, they had seen nothing but large buildings and throngs of people. Sequoyah wished fervently that he had not agreed to make this trip. He longed to be back in Arkansas. He began to fear that many of these whites would be there before he could get back. In one of their hotel rooms, they talked, and they drank whiskey, generously provided for them by the government officials.

"What are they going to do to us?" asked John Looney.

"Ah," said Thomas Graves, a white man who had lived among them for most of his life, "they'll take us to some government office in the morning to talk. That's all."

"To talk about what?" asked Thomas Maw.

"They'll try to get us to sign a new treaty," said James Rogers. "That's what. They'll want some of our land."

"We're here to talk about what we want," Graves said. "We want the white people out of Lovely's Purchase. We want our lands surveyed, and we want the money they owe us. That's all."

"That's what we want," Black Fox said. "But what do they want?"

Sequoyah drank his whiskey and did not say anything. He listened to the others argue and speculate about what was about to happen. He heard his name, and it was almost as if someone had roused him from a sleep. He jerked his head up.

"What?" he said.

"What do you think, Sequoyah?" Thomas Maw asked.

"I want to get this over with and go home," he said.

They did not even talk the next day. The government men drove them in carriages around the city, showing off the strength and might of the United States, driving past opulent buildings, private mansions, military installations, statues of prominent Americans. It was all impressive, but the thing that impressed Sequoyah the most was the population. There were so many white people. He was stunned the whole time. He was impatient. But he kept his feelings and his thoughts to himself. He did not share them even with his companions. He did drink the whiskey the white men gave him.

Sequoyah was surprised at the personal attention paid to him by the whites. He was astounded to discover that his fame had spread even to this white man's capital. He was constantly being introduced as "George Guess, the Cherokee Cadmus. The native genius who raised his people from illiteracy. The inventor of the Cherokee alphabet." When there was time for chatting, they asked him questions. What was it that had caused him, a dark child of the forest, to entertain such notions in the first place? How had he gotten the idea that he could create a writing system for his people? What had been his process of discovery?

Of course, these questions had to be asked him through an interpreter, and Thomas Maw usually found himself in that position. The evening social occasions were the worst. Sequoyah, dressed as he had become accustomed to of late, in his leather moccasins, leather leggings and breechcloth, white trade shirt with ruffled cuffs and collar, hunting jacket made of a trade blanket and colorful turban wrapped round his head, would find himself in a corner with a drink in his hand. Two or three white people, men and women, in their fancy dress, would close in on him. There was no escape.

They would start talking at him, and he, of course, would not understand a word they said. Maw would miraculously appear and speak to the whites. They would giggle politely and then speak to Maw, and then look at Sequoyah with simpering expressions on their pale faces. Maw would nod and then turn to Sequoyah.

"They want to know how you happened to learn to write," he would say.

"I saw that white people could do it," Sequoyah would say, "and so I thought, we Cherokees can do it too."

"But how in the world did you go about it?" a matron would ask. Maw would translate.

"I went hunting in the woods one day," Sequoyah would say. "I thought I saw a strangely shaped rock on the ground, but when I picked it up, I discovered that it was a book. I took it home with me to study the marks inside." Or he might say, "I have a nephew who was going to the white man's school. One day I went with him, and I watched his teacher mark down words. I decided that I could do it too."

"But where did you find pen and paper in the wilderness?"

"I made my marks on the bark of trees. I carved them in stone.

I painted on the hide of deer and buffalo. I made ink from berries, and I made tiny brushes from the hair of a horse's tail. Then I painted my signs on the leaves of trees."

"Have you always been lame?"

"I was shot helping your president fight the Indians," he might say, or, "It was an unfortunate hunting accident."

"But what did your people think when you were busily engaged in your studies?"

"At first they thought I was crazy, and they laughed at me. Then when the roof was falling in on my house, and the bears had moved in with my wife and children, they thought that I was worthless and lazy. They took pity on my wife and tried to find her a new husband, but she wouldn't have any they offered. At last they believed that I was engaged in black magic. They were afraid that I was trying to turn them all into mice. They threw stones at me and tried to cut off my ears. You see how far they succeeded."

He made a point to show off his ears, which had been slit, the loose skin of his lobes hanging down as far as his jawline. The white women gasped. The men looked fascinated. Of course, his ears were only slit that way because it had once been the fashion of Cherokee men. It was a tradition, like many, that was fading, and Sequoyah was sorry to see it go. His cousin Agili had ears slit in the same way, but not many sported them in that manner any longer. For a while, Sequoyah enjoyed telling his tales to the white people, having them alternately fascinated, horrified and amused, but even that grew tedious.

But the official talks when they began were even worse. James Rogers had been right, of course. The U.S. wanted a new treaty. When they told the people in the east that they should move west where they would never again be bothered, they lied. They couldn't even wait to get all the Cherokees moved west before they wanted the lands in the west and wanted them to move farther west. The government agents had been clever. They had waited for the Cherokees to say that they wanted the whites off of Lovely's Purchase. Then they had said, if you want the whites off of that land, why don't you move on over there yourselves and leave us the Arkansas land for whites?

The Cherokees refused. "We don't want to move," Black Fox

said. "We want the whites out of Lovely's Purchase. That land was bought for us to use for hunting. We want our land in Arkansas surveyed, and we want the money you owe us. We don't want to make any new bargains. That's not what we came here for."

But each day came to an end with no resolution. Each morning brought a new meeting. Each evening brought new parties. Sequoyah began to think that he had seen enough of white people to last him for the rest of his life. He was fifty years old. That might not be too far in the future.

14

r. Knapp would like to know," said Thomas Maw, "just
how you came to distinguish all the sounds in the Cherokee language."

This was not the first interview Sequoyah had granted while in
Washington, and he was beginning to tire of the all the questions,
many of them he considered foolish, that the white men were
asking him. How had he, a rude child of the forest, managed to
accomplish this great deed? The first copy of the new *Cherokee
Phoenix* had appeared in Washington and it had made Sequoyah
a much sought after celebrity. He wanted to go home.

"Tell him," he said to Maw in Cherokee, "that I listened to the
sounds of the birds and the animals in the forest." Maw gave Sequoyah a curious look. "Tell him that," Sequoyah said, and Maw
repeated in English what Sequoyah had said. Other questions followed which Sequoyah answered with more or less truth until the
white man began to ask about Sequoyah's home life and family.
Sequoyah leaned back in great dignity and puffed on his pipe. "Tell
him that I have five wives and twenty children," he said, "and I
cannot recall all their names."

While Sequoyah had grown weary of all the questions and the
interview, he did find it fascinating to learn that there were white
men who not only earned their livings but also gained great respect
among their people for writing down their thoughts and feelings.
And he heard about the writing down of history. The thought grew
in his mind that he could write down the history of the Cherokee
people. It would be a great undertaking, but it would be well worth
the effort if he could do it. He made up his mind that he would

take on the task, and he bought pencils and paper to take home with him.

One morning at the hotel, one of the government men came. Sequoyah thought that they would be taken back to the government offices for more talks. He knew what the talks would be like. They had already disintegrated into long harangues by the government men about selling the Arkansas land and moving onto Lovely's Purchase. The Cherokees kept saying no, and the white men kept asking why not. Sequoyah was surprised when Maw turned to him and said, "There will be no talks today. But a famous white artist wants to paint your picture."

Sequoyah was fairly well known among his own people for his paintings as well as his silver work, so he understood that an artist could be respected. Still he was amazed when he arrived at the studio of Charles Bird King. He wandered around looking at the paintings on the wall and the unfinished work standing on easels in the middle of the huge room. He looked with wonder on the daubs of different colored paints on the palette. At last, he sat for the portrait. King asked him to pose holding up a copy of his syllabary, and he gave Sequoyah a pad on which to write the syllabary chart.

When Sequoyah had finished drawing all the symbols, he sat again, held the chart up in one hand and pointed to one of the symbols with the other. His pipe was in his mouth. He found it difficult to hold the pose, but King sketched as quickly as he could. At last, he told Sequoyah, through Maw, of course, to relax. He had gotten the pose down in his sketch, and he began to lay on the colors. Sequoyah watched him closely.

King was still not finished with the portrait when Sequoyah was taken away in the late afternoon, but the work was far enough along that Sequoyah was marveling at its accuracy and realism. Just before leaving, he told King through Maw that he hoped to be able to return and view the finished product.

"I certainly hope so as well," said the artist.

Time seemed to drag on for the Cherokee delegation. The talks seemed to go nowhere. The government men had their hard line: "Move to Lovely's Purchase." The Cherokees had their own: "We don't want to move. We want our lands surveyed, and we want the money you owe us." Each day was like the last, and the government men grew tired of wining and dining the Cherokees. They had them taken back to the hotel after their day's negotiations were done. The long evenings in the hotel rooms were dull. Sequoyah and some of his companions tried to make them pass more quickly by drinking whiskey.

May 6

They had been living in the hotel rooms in Washington City for well over two months, and all of them felt worn out. They were tired, and they were homesick. They had reached the conclusion that the government men were not going to let them leave until they had signed the new treaty. But if they signed what the government men wanted, their own people might kill them when they got back home.

"I'd rather be killed at home than waste away here," Thomas Graves had said.

The government man had a long paper in his hands, and he droned on reading it in the ugly sounds of the English language. Now and then, he would pause to allow Thomas Maw to put the words into the Cherokee language for Sequoyah and the other members of the delegation who did not understand English.

"They wish to secure a permanent home for us and for those in the east who might join us," Maw said. "The land will be ours forever. No state can be made over us or around us. He says, our present location is unfavorable to us. He wants us to avoid trouble with Arkansas in the future."

Maw paused, and the government man read on.

"They're drawing a boundary line," Maw said, "from the eastern Choctaw line on the Red River due north to the Arkansas River, then straight to the southwest corner of Missouri."

Again he paused for the white man to read, and again, he translated. The government was promising them seven million acres of land which encompassed the so-called Lovely's Purchase and further guaranteed them a perpetual outlet west and "free and unmolested use of all the Country lying West of the Western boundary of the above described limits, and as far West as the sovereignty of the United States, and their right of soil extend." The government man read further that the boundary lines would be run and any white people or any others "who may be unacceptable to the Cherokees" would be removed.

"They will also value all our improvements and pay us for them," Maw interpreted. "And they will pay us fifty thousand dollars and another two thousand dollars a year for three years. Another eight thousand seven hundred and sixty dollars for any damages done to us by Osage or white people. They agree to pay Thomas Graves one thousand two hundred dollars for his losses while falsely imprisoned, five hundred dollars to George Guess for his invention of the writing, and to give him the use of a saline Spring on Lee's Creek because of the saline he'll be giving up in Arkansas. They want to spend two thousand dollars a year for ten years for the education of our children and one thousand dollars towards the purchase of a printing press and type."

There were a few other minor details, and then there was a long pause. The government man read again. The Cherokee delegation waited. Finally Maw translated.

"For all of this," Maw said, "we 'chiefs and headmen,' as he calls us, promise to give up to the United States all of our land in Arkansas and get out of there in fourteen months. Then he promised some things to any Cherokees who leave Georgia and come out to join us. They want to keep the land where Fort Gibson is. There is five hundred dollars for James Rogers for the horse he lost and for his services in the past to the United States."

Maw paused, and the government man said, "That's all except for your signatures."

"Give us some time to talk this over," said Thomas Graves.

"I'll return in a few minutes," the government man said, and he left the room, shutting the door behind himself. The delegation sat silent for a long moment.

"They told us not to do this," Sequoyah said.

"If we sign this paper," said Black Fox, "they'll kill us when we get back home."

"If we refuse to sign it," Sequoyah said, "we may never see home again."

"Sequoyah's right," said James Looney. "I don't believe they mean to let us leave this city until we've signed this treaty."

George Marvis said, "The offer is generous. We'll have even more land than what we have in Arkansas. And the use of all that land to the west. They'll pay us to move and for our improvements. It's a lot of money, what he offered."

"They won't keep those promises," Sequoyah said. "They've never kept one yet."

"So what do you suggest?" asked Black Fox.

Sequoyah shrugged. "Let's sign it, go home and take our chances."

"They put it in that treaty that they'll pay us for different things," said Graves. "They owe us that money, but why should they put it in that treaty? When the council at home finds out about that, they'll believe that we were bribed to sign the thing. We should tell them to pay us what they owe us and take all that out of the treaty."

"I don't believe the white men will change any of the treaty now," Maw said. "They think they have the final copy, just what they want. Now they want us to sign it."

"I don't think we should sign it," James Rogers said.

"Do you want to live the rest of your life here?" asked Black Fox.

"Die and be buried here?" said Graves.

"Sequoyah," said Black Fox. "Will you sign it?"

"Yes," Sequoyah said. "I want to go home."

Black Fox, Thomas Graves and James Rogers each made an X beside his name. Sequoyah wrote his name, 'Si kwo ya,' in his own symbols beside the words, 'George Guess.' Thomas Maw, George Marvis and John Looney also signed in the letters of Sequoyah. The delegation was solemn. The agents of the United States were delighted.

Sequoyah was not anxious to face the people back in Arkansas and try to explain what they had done and why they had done it.

He knew, as did the other delegates, that there would be those who would say they should be killed. He contemplated that possibility, and asked himself what he would do if it should come to that. He decided that he would not argue and would not resist. If his own people decided that he should die, then he would die. At least he would be free once and for all of the ever-advancing white hordes.

He studied those seemingly endless whites as he and the others were driven out of Washington City. If those back home could see this, what we have been facing here, he thought, then perhaps they would understand, but he knew that there was no way he nor any other man could describe it adequately to anyone who had not seen it.

Soon they were out of the city, and Sequoyah felt a sense of relief, but at the same time, he seemed closer to home, and felt a corresponding sense of impending doom. The delegation was loaded into a stagecoach and started on the trip west to the Ohio River. The stagecoach trip seemed endless. It was a rough ride, jouncing and bumping all the way, and dust from the road was constantly filling the small coach and the lungs of its passengers. Sequoyah was glad when it was over, even though it meant they were that much closer to home, and perhaps, to the end of the line, in more ways than one.

Not even the great paddles on the river boats could distract Sequoyah's mind from the danger that was ahead of him. The days of the trip seemed to pass by much faster than had the days of the trip to Washington City. Almost before he knew it, they were changing from one boat to another, from the Ohio River to the Mississippi. He would be facing the angry council and people of the Cherokee Nation West before he knew it. He was standing at the rail staring at the big wheel when Thomas Maw stepped up beside him.

"Sequoyah," said Maw, "what will we tell them?"

"The truth," Sequoyah said.

"Of course," said Maw. "We'll have to tell them what we signed, but they'll ask us why we did it. What will we say?"

"I can only answer for myself," Sequoyah said, "I had my reason for signing. You had yours. Each of us had a reason. We can only tell the truth. Or keep quiet about it. It's up to you what you decide to tell them."

"Do you know what you'll say when they ask you?"

"No."

"But—"

"You know," Sequoyah interrupted, "we might not have a chance to say anything. They might just kill us."

They gathered in a stateroom on the river boat. Thomas Maw had talked with the others, and they had decided to call a meeting. Reluctantly, Sequoyah joined them. The meeting began with the same questions Maw had been asking Sequoyah.

"They can't know what we were facing there," John Looney said.

"Then we'll have to tell them," said James Rogers.

"Tell them what?" Graves asked. "That we saw more white people than they can imagine? That we saw the strength of their army? That they kept us prisoners until we signed?"

"Yes," said Looney. "Prisoners in a white man's big comfortable house with fine meals and expensive whiskey every night."

"That's not the point," said Rogers. "If we hadn't signed, we'd still be there."

"Every Cherokee in Arkansas will have to move because of what we did," said Thomas Maw. "They won't care about what it was like for us. They'll only think about the move they have to make."

"What will you say, Sequoyah?" Looney asked.

"That I signed," Sequoyah said.

"Why did you sign?"

"Because I want to go home."

"I'm afraid we'll all be killed," Rogers said.

"Well," said Graves, a burly man, "let them have at it. I'll take a few with me. I'll crack some skulls."

"When we get back," Sequoyah said, "if they allow us to appear before the council, let me speak for all of us. Perhaps I can think of the right things to say. Perhaps I can convince them that we did the only thing we could do, and that any one of them, had he been in our place, would have done the same thing."

The others looked at one another, and because no one else knew what he would say, and none was anxious to be put on the spot before the council, and because they were all aware that Sequoyah had become a big man among them, they all nodded and readily agreed. They seemed to relax after that, seemingly placing a tremendous confidence in the abilities of Sequoyah. After all, they thought, there was a time when all Cherokees thought that he was crazy or lazy or evil, and he had managed to persuade them otherwise. He had gone from being one of the most scorned Cherokees of all time to one of the most revered. If anyone alive could save them, they reasoned, it would be Sequoyah.

Sequoyah could sense their feelings, and he asked himself why he had stuck his neck out in that way. He had a fair notion of the high esteem in which he was suddenly held, and he was not at all certain that he was deserving of it. Looking back over the development of the syllabary, it seemed to him that any man of good sense could have done the same thing had he put his mind to it. All the praise and all the celebrity were wearing on him. In his own mind, he was like any other Cherokee man of middle age. No more, no less.

Yet he had jumped into this new and precarious situation. He had volunteered to be the spokesman for the group, to stand before the angry council and take all the questions, all the accusations, all the abuse. And once he had taken on that role, his fellow delegates all seemed confident that he would save them. Sequoyah did not feel so confident.

It would take more than his writing to pull his feet out of this fire. As Agili had said some time ago, the writing was not even his any more. Soon, the Cherokees would act as if they had always been writing, and they would forget his name. Unless the story was written down. He thought again of writing the history of the Cherokees, but almost as soon as he thought of it, he pushed it back out of his mind. There were more immediate things to be thinking about. He got himself off alone, and he took out his pad and his pencil. At the top of a clean sheet, he wrote, "To tell the council."

Then he began a list.

We got more land
We'll get much money
The whites won't come on our new land
We're free to roam as far west as we like
No states will surround us
We have fourteen months in which to move
It's a good bargain

He sat and looked over his list, and he felt like the government man trying to convince the delegation that they were being presented with the best of all possible deals. He told himself that would not work with the council or with the people. It had not worked with the delegates. They had said "no" to those same arguments for over two months. It was not the details of the bargain that had finally forced them to sign the treaty. Not at all. They had simply been worn down by the whites, and they had wanted to get out of Washington City and get back home.

Sequoyah knew that he would not save himself and the others by outlining the terms of the treaty. He would have to come up with something else. He thought about trying to describe the sights they had seen, trying to convince the people of the might of the United States, of the enormity of their population and the power of their military. He considered attempting to convey to the people the loneliness and the homesickness the delegates felt in the white man's capital for such a long time. He thought about a great many things he could try to explain, but nothing he could come up seemed adequate. There was whiskey on board the boat. He decided to get drunk.

15

Arkansas,
September, 1828

When Sequoyah arrived home, he saw that a pole had been set up in the yard in front of his house. It was curious, but it did not seem of any real importance. He walked toward the door, but just then, Sally came running out to meet him. "Sequoyah," she said, "run away fast. You can't stay here."

"I just got home," he said.

"But it's not safe for you here."

"Why not? Do you have another man in there?"

"Don't make jokes," she said. "You see that pole standing there? Some men came and put it there, and they said, 'It's for his head when he gets back home.' They did the same thing to the others, the ones who went with you. They mean to put your heads on the poles. You sold our land, they said. Is it true? Did you sell our land?"

Sequoyah sighed. He was tired from the long ordeal. "Yes," he said. "We did, and if they want my head for it, they can have it. Right now, I'm too tired to worry about such things. I want to rest."

But they did not cut off Sequoyah's head nor those of the other delegates. They called a council meeting and ordered the beleaguered delegation to attend. "Be ready to explain your actions," Ooloodega had said. "Sequoyah, when the arguments begin, I won't be able to help you. I'm your uncle, so I'll have to step aside."

Sequoyah got himself ready for the meeting. When he was fully dressed and ready to go, he tucked a folded-up newspaper under his arm. As he headed for the front door of his cabin, Sally rushed to him and threw her arms around him. She held him tight for a moment.

"Don't worry," he said. "What will happen will happen. But for now, my head is still on my shoulders."

"I don't want to lose you," she said.

"I'll do my best to stay around for a while yet."

Outside, twelve-year-old Teesee helped to saddle the horse.

"Do you want me to go with you and help fight them?" he asked.

Sequoyah smiled and rubbed the boy's head. "No," he said. "I don't think we'll have to fight them this time."

When he arrived at the meeting, an angry crowd was already gathered. The other delegates were seated in front of the crowd, and the chief and the council members faced them. Sequoyah took his place in the front row. Ooloodega called for order, and the angry voices died down.

"We sent you to Washington City to do a job for us," Ooloodega said to the delegates. "We told you to try to get our money for us, the money the government owes us already. We said, ask them to survey our lands, so we'll know exactly where our boundaries lie, and we said that we wanted the whites out of our hunting grounds, the land they call 'Lovely's Purchase.' We also said 'do not sell any land.' You had those instructions. You understood them. Now we find out that not only did you sell some land, you've sold all of our lands in Arkansas. Voices have been raised calling for your deaths. You know that's the penalty for selling our land. But we've brought you here today so that you may speak for yourselves—if you have anything to say."

Thomas Graves, the white man, stood up, and Ooloodega acknowledged him.

"We did what we had to do," Graves said. "If any of you had been there, you'd have done the same thing. So if you want to kill me for what I did, have at it, but it won't be easy. I may take a few with me." Graves sat back down.

John Looney stood up. "The white men just wouldn't listen to us," he said. "They just kept saying the same thing every day. Day after day."

"They wouldn't listen to us," said James Rogers.

Black Fox, Thomas Maw, George Marvis and James Looney sat silent. Ooloodega looked at Sequoyah. "Have you anything to say?"

Sequoyah stood up. The folded newspaper was tucked under his arm. He casually tossed it on a table at the side of the room. "I don't know what to say to you," he told the gathering. "When I got home, my wife showed me the pole in my yard and said that you mean to set my head on it. It will make a poor decoration for my house, and I think my wife will have to move and take my children to some new house. But then, after what we did in Washington City, we all have to move anyway, so I guess it won't matter much.

"It's true you told us not to sell any land, but you also told us to get the whites out of Lovely's Purchase. The only way the government would agree to get the whites out of Lovely's Purchase was if we sold this land. We could not do both. It was not possible to do one thing and not do the other. We held out as long as we could. We went to the talks for sixty days or more. We were homesick for our wives and children. We were surrounded at all times by ugly white men and white women."

He paused, and he took note of a man in the crowd moving over to the table and picking up the newspaper.

"We were alone there in that big city with thousands of ugly whites who were constantly going someplace or coming back from someplace. They showed us their army and their navy, their big guns and their big boats. We listened to their loud noises all day and all night with no rest. They told us the white people are pressing into Arkansas already, and they said they can only keep them off of our land if we move into Lovely's Purchase."

The man with the newspaper had opened it, and the others on both sides and behind him were looking at it, leaning over or craning their necks over his shoulders.

"We're not the wisest nor the best men among you," Sequoyah went on, "and we sorely needed your comfort and your counsel, but we were far from home and alone and crushed in on all sides by the enemy. So in the end, we did what we did, and if we must pay for it with our lives, so be it. I have no more to say."

He went back to his chair and sat down. Behind him, he could hear voices muttering on two different topics.

"This newspaper is written in Cherokee."

"In the symbols Sequoyah made."

"It's from home. From the old country."

"Let me see it. Pass it over here."

"But the treaty paid Sequoyah five hundred dollars."

"That was not for selling the land. It was for his letters."

"What about the twelve hundred for Graves?"

"That was for the time he spent in jail—falsely accused."

Ooloodega called for order again. "We'll meet again in four days," he said, "to have a trial. Then we'll determine what to do. Now everyone can go home. Be back here in four days."

The trial four days later was quick and easy. The decision seemed to have been made before the meeting started. The verdict was 'not guilty.' The lives of the delegation were spared. Heads were not placed on the poles in their yards. Black Fox said to Sequoyah, "It was you who saved us all. Your words were good. And the people were all excited by the newspaper printed in your signs."

Sequoyah smiled. "Yes," he said, "I guess they were."

1829

Once again, they packed to move, leaving behind the homes they had built, leaving behind the things that they had no way to pack and haul. The saline that had been promised to Sequoyah was located on Lee's Creek, and he found it and settled there, building a new cabin and establishing a new salt works. Sequoyah managed to transport his salt kettles and his blacksmith's tools. There was little time for visiting, for everyone was busy relocating and rebuilding. Reverend Washburn moved Dwight Mission across the line too, settling not far from Sequoyah.

Soon, though, Sequoyah was selling salt again, and now and then, visitors came by. But his fame had a new and permanent impact on his life. For now, traveling white men stopped by to see and visit with the famous Sequoyah. He treated everyone with friendship and respect. He enjoyed talking about his syllabary, even though, now and then, he embellished or changed the details of his stories. He was boiling salt water in his large kettles when he saw Ooloodega coming, bringing along another man. Sequoyah called out a greeting, and as the others drew closer, he recognized the chief's adopted son, Golanuh, the Raven, known to the whites as Sam Houston.

"It's good to see you, Sequoyah," said the Raven.

"It's good to have you back among us," said Sequoyah.

"It's been eleven years," Ooloodega said. "That's much too long."

"And much has happened," said the Raven. "Sequoyah, you've become a famous man. And you deserve to be. Why, what you've given your people with the syllabary is worth more than two hands full of gold given to every Cherokee man, woman and child."

"So much?" said Sequoyah, with a smile.

"I believe so," the Raven said.

"And what about you?" said Sequoyah. "I heard that you had become a big man among the whites back east."

"Well, my friend, that's all over. I've left it all behind me and come home to live with my father and my brothers and friends right here in the Cherokee Nation West. There is no place else on earth I would rather be."

"And my son will be a big help to us, Sequoyah," Ooloodega said. "You know, Jackson has become the president, and the Raven knows him as well as any man."

"Jackson is a great man," said the Raven, "and he'll be a staunch ally for us in Washington City. I'm proud to call him my friend, and I'll be honored to work on behalf of the Cherokees in Washington City anytime the need should arise."

"You know," said Ooloodega, "they want to move all the Cherokees out here with us. We don't have enough land for that. We'll be sitting on top of each other."

"We'll get more land out of Jackson," the Raven said. "We'll make sure there's plenty of room for all."

"I, for one, will be glad to see you take on the job of dealing with those men in Washington City," Sequoyah said. "When I went there, I almost lost my head."

"I heard about that," the Raven said. "I'm glad to see that it's still firmly fastened to your neck."

"Let's go back to my house," Sequoyah said. "Sally will fix us some coffee, and we can sit down comfortably to visit."

"I have a better suggestion," the Raven said. "Come along with me. Let me show you where I've settled. I have a good supply of whiskey there, and we'll have us a few drinks together."

"That sounds good," Sequoyah said. "I'll tell Sally on the way by the house."

Sequoyah and the Raven sat outside in front of the Raven's cabin sipping the whiskey the Raven had brought with him. The night was cool, and the fresh air was crisp and exhilarating. Bugs and birds sang their night songs.

"I was governor of the state of Tennessee," the Raven said. He was already feeling his cups. "I made it that far. General Jackson spoke up for me and had me appointed sub-agent to the Cherokees back in 1817. That was the beginning of my career in politics. I resigned that position to study and then to practice law, and I became district attorney, adjutant general and major general of state troops. In 1823, they sent me to Congress for two terms. Then in 1827, when I was but thirty-four years of age, I was elected governor of the state."

He paused and took a long drink.

"So why did you leave when you were doing so well?" Sequoyah asked.

"My brother," said the Raven, "that's something I never speak of. It has to do with the honor of a lady, my wife."

"Oh," Sequoyah said, and he drank.

"My once wife," the Raven said.

"But after you've been such a great man among the whites," Sequoyah asked, "how can you be satisfied to settle here among us Indians and live the life of—what?"

"I'll take up storekeeping," the Raven said. "It's an honorable and profitable profession."

"I've done that," said Sequoyah. "I don't think you'll like it."

"Perhaps my father, Ooloodega, will find reasons to put me to work at more adventuresome tasks from time to time. He's already talked of sending me to Washington City as a delegate from this nation."

"Yes. I heard that."

"I should find plenty to occupy my time here. For one thing, my friend," the Raven said, leaning close to Sequoyah with a lecherous look on his face, "I have to find myself a new wife."

"Get a Cherokee woman this time," Sequoyah said.

"Yes. I think so too. I should. Maybe I'll start looking around in the morning. First thing."

Sequoyah took another drink. "Not *too* early in the morning," he said. The Raven stood up and staggered a few feet away to relieve his bladder on the ground. "If you let the women see that thing," Sequoyah said, "you'll have them all around you."

"Ha," the Raven said, putting himself back together and moving back to sit down near his friend. "But you know, I did see a lovely thing at the recent green corn dance. I asked about her. Someone told me her name is Diana Gentry. Do you know her?"

"I know who she is," Sequoyah said. "She is Diana Rogers, the daughter of John Rogers, the white man."

"Hellfire Jack?" the Raven asked.

"I think they call him that," Sequoyah said. "Anyway, she was married to David Gentry. He was killed fighting the Osages."

"Ah, a widow. Children?"

"I think so."

"I'll raise them as my own. I love her, Sequoyah. I'll find a way to meet her. I'll court her and marry her. I've made up my mind."

Sequoyah nodded a bit drunkenly. "She'll be a good one for you," he said.

Then the Raven changed the subject abruptly, asking, "What do you hear from our friends in Texas?"

"Nothing for some time now," Sequoyah said. "You know, Tahchee has gone down there now too."

"So Captain Dutch has gone to live with the Bowl."

"No, I don't think so. I think he has his own towns along the Red River. Sometimes I think I'd like to go down there. I'd like to show the Cherokees down there how to write my—syllabary. If they could read and write, maybe we'd get letters from them. Maybe we'd know what's happening with them."

"That's a fine idea," the Raven said.

Sequoyah took another drink. "Maybe one of these days," he said. "Tahchee's an outlaw, you know. He won't stop killing Osages."

"He should," the Raven said. "It's time for that to stop. That might be something I can help with. Maybe I can talk to Dutch, the Osages and the army at Cantonment Gibson and help to bring about a peace."

"That's a worthwhile task," Sequoyah said.

"Well, I'll talk to Ooloodega about it in the morning."

"Yes, but not too early."

They laughed and drank some more, and Houston said, "I saw that the white preacher has set up shop not far from your home. Will he be trying to convert you to his way of thinking?"

"He may try," Sequoyah said. "He's changed Agili."

"He's had far-reaching effects, all right, and he won't rest until he's Christianized all Cherokees."

"His reaching won't reach me."

"Maybe you'll have to go to Texas just to get away from him," said the Raven. "You're a favorite target, you know. You're a celebrity, and you're known far and wide as a native scholar and philosopher. The preachers want very badly to put you on their list."

"They're using my own work and turning it against my people," Sequoyah said.

"Of course. They'll use anything they can sink their teeth in. They're leeches. They'll suck the blood right out of your way of life. I have an idea. Let's go over to Dwight right now and shout curses at the preachers and tell them to pack up and go home."

"Yes," Sequoyah said. "Let's do that."

Houston lurched to his feet and staggered over to his horse's side. He bent to pick his saddle off the ground. Heaving it up, he staggered backward. "Let's go," he said. Sequoyah had to use his walking stick to help him stand, but he made his unsteady way to where his own horse waited. Balancing himself carefully, he picked up his saddle. Houston walked back to his horse. He stood there staring and holding the saddle down at arms' length. He took a deep breath in preparation for heaving the saddle up and onto the horse's back, but instead of heaving, he fell, landing flat on his back. He did not move, he did not speak; he did not even moan. Sequoyah looked at him lying there. He looked at his horse. He dropped his saddle to the ground, and then he too fell over. He was out as soon as he hit the dirt.

16

Some Creeks moved in from their old country in the east to new homes just south of the Western Cherokees that year. They were being subjected to the same pressures back east as were the Cherokees. The vast, wide-open freedom the Cherokees had been promised if they would move to Lovely's Purchase was already being closed in on. However, the U.S. government did actually keep one promise. They made the whites move out of Lovely's Purchase. Most of the squatters had moved just across the line into the newly created Washington County, Arkansas, where they stared back at the coveted Cherokee lands with hateful looks on their pinched faces. It was also the year that some Tawakoni Indians in northern Texas killed some Cherokee hunters and amused themselves with the bodies. The insult was felt keenly by Captain Dutch and others, who were still living along the Red River on the Texas side. Clermont, the great Osage leader, died that year. Sam Houston said that it would be a good time to make a final peace with the Osages.

1830

The Osage peace had to wait. Everything hinged on Dutch; without his agreement, there could be no peace with the Osages. Everyone involved knew that. But Dutch was occupied with other things. He was busy in Texas. Following a four day war dance, Dutch led a large force of Cherokees to the Tawakoni village where the killers of the Cherokee hunters lived, and there he took terrible revenge, destroying the village and killing nearly everyone there. It was the following year before the efforts of Houston and the U.S. Army officers at Fort Gibson were able to secure a peace agreement between the Osages and the Western Cherokees. Still it hinged on the cooperation of Dutch.

Desperate by now for a final conclusion to the war, the Western Cherokee Nation sent a delegation to Dutch's settlements on the Red River. They told him that Clermont was dead, and that he was wanted back home. They told him why. To everyone's surprise, he agreed. He packed up his entire settlement and moved north to the Cherokee lands up there, settling on a creek that would ever after bear his name: Dutch's Creek. The long and bitter war with the Osages was actually and finally at an end.

Sequoyah was fifty-three years old. He stayed at home minding his own business. Sometimes he spent several consecutive days at his salt works, other days he worked at his anvil. There wasn't much call for his silver work or for teaching. Nearly all of the Cherokees could already read and write. He tried to put all the troubles that were plaguing the Cherokees out of his mind, but from time to time, someone came by to visit, and often they brought news of what was going on.

1832

It was a busy year. The Cherokee Nation back east had taken a case clear to the U.S. Supreme Court and won. The Cherokees had been elated at the news, until they heard that President Jackson openly defied the Court's ruling. He would not enforce it. At that point, some of the powerful and influential Cherokees who had been in the forefront of the resistance to removal gave up the fight. Where was there to go, having already gone to the highest court in the land? Major Ridge, his son John and his nephew, Elias Boudinot, the young editor of the *Cherokee Phoenix*, all began advocating that the Cherokees sign a treaty of removal. The Cherokees back east became divided into two camps, the Ridge Party and the Ross Party. The Ross Party was by far the largest, and its leader was Principal Chief John Ross. Feelings were bitter and often hostile. All of this news reached Sequoyah and others in the West.

The other big news of the year was local. Sam Houston, in a drunken and stupid state, had angrily struck old John Jolly, Ooloodega, his adopted father. The next morning, sober and ashamed for what he had done, he presented an abject, public apology to the old man, and left the Cherokee country for good, his head hanging. He was on his way to Texas.

In his leisure hours, Sequoyah wandered the woods in search of bee trees to gather wild honey, a delicacy he dearly loved. Or he fished. He did not hunt much anymore, because of trouble with his leg. He left the hunting to Teesee, who, at sixteen years of age, was plenty big, and he was getting to be good at it as well. And he kept his eye on the young men who lurked around his daughter. He knew what they were thinking. That was mainly Sally's job, though, and he largely left it to her. In the old days, he, as husband and father, would have been almost irrelevant to the family, and although the old clan structure was slowly giving way to the new European-style family, old habits die hard, and Sequoyah remembered what the old days had been like. He had never even known his own father—was not really sure who the man had been—and that fact had never bothered him at all.

Sequoyah was sitting in the house sipping his coffee when Sally came inside with a strange man. She introduced him to Sequoyah as Charles Vann. He had come specifically looking for Sequoyah. Vann was a mixed-blood, Sequoyah figured, for when he spoke to Vann, Vann answered in Cherokee.

"I've been sent by the principal chief and the council of the Cherokee Nation to see you," Vann said. "I'm sure you're aware of the fact that a medal was made to be presented to you in 1824, and, of course, you've never received it after all this time. Please read this. It's a letter from our principal chief."

Vann handed Sequoyah a folded and sealed paper. Sequoyah studied it for a moment, then broke the seal and unfolded it. He studied the paper for a moment, then handed it back to Vann.

"I can't read the English words," he said. "I don't even understand the language. Will you interpret it for me?"

"Oh, yes," said Vann. "Of course," and he began to read.

Mr. George Gist, My friend, The Legislative Council of the Cherokee Nation in the year 1824 voted a medal to be presented to you, as a token of respect and admiration for your ingenuity in the invention of the Cherokee Alphabetical Characters; and in pursuance thereof, the two late venerable Chiefs, Path Killer and Charles R. Hicks, instructed a delegation of this nation, composed of Major George Lowrey, Elijah Hicks and myself, to have one struck, which was completed in 1825. In the anticipation of your visit to this country, it was reserved for the purpose of honoring you with its presentment by the Chiefs in General Council, but having been so long disappointed in this pleasing hope, I have thought it my duty no longer to delay, and therefore take upon myself the pleasure of delivering it, through our friend Mr. Charles H. Vann who intends visiting his relatives in the country where you dwell. In receiving this small tribute from the people of your native land, in honor of your transcendent invention, you will, I trust, place a proper estimate on the grateful feelings of your fellow countrymen. The beginning, the progress and the final completion of the grand scheme is full of evidence that the efforts of all the powers of a man of more than ordinary genius were put in action. The present generation have already experienced the great benefits of your incomparable system. The old and the young find no difficulty in learning to read and write in their native language and to correspond with their distant friends with the same facility as the whites do. Types have been made and a printing press established in this nation. The scriptures have been translated and printed in Cherokee, and while posterity continues to be benefited by the discovery, your name will exist in grateful remembrance. It will also serve as an index for other aboriginal tribes or nations similarly to advance in science and respectability; in short, the great good designed by the author of human existence in directing your genius in this happy discovery cannot be fully estimated. It is incalculable.

Wishing you health and happiness, I am your friend, John Ross.

Sequoyah stood silent, almost as if stunned. Sally looked at him with clear admiration. Vann folded the letter and handed it back to Sequoyah. Then he reached into a pocket and withdrew a small packet which he unwrapped to reveal a silver medallion attached to a colorful ribbon. He showed the medal to Sequoyah and to Sally. The bust of a male Cherokee in a turban was on one side, along with the inscription, in Cherokee, "Presented to George Gist by the General Council of the Cherokee Nation for his ingenuity in the invention of the Cherokee Alphabet: 1825."

Vann turned the medal over to show two pipes crossed and English writing above them. "It's a translation," he said, "into English of the words on the other side. May I?"

He held up the medal by the ribbon, and Sequoyah leaned his head forward so that Vann could place the ribbon around his neck, leaving the medal to hang down on his chest.

"Thank you," Sequoyah said.

"I'm only doing my duty," said Vann. "It was a great pleasure for me to present this well deserved medal to such an honored man."

When Vann had left the house, Sally stared at her husband and at the medal on his chest. "It's beautiful," she said. "And you are a great man. Even John Ross knows it now."

1834

Captain Dutch found Sequoyah outside his smithy splitting short logs into sticks suitable for use in his forge. Sequoyah paused in his work to say hello, and to meet the young man Dutch had brought along with him. "This is Ujiya," Dutch said. "He's an admirer of yours, so I brought him out to meet you." Ujiya, or Worm, practically groveled before the great man, Sequoyah, so much so that Sequoyah was beginning to be embarrassed. Dutch sensed that fact and suggested that they help him split the wood. Ujiya was eager to help. He stepped in front of both of the older men and went right to work, thrilled to be doing something for Sequoyah. Sequoyah called out to Sally and asked her to prepare something for his guests. By the time Ujiya had all the wood split, Sally brought kanohena and coffee. The three men sat down to visit.

"Ujiya's going with me on a long trip," Dutch said. "The army at Fort Gibson wants to go west and meet some of the wild Indians they've never met before: Comanches, Wichitas, some others. Jesse Chisholm will be their chief guide, and he's asked me to go along. Ujiya's going with us too."

"It should be an interesting trip," Sequoyah said, and he felt a pang of jealousy. If only he were younger, and his leg did not bother him so. "I almost envy you," he said, understating his feelings.

Ujiya beamed with pride. Dutch was a hero because of his war exploits. Chisholm was known far and wide for his explorations and his familiarity with many different tribes of Indians. It was said that Chisholm could speak fourteen different languages, Cherokee and English being two of them. Maybe Spanish and French. The rest were the tongues of various plains Indian tribes. He had taken wagon trains to California, and he had ransomed many captives from the Comanches, returning most of them to their families. When their families could not be found, Chisholm kept them and cared for them in his own home. But Sequoyah, now there was the man.

Sequoyah, with his syllabary, had done more for the Cherokees than any other one man. All Cherokees made use of Sequoyah's syllabary. Ujiya felt like he was in the company of three of the greatest men alive. He was about to embark on a major adventure with two of them, and the third, the greatest of all, had actually expressed some envy of his position. They discussed the upcoming westward expedition for a while, but, since it had not yet occurred, there really wasn't much to talk about. Dutch changed the subject.

"Have you heard the latest news from back east?" he asked.

"I don't know," Sequoyah said. "What is it?"

"They had a big meeting back there, and some of the people spoke for removal and others spoke against it. When the talk was all over, some men killed John Walker Jr., just for expressing his opinion that it would be best to go ahead and move."

"It had almost gotten that far a time or two while I was still back there," Sequoyah said. "It's not safe to even say what you believe in times like these. What do you think will happen, Tahchee?"

"The government will move them all out here with us," Dutch said. "Sooner or later, they'll move them all out."

"And then what?" Sequoyah asked. "Will there be room for everyone? Will the argument continue out here? Will they still kill one another?"

Dutch shook his head. "I don't know. We can't know that until the time comes. You know, I used to be envious that I had never known the old country. That's no longer true. I'm glad that I grew up away from it."

"The times are hard," Sequoyah said.

The Dodge Expedition, as it came to be called, because it was led by Colonel Dodge, went out of Fort Gibson and returned some months later. They did indeed meet Comanches, Wichitas, Kiowas, Caddoes and other plains tribes. They escaped several near fights because of the linguistic abilities of Jesse Chisholm, but many of the soldiers came down with a mysterious prairie sickness, and many of them died, including Dodge himself. The Cherokee scouts somehow managed to avoid it. Sequoyah heard the story later. He was most interested, though, when Dutch told him about the white man from St. Louis named Catlin who had made sketches of him and others along the way.

The following year, a group of Cherokees back east, headed by Major Ridge, John Ridge and Elias Boudinot, signed a treaty of removal with agents of the United States. The treaty was fraudulent, as none of the signers were elected officials of the Cherokee Nation, but the U.S. government chose to treat it as valid and chose to enforce it. A deadline was set for the total removal of the Cherokee people from their eastern lands. Those who had been known as the Ridge Party were suddenly being called the Treaty Party, and they were being called traitors. There were many voices calling for their deaths. Shortly after the signing, the Georgia Guard seized the Cherokee Nation's press and newspaper offices.

Groups of Treaty Party members began moving west in 1836, where they expressed their willingness to live quietly under the government of the Western Cherokee Nation. That same year, Ooloodega's son, the Raven, Sam Houston, was involved in a revolution in Texas against Mexico. Davy Crockett, who had defended the Cherokees in Congress, and who earlier had also fought with them at Horseshoe Bend, was killed at the Alamo.

The news from back east was terrible. Georgia had passed a series of anti-Cherokee laws. They forbade Cherokees to dig gold on their own land. Georgians drove Cherokees from their homes and then moved in to take the homes over as their own. The Cherokee victims had no recourse, for the federal government under the leadership of Andrew Jackson, the chicken snake, refused to interfere, and a Cherokee was not allowed to testify in a Georgia court. From all reports, life in the old Cherokee country had become almost unbearable. Yet Chief Ross held out, refusing to move.

Each time he heard news from the east Sequoyah contemplated the events. He recalled the time just before he had decided to make the move. He remembered that his own life had been threatened for even considering such a thing. He wondered what life would be like back there had he not made the move when he did. He hated to think of his own people, many of them his friends and relatives, enduring all those injustices he was hearing about, and he wished that there was something he could do to help. Of course, he knew there was not. There seemed to be no end to the invasion of the ugly hordes of white people. He wondered if one day they would completely overwhelm and smother the Indian people.

1838

Ooloodega was dead. The Western Cherokees had elected John Brown their new chief. John Looney was second chief, and John Rogers third. The three chiefs was an old practice, left over from the days of the Osage war. It was a way of insuring that they would not be left without a chief in case of some unforeseen disaster.

And that was the year the United States, tired of waiting for John Ross to acquiesce, had sent the Army to round up Cherokees in the old country and begin forcing them west.

It was a terrible ordeal. People were dragged from their homes or from their fields. Families were separated. They were marched down out of the mountains, leaving behind most of their belongings, to holding pens, stockade fences, where they were held like cattle. In these prison camps, people sickened and died. Food was insufficient and often barely fit to eat. Sanitary conditions were nonexistent. White men came by to sell whiskey, and those who could buy it stayed drunk. Soldiers enticed young Cherokee women out of the stockade with the promise of whiskey in exchange for their favors. Children cried. The sick moaned. People waited, enduring the hunger, the pain, the stench and the uncertainty. They waited, for there was nothing else they could do. They were prisoners.

At long last, some were taken out of the stockades and started by the army on the long march west. The weather was unbearably hot. There were some wagons and some horses, but mostly the Cherokee people walked. At night, when they camped, some ran away. No one knew where they went or what became of them. Babies were born along the way. Babies and old people died and were buried along the way in unmarked graves. In the humid, swampy parts of Mississippi and Arkansas, people sickened from the stifling, muggy heat. When they arrived at last at Fort Gibson, there were several hundred less than there had been when they had departed the old country.

Chief Ross, seeing the horrors of the forced removal, proposed to the army that the Cherokee Nation be allowed to contract for the rest of the move and do it themselves. He was successful. Because of the unhealthy atmosphere of the summer, he held up the remaining waves of immigration, but he held them up too long. Many of the people were caught between the frozen waters of the Mississippi and Ohio Rivers in Southern Illinois in one of the worst and earliest winter storms in memory. They could not move in either direction. They froze. They starved. Again, they sickened and died.

When it was all over at last, the immigrants who arrived at Fort

Gibson were a sorry and wretched lot. It was said that of all those who left the old country, one-fourth had died along the way. Sequoyah watched the newcomers straggle in. He saw the pain and misery and bitterness on their faces. So did Dutch and Ujiya, and young Teesee. Teesee and Ujiya had become close friends. There wasn't much that Sequoyah could do. He helped with expenses until his own funds were depleted. But Dutch and the two young men did more. They helped the newcomers to locate home sites and to get started on their cabins. They hunted. Dutch provided beef, and no one asked him where he had gotten it. No one cared.

But something else was going on, and it was the very thing that Sequoyah had feared the most. There was a seething anger, a hatred born of suffering, a desperate desire to seek revenge or justice, to balance things out. It was no use aiming all of the frustration at the United States. Nothing could be done about that. And so it was focused on the Treaty Party, the traitors.

June 3, 1839

They met at a place called Double Springs, the site designated by the Western Cherokee Nation as its capitol. Six thousand Cherokees gathered there, as well as interested whites, mostly the missionaries. John Ross was there as the leader of the recent immigrants. Sequoyah was in the crowd. Members of the Treaty Party, including the Ridges and Elias Boudinot, showed up, but when they saw the looks they were receiving, they left. On the speaker's platform, Chief John Ross and Chief John Brown congratulated one another as heads of a reunited people. Chief Brown was about to call the meeting closed when Ross stepped forward to speak.

"On what terms will we, the recent immigrants, be accepted by your government?" he asked.

"You have been accepted," Brown responded. "We are one people."

"But to what privileges are we entitled?"

Brown thought that he had said it all and said it satisfactorily. He tried to hide his exasperation as he turned again to address the crowd. "We cordially receive you as brothers," he said. "We joyfully welcome you to our country. The whole land is before you. You may freely go wherever you choose and select any places for settlement which may please you, with this restriction: that you do not interfere with the private rights of individuals. You are fully entitled to the elective franchise, are lawful voters in any of the districts in which you reside, and eligible to any of the offices within the gift of the people." He went on to say that elections were coming up soon, and as the new immigrants far outnumbered the "old settlers," they would very likely prevail in those contests. In the meantime, he said, "It is expected that you will all be subject to our government and laws until they shall be constitutionally altered or repealed."

John Ross was not satisfied. "It is imperative," he said, "that we remain as an organized body politic for the purpose of settling our accounts with the United States."

By all means, Brown told him, keep your government for those purposes. Still Ross was not satisfied. He objected to the laws of the Western Cherokee Nation. "They are modeled after your own," said Brown. "Change them at election time." Even that was not good enough for Ross. Brown, disgusted, adjourned the meeting and left, but Ross called on his followers to stay. They met for two more days, and then Ross sent a letter to the United States Agent to the Cherokees.

"Reasonable propositions submitted to the consideration of the representatives of our western brethren," he wrote, "have not been received by them in a manner compatible with the wishes of the whole people." He wrote further that he was afraid their attitude would "disturb the peace of the community, and operate injuriously to the best interests of the nation."

Sequoyah worried. He felt that he could see that the animosities toward the treaty signers were being extended to include all those who had left the old country before the forced removal. It was almost as if the Western Cherokee Nation and the Treaty Party had become one and the same in the minds of John Ross and his followers. If trouble is coming, Sequoyah thought, it will come to us all.

Four days later, twenty-five men rode to the home of John

Ridge. They pulled Ridge out of his bed in the wee hours of the morning, dragged him outside, and in view of his wife, his children, his wife's sister and her husband, stabbed him numerous times, tossed his body into the air, and, when it landed, stamped on it. They left him there, not quite dead, and his wife and children watched him slowly expire.

Thirty riders waited in the woods near the home of Reverend Worcester, with whom Elias Boudinot and his wife were living. Four of the thirty went to Boudinot and said they needed some medicine for sick members of their family. As Boudinot walked with them toward the mission, the men came out of the woods and stabbed and hacked him to death.

Major Ridge was riding along a lonely stretch of road in Arkansas just outside the Cherokee boundary. From the woods on both sides of the road, a dozen shots rang out. The old man, hit several times in the head and body, tried to hold on to his horse. It reared and threw him. He fell to the road dead.

17

Sequoyah rose early and dressed himself, casually, almost carelessly, as usual. He wrapped his turban around his head, and then pulled on his once colorful but now faded hunting jacket. He still wore leather leggings and moccasins. Sally gave him a concerned look.

"Where are you going?" she asked.

"Little John has called a meeting over near his new home," he said. "Everyone's invited."

"Don't go, Sequoyah," she said. "It's not safe."

"If someone wants to kill me," he said, "then it's not safe anywhere. Where was John Ridge killed? Right in his own home. Besides, I'm not one of that party."

"They're acting like all of us belong to that party. The treaty signers and those of us who were already out here. They're calling us 'old settlers' now, and they're lumping us all together: old settlers and Treaty Party."

"That's why this meeting is so important," Sequoyah said. "It's a chance to set aside all the differences and get all the people back together. We're all Cherokees. One people. Someone has to make everyone see that."

So he mounted his horse and rode toward the home of John Ross, Little John, for the big meeting. Nothing his wife could think of to say made any difference. His mind was made up. He was aware of his status among the Cherokees. Maybe it would do some good for him to be there and to present a voice of reason.

July 1

He found that he was one of the few at the meeting representing the old settlers, and members of the Treaty Party were even more scarce. It seemed that everything proposed by John Ross was endorsed by the people. Amnesty was declared for all crimes committed by anyone since the end of the long trail, the Trail of Tears. That meant that no one would ever be prosecuted for the killings of Major Ridge, John Ridge and Elias Boudinot. Stand Watie and others were not going to be pleased at that.

John Ross announced from his platform that any treaty signer would be forgiven if he would publicly profess his sorrow at a council meeting and consent to being ineligible to hold office for a period of five years. Sequoyah thought that some of them would do it to protect themselves, but others, like Stand Watie, would never submit to such humiliation. The times were seeming more and more dangerous. During a break in the proceedings, Chief Ross sought out Sequoyah.·

"It's good to see you here, my friend," he said, speaking through an interpreter, for the chief's command of the Cherokee language was severely limited.

"I thought I should come," Sequoyah answered.

"I'm glad for two reasons," Ross said. "I'm pleased to see you and be able to greet you as an old and dear friend. And I'm happy to see the token of our respect hanging around your neck. You must know how much all Cherokees honor and respect you for what you've done. The other reason that I'm pleased to have you here is that many of the old settlers and the members of the Treaty Party seem to mistrust our motives. We want nothing more than to bring our people all back together in peace and harmony and proceed with the business of rebuilding our great nation. Your appearance here can only help us in that respect."

"I want the same thing," Sequoyah said. "I'll do anything I can to help."

Later in the day, John Ross formed a committee of men to

gather on the platform. Then he called Sequoyah forward. He made a long speech which Sequoyah did not understand until it was repeated for him and others who did not know the English language. It praised Sequoyah for all his hard work in the face of such difficulties, and it praised him further for the wonderful results of that work, the syllabary. It said that no other man in the history of the world had done such a thing as Sequoyah had done for his people, and at one point in his speech, Chief Ross reached for the medal around Sequoyah's neck. "This," he said, "is the very token of appreciation which the council of the Cherokee Nation presented to this fine man. It says," he looked closely at the medal and turned it over so that he could read the English, "It says, 'Presented to George Gist by the General Council of the Cherokee Nation for his ingenuity in the Invention of the Cherokee alphabet: 1825.' " Ross then released the medal and stepped to Sequoyah's side. "He has already done much for his people," he continued, "and he is here today to show his support for the unity of our nation."

Sequoyah looked down at the medal on his chest. He waited for the chief's talk to be repeated in Cherokee. Then he stepped forward proudly. "I thank the council for this honor," he said. "This is the first chance I've had to do so. Everything I have done is for my people. I want all Cherokees to live together in peace and brotherhood. And when we are separated for any reason, I want us to be able to send talks to one another, so that we may at least remain together in spirit."

July 5

The council reconvened, and this time Sequoyah and Agili were named co-presidents of the convention. As before, there were few old settlers and fewer Treaty Party members in attendance. Chief Ross wrote a letter to the chiefs of the Western Cherokee Nation inviting them to the meeting. The purpose, the letter said was to promote "peace, tranquillity, and the future prosperity and happiness of our common country." The letter was endorsed by Sequoyah and Agili and delivered to Chiefs Brown, Looney and

Rogers, where they were holding their own separate meeting. There was no response. Sequoyah composed a second letter and wrote it in his own hand.

"We, the old settlers, are here in council with the late emigrants, and we want you to come up without delay, that we may talk matters over like friends and brothers. These people are here in great multitudes, and they are perfectly friendly towards us. They have said over and over again, that they will be glad to see you, and we have full confidence that they will receive you with all friendship."

This time, John Looney came, and others came with him. Sequoyah embraced Looney and took him to meet John Ross. "Where are Chiefs Brown and Rogers?" Sequoyah asked.

"They refused to come," Looney said. "I reasoned with them until I was out of breath. They insist that we'll keep our own government, separate from the government of John Ross. Treaty Party men are aligning themselves with them."

"We must hold this nation together at all costs," Ross said.

Sequoyah pulled Looney aside and whispered in his ear. "Are there enough of us here to do something?" he asked.

"Like what?" Looney asked.

"Can we put those other two chiefs out of office?"

Looney looked around and considered for a moment. "Yes," he said. "I think we can."

Sequoyah went back to Chief Ross and spoke through an interpreter. "We're going to have our own meeting over there aside from the rest of you," he said, "but I don't want you to be alarmed. We're going to discuss what we can do about this situation when two of our three chiefs refuse to join us here. We'll come back to you soon with our decision."

Ross nodded his understanding, and Sequoyah and Looney withdrew with all of the old settlers who were present. There were about two-hundred and fifty there. When they had everyone's attention, Sequoyah stood before them.

"Our whole Cherokee Nation is gathered here," he said. "Little John wants us to be united again under one government. That's as it should be. We're one people. All of us have friends and relatives on both sides. There should only be one side. But our other two chiefs don't agree with that. They want to keep our old government, the Western Cherokee Nation. I believe that's a dangerous attitude to hold. I think we need to unite."

As Sequoyah stepped back, Looney moved up to take his place. "We can do as Sequoyah suggests," he said. "We can vote right here to disband our Western Cherokee Nation government and reunite with the greater Cherokee Nation, but in order to do that and for it to be official, we must first vote to depose Chiefs Rogers and Brown. If they are no longer our chiefs, then the only one left is me, and I'll vote with you to conclude this act of union."

There was some discussion, but soon everyone agreed to follow the advice given them by Sequoyah and John Looney. They seemed to be voices of reason. There was too much dissension in the nation. There had already been violence, and the potential for more was great. Looney and Sequoyah went back to John Ross and told him what they had done.

In Sequoyah's mind, all that was left to do was to bring the Cherokees in Texas back into the fold. He wrote a letter to Chief Bowles urging him to return to the Cherokee Nation.

August

Sequoyah was lounging in a hand-made chair in front of his cabin. Sally had just brought him a cup of coffee. She glanced up to see a rider coming. "We have a visitor," she said.

Sequoyah looked up. "It's Tahchee," he said. "Bring another cup."

Captain Dutch rode up and dismounted, and he sat down in another chair at Sequoyah's invitation. Sally brought him coffee.

"I came with some news," Dutch said. "It's not good news, but I know you're interested. I know about the letter you sent to Texas to Chief Bowles. A few days ago, John Bowles and some others came to my house."

"John Bowles?" Sequoyah said.

"The son of the old chief," said Dutch.

"Ah."

"He and the others with him had just come from Texas. He told me that the Texans had told the Cherokees to get out of Texas. Bowles argued with them for a time, but at last he agreed to get out."

"What about the Raven?" Sequoyah asked.

"Now that Sam Houston has won their independence from Mexico for them," Dutch said, "the Texans have turned on him too. He defended Bowles, but his words fell on deaf ears. The Texans told Bowles to give up all his gun locks, and they would escort him and his people to the border. Bowles said they would not give up their gun locks, and they needed no escort to ride out of Texas. He and his people left in the night, meaning to come up here and join us.

"The Texans attacked them without warning. They had a bloody battle, and many of our people were killed. The old man was riding his white horse, and a Texan shot the horse. Bowles was thrown to the ground. He got up to his knees, but a Texan came up close behind him and shot him in the head. Bowles is dead. He was carrying the treaty he had signed with the Raven, and he was wearing the sword the Raven had given him. The ones who survived scattered. Some went south toward Mexico. Others came up here. They stopped with me. They have nothing. Jesse Chisholm has been providing beef to help feed them."

Sequoyah thought long and hard. At last he said, "Of course, I'll help you to provide for them," he said. "The news about Bowles is hard news. I'm glad for those who came back home to us, but I'm worried now about the others, the ones who went to Mexico."

"If that's really where they went," said Dutch. "Of course, there's no way we can tell for sure."

"Hmm," Sequoyah murmured.

September 6, 1839

They gathered at Tahlequah, the newly laid out capitol of the Cherokee Nation, and there they formed a new government embracing all Cherokees. A formal Act of Union was signed between the Cherokee Nation and the Western Cherokee Nation, with John Looney, Sequoyah and others acting on behalf of the former Western Cherokee Nation. John Brown and John Rogers, it was said, were still firmly in the camp of Stand Watie.

"There's going to be trouble, Sequoyah," John Looney said. He was right.

1840

In the next several months, killing followed killing. Archilla Smith, a follower of Watie, stabbed John McIntosh to death. Smith was arrested, tried in a Cherokee court and hanged. David Miller killed John Phillips. Ellis Phillips and others, in retaliation, killed Miller. Stand Watie gathered together a small army and holed up in Arkansas. Another small army formed around the home of Chief John Ross. No one was safe. It was said that Stand Watie had offered ten thousand dollars for the names of the men who had killed his brother, and everyone knew why he wanted those names. It was said that John Ross wanted Stand Watie killed. It was said as well that Stand Watie had the list of names he wanted. More killings were bound to come. Each killing seemed to lead to another.

"Sequoyah," Sally said, "I don't think it's safe for you around here."

"Why not?" he asked.

"John Brown and John Rogers and Stand Watie might call you a traitor for doing what you did. They've killed others for less reason."

"You mean for signing the Act of Union?" he said.

"For kicking out those two chiefs," she said. "For going against the government of the Western Cherokee Nation."

"I don't think they'll bother me," Sequoyah said.

"Don't be so smug just because you have that medal hanging around your neck. Don't think you're such a great man as to be above anyone else. You've escaped a killing several times already. There were those who wanted to kill you because of your symbols. Then they wanted to kill you for signing that paper with Ooloodega and the Raven. Even out here, when you went to Washington that time and signed that paper, they put a pole in front of the house to stick your head on. You're taking too many chances, Sequoyah. The next time, they might do it. And that could be just any day now."

Sequoyah filled and lit his pipe. Then he took his walking stick and hobbled away from the house to sit beside Lee's Creek and think about what his wife had said. Was he getting too puffed up with pride? he asked himself. Was he, as she had said, smug? Had he allowed himself to believe that he was such a great man and so highly respected that he could do whatever he wanted to do and not expect to have to account for his actions to anyone? She was right, of course. There was a conflict, a serious one, and he had changed sides. If anything, the fact of his fame would place him in even a more precarious situation than if he were unknown. People paid attention to him. They took note of his words and deeds.

Had not Chief John Ross been pleased to have Sequoyah join him in his cause? Had not John Looney and over two hundred others taken his advice and followed his lead? And now, he had heard, even Dutch had joined with Rogers and Brown, and they were saying that Dutch was the third chief of the Western Cherokee Nation. Dutch was a dangerous enemy for anyone to have.

There was no safe way to turn, it seemed. The feelings were too hard and bitter on all sides, and they would not easily be reconciled. Sequoyah had thought that the best course would be to get all sides back together under one government, and the largest and most powerful group was that of the recent emigrants under the leadership of Little John. He had done what he thought was best. But then, so had the Ridges and Boudinot. Would the Cherokees never get back together in peace?

All of these problems, of course, were the result of the interference of the white man in the affairs of the Cherokees. As he contemplated the conflicts and all the complications of Cherokee life, Sequoyah hated the whites. He recalled the days in his childhood when his mother had clutched him close to her breast, huddled on the steep side of the mountain, watching as white men burned their town below them, destroyed their home and their food supply, killed any stragglers who had remained behind. He recalled those horrors and others that had followed.

The white men no longer rode into Cherokee towns burning and killing. Their tactics had changed. They came instead with papers and bribes. They came asking for land, and they found some who would sign the papers. They no longer needed to kill Cherokees, for once they had gotten the signatures on the papers, Cherokees would begin killing Cherokees. He thought that he preferred the old way. The enemy was plain to see. The fight was straightforward. This new way, one did not know what to expect.

Who might kill him? John Rogers? Stand Watie? Captain Dutch even? Certainly not a white man. But if some assassin should come for him, the fault would be that of a white man. Sequoyah tried to think ahead, tried to see what might become of all this. He could not see the future for the Cherokees, or if he could, he did not like what he thought he could see. If anything, the hard times were getting worse. Life among the Cherokees was becoming more dangerous with every day.

"Sequoyah!"

He looked around with a start, but it was only Sally calling to him.

"I'm here," he answered. He stood up with a groan and started back toward the cabin. Sally was coming to meet him, and a man was walking beside her. The man, a Cherokee of mixed-blood who could speak Cherokee, introduced himself and shook hands with Sequoyah.

"It's an honor to make your acquaintance," the man said. "I've been sent by Chief John Ross to invite you to be a guest at his home. There's an important white man named John Howard Payne staying at the chief's house, and he wants to meet you. He's a famous writer among the whites, a writer of plays and poems and songs, and he's an actor as well."

Sequoyah did not quite understand the actor, and the writer of plays. He only understood the fame.

"John Howard Payne is known around the world," the young man continued. "He's staying with our chief to write things about the Cherokees, things about our history and our way of life. He wants to write these things down before they're all forgotten, and

Chief Ross told him that he should talk to you. He said you're one of the wisest of all the Cherokees."

"Tell Little John for me that I'll be there," Sequoyah said, and he asked himself, did I agree to that so readily because of the way in which he appealed to my puffed up pride?

18

December,
1840

S equoyah," Sally said, "you didn't even know that young man. How can you trust him?"

"He came from Little John," Sequoyah said. "They want me there."

"Some men told Boudinot that they wanted medicine," she said. "Along the way, they killed him."

"You think they'll kill me along the way to Little John's house?"

"Do you think they won't?"

He finished packing, went outside, saddled his horse and left. He knew that there was wisdom in her words. He knew that Boudinot had been led away down a lonesome path by lies, so that they could waylay and kill him. He even knew that there were likely some men out there somewhere who would think that he should be killed for his role in the Act of Union. Even so, he was not terribly worried. Somehow, he did not think that any Cherokee would actually try to kill him. Even so, he watched both sides of the trail as he rode, and now and then, he looked back over his shoulders.

He was startled by the sight that greeted him as he rode toward Rose Cottage, the southern plantation–style home of the principal chief, for it was surrounded by armed guards, a small army of full-blood Cherokees. He had not seen anything like it since the days of the Red Stick War. He hesitated, and thought about turning around to ride back home, but one of the men spotted him and waved to him to ride ahead. As he drew closer, he heard the man call out, "It's Sequoyah. Cooweescoowee is expecting him. Let him ride through."

Sequoyah was welcomed into the fine home of Cooweescoowee, Principal Chief John Ross, ushered in by a Black slave dressed in fine clothes. He was pleased to see young Ujiya there. "They asked me here to interpret," the young man said. "It's an honor." Through the translations of Ujiya, Sequoyah was introduced to the white man, John Howard Payne. Then he was escorted to a special seat beside the fireplace. It was comfortable there before the blaze. A female Black slave brought coffee, and Sequoyah filled his pipe and lit it. Payne placed himself at a small desk, prepared to take notes. Ujiya took a seat between Sequoyah and Payne, but he pushed it back so that the two great men could still see one another. Ujiya was at least as anxious as was Payne.

"Now," Sequoyah said, "I'll tell some ancient memories. I'll start with everything I can recall from my earliest childhood about the town of Taskigi where I was born. Things have changed since those days. Nothing is recognizable any more. I was born in Taskigi, an old Cherokee town. You couldn't find it today. It's in the state of Tennessee, and white men have destroyed everything and built their own towns and farms. Even in my childhood, they came, many of them, mounted on horseback, and they rode through Taskigi screaming and laughing and burning all the houses and trampling and cutting the corn. If they found any people there, they killed them. My mother had taken me up the mountain before they came, and we watched it all. I can still see it in my mind."

Ujiya leaned forward in his chair, staring at the floor between Sequoyah's feet, listening intently. Payne sat poised with his quill, fascinated by the voice and gestures of the great man, waiting patiently for the words to be put into English by the young translator so that he could write them down.

Sequoyah talked on. He talked about the great men of the Cherokee during his childhood and youth, several of them his own uncles. He talked about the rumors that his father had been a white man named Gist or Guess, but he said that he did not know. He had never met the man. Besides that, he said, it was not important. He talked about the great Dragging Canoe and his followers, called the Chickamaugas, and how they had fought for

Cherokee land and the Cherokee way of life, and he talked about the way things had changed for Cherokees during his own lifetime of sixty-two years.

"Sixty-two years," he said. "It's a long life for a man, yet it's a brief time in the life of a nation of people, a very short time for such sweeping changes as we have seen."

Sequoyah talked about the old ceremonies and about the time the missionaries came in and began trying to change the way the people believed and behaved, and he talked about his own feelings regarding that conflict of beliefs. He stopped short of saying that he hated the missionaries for their work, but he did say that he found them unbearably arrogant, and he said that they must not be very effective, because so many white people behaved so badly.

"Perhaps," he said, "they came among the Indians because they were unsuccessful among their own kind. They were looking for someone who would listen to them. Sometimes, I think, we're too polite for our good. We'll listen respectfully to any stupid thing that anyone wants to tell us."

At last Sequoyah paused to refill his pipe, and Payne seized the opportunity. He turned to Ujiya, and said, "When will you translate for me what he's been saying? You've waited too long."

"Oh," said Ujiya, "I couldn't interrupt him. It wouldn't be polite."

"Ask him," said Payne, "if he'll start over and pause now and then so that you can tell me what he said, and I can write it down."

Ujiya asked the question of Sequoyah. Sequoyah puffed at his pipe until it was well lit. "I'm tired now," he said. "Tell the white man we'll talk again in the morning."

The slave returned with some venison, cornbread and coffee and passed it all around. Sequoyah ate a little. Then he was taken to a corner of an upstairs room where he was a shown a cot on which he could sleep. He took off his turban and his jacket and stretched out to rest. He thought about the white man downstairs. He knew that he had frustrated the man. He considered the things he had said about the white men attacking his town, about the missionaries and their goal and what he thought about it and about them, and he wondered if maybe it had all been for the best that his words had not been interpreted for the white man to write down. Perhaps the white man would not have written down what he had actually said.

So the white man wanted to write about Cherokee history and the Cherokee way of life. Well, Sequoyah thought, he himself had thought about writing those things down. Now he would do it. He would write it all down, and he would write it in the Cherokee language. There would be no chance for his words to be changed by the process of putting them into English and having them written down by a white man. With those thoughts, he drifted off to sleep with a smile on his face.

They ate breakfast and drank coffee in the morning, and when they had finished, Payne spoke to Ujiya, who then turned to Sequoyah and translated. "He would like to know if we can begin again this morning and let him take notes this time," Ujiya said. Sequoyah thought for a long moment.

"Tell him," he said at last, "that my memory is not so good as it used to be. Tell him that I have to think about those things. I'm afraid that I might have recalled some things imperfectly."

Having heard Sequoyah's response, Payne asked, "But when?"

"I have to think about it for a while," Sequoyah answered.

In a short time, he had saddled his horse and was riding back toward his home. Ujiya rode with him.

"The white man was disappointed," he said. "He wanted to write down your words."

"There are plenty of others who'll tell him tales," Sequoyah said.

They rode on in silence. Sequoyah was thinking about the history he would write.

They were getting close to Sequoyah's home. In another half day's ride they would be there. Ujiya had been a good traveling companion. He was respectful of Sequoyah's age and position. He did not talk too much, and he did what he could to make the old man's travel as easy and comfortable as possible. It was near noon when the young man spotted something ahead on the horizon.

"Sequoyah," he said. "Look."

It was the silhouette of a man on horseback holding a rifle.

"Don't worry," Sequoyah said. "Ride on."

They continued along the road, and the man on the horizon did not move. At last they were close enough that Sequoyah recognized the figure as Captain Dutch. Of course, Dutch would have recognized him as well. As they drew closer, Dutch was off to their left on the horizon on a rise overlooking the road. They continued along until they were nearly below Dutch, and Dutch raised the rifle to his shoulder. He aimed at Sequoyah.

"He's going to shoot," said Ujiya.

Sequoyah stopped his horse and looked up at Dutch. "Be still," he said to Ujiya. "He won't shoot you."

It was all Ujiya could do to sit still. He wanted to kick his horse in the sides and race ahead to safety, but he could not bring himself to ride away from Sequoyah. Sequoyah sat still looking at Dutch. Dutch's rifle remained trained on Sequoyah. At last, Dutch lowered his rifle, waved an arm, turned his horse and rode away. Ujiya breathed a long sigh of relief. Sequoyah urged his horse forward.

"Let's go," he said.

Back home in his own bed, Sequoyah did not sleep. He lay awake thinking. Sally had been right. There was no doubt about it now. Even Tahchee had thought about killing him. He had taken aim, but he had thought further about it and decided against it. If he had squeezed the trigger faster, not taken the time to think, Sequoyah might be dead already. He was not afraid of death. In fact, at his age, he considered that it was not far off. But he did not like to think about being killed by one of his own people, especially by an old friend. And all because of troubles stirred up by white men.

He made up his mind to stay at home, to work at his trades and make a living. If he kept to his business and did not show himself around, perhaps he would not be in peoples' minds so much, and he would be safe. He would not go to public meetings. He would not respond again to invitations to be a guest at the home of the principal chief. He would work very hard at being nothing but a private citizen. He would practically become a hermit.

And he did stay home, but he was not forgotten. People came looking for him. Sometimes his Cherokee friends and relatives came for a visit. That was all right. Other times, Cherokees came to ask him to attend a meeting or to use his influence to help this or that cause. He made excuses. And because it was difficult for him to say "no," his standard answer became, "Well, I might," and then he would not, but at least, he had not told a lie. And there were the white visitors, people who stopped by to get a chance to meet the famous "Cherokee Cadmus."

Sometimes he enjoyed these visits, and other times, he wished that people would leave him alone. And then, too, he heard reports of continued killings, the followers of John Ross killing the treaty men or their allies, the treaty men killing Ross men. Cherokees killing Cherokees.

He tried to put the troubles out of his mind, and one of the ways he chose to do so was by beginning work on his history of the Cherokees. He began in the beginning, with the telling of the creation of the Cherokees and of the way in which they learned their life ways. He described a long migration which eventually brought the Cherokee people into the country in which the white people first encountered them. "In those days," he wrote, "our priests could read and write." He went on to explain how the Cherokees settled into their new land, how they built their houses and the way in which their villages were laid out.

He explained the annual cycle of ceremonies, the rituals and rites which made the crops grow and which kept the world in balance and the Cherokees in harmony with the world. He told a story that explained the coming of death into the world of the Cherokees and another which showed how diseases came about, and then, how the Cherokees learned about the plants and ways in which they could be used to cure disease.

He wrote of the wars between the Cherokees and the Shawnees that took place before the coming of the white man, and he named the names of the great heroes on both sides of the wars. He told about the time when the priests, who were all-powerful because of their vast knowledge, came to take improper advantage of their power. They became tyrannical rulers who took anything they wanted from the people until at last, the people had taken all they could from these despots, and they rose up and slew them, almost to a man.

That was why and when, he wrote, the Cherokee towns became

independent of one another. That was the end of any semblance of central government among the Cherokees. From then on, they would not have it. Each town was its own. And he detailed the structure of the town governments and explained the way in which they worked. He wrote of the Cherokee clans and the importance of the mothers of the people, and he told about the War Women, how they achieved their status and what their powers were.

Now and then, he would become weary and put aside his pencil and his pad and rub his tired eyes. He would begin to think that he had taken on a task so monumental that it could not ever be completed. But then he would think back to the days when he had been struggling with the symbols, trying desperately to find a way to write down the language. He recalled the long hours of often wasted labor, the ridicule, the threats, the disruption of his home life. And then he would look at the medal hanging around his neck, and he would recall with pride that he had accomplished that seemingly impossible task.

Well, he could accomplish his new task as well. This time, he thought, if he were to tell people what it was he was doing, they would likely say, "Of course, Sequoyah can do it," but this time he would not tell them. He would work away in secret, and when it was done, he would present it to them and let them be amazed all over again. When Sally would ask him what he was doing, he would simply say, "Just writing."

At last, he had dealt with all the early stories that explained why things were the way they were, and he had told how the Cherokees lived and believed. He had gone through the early history of the wars with other Indian tribes, and he had shown the way the Cherokees were living. He sat back and looked at his work. He read over the last few pages. He thought long and hard, and then he wrote, "And then the white man came."

19

James Foreman stood at the bar in the small store in Arkansas just across the line from the Cherokee Nation. The others in the small room were quiet, tense. It was rumored that Foreman had been the leader of the group of killers who had taken the lives of the Ridges and Boudinot. Foreman had friends in the room, and he had enemies. There were white men there too, men not on either side of the Cherokees' quarrel. But Foreman was known to be dangerous, and no one wanted trouble with him. No one, that is, except Stand Watie, and as chance or fate would have it, Stand Watie walked into the room.

Just inside the door, Watie stopped still and stared hard at Foreman. James Miller, a friend of Watie's who happened to be in the store, sensed the danger in the air and broke the ominous silence. "Stand," he said, "let's go someplace else."

"I think we should stay and have a drink first," said Watie, never taking his eyes off Foreman. Foreman called for a fresh glass of whiskey. When it was poured, he lifted the glass.

"Stand Watie," he said, "here's wishing you may live forever." Then he held the glass out toward Watie. Watie took it and smiled.

"Jim," he said, "I suppose I can drink with you, but I heard a few days ago that you meant to kill me."

Suddenly Foreman came up with a whip in his right hand and turned to face Watie. Watie threw the whiskey glass past Foreman's face and lunged at him, grabbing him by the throat. Foreman flailed at Watie with both arms, the whip still in his right hand. One of Foreman's cronies began to work his way around behind Watie, but Miller saw it and jumped on the man, flinging him through the front door out into the yard.

Foreman at last managed to wrench himself free of Watie's grasp, turned and ran out the door. Stand Watie followed, but just as he stepped outside, Foreman swung a board he had picked up out there. Watie raised an arm just in time to deflect the blow. Then he pulled out his hunting knife, moved in low and stabbed Foreman. Foreman jumped back, turned and ran. Then he stopped and turned again to face Watie. Clutching at his stomach, blood running out between his fingers, he snarled, "You haven't done it yet."

Watie walked to his horse and opened the flap of his saddle bags. He reached in and pulled out a pistol. Climbing into the saddle, he cocked the pistol, twisted to face Foreman, and fired. The ball smashed into Foreman's chest, and Foreman dropped to the ground dead.

Sequoyah was seated at the table in his cabin working on a pair of silver spurs when Jesse Chisholm walked in. He looked up from his work and invited Chisholm to sit. "Just a minute and I'll pour us some coffee," he said. "Sally's down at the creek doing something."

Chisholm took a chair just across the table from Sequoyah. Sequoyah made a few more strokes on the spur in his hand, put it down along with the tool he was using, and stood up. He turned, hobbled across the room without the use of his cane, and came back with a coffee pot and a cup. The cup he was using was already on the table. He poured both cups full of coffee, put down the pot and resumed his seat.

"It's good to see you," he said.

"You might change your mind," said Chisholm, "when I tell you why I've come."

Chisholm was a much younger man but already wise beyond his years in the ways of the west. A veteran of the ill-fated Dodge Expedition, Chisholm was said to have command of fourteen languages and to know his way around from North Carolina to California, from Kansas to Mexico. A mixed-blood, he had more the look of a grizzled frontiersman than of a Cherokee, but he was well known and liked among the old settlers.

"What is it?" Sequoyah asked.

"Things are beginning to boil again," said Chisholm. "Have you heard the news from Arkansas about Stand Watie?"

"I don't think so."

"Watie killed James Foreman. Stabbed him and shot him. He's been arrested in Arkansas, and there will be a trial for murder, but it looks like he'll get off on a plea of self-defense. It's starting up again, Sequoyah. Foreman's friends will be after Watie, those who are bold enough, and Stand Watie and his bunch will be looking for the rest of those on their list. John Ross is at the top, of course, but you helped to depose Brown and Rogers, and there's still hard feelings about that."

Sequoyah took a sip of hot coffee. He put the cup back on the table and stared at it for a long moment. At last, he said, "My friend, you know, I've been thinking much lately about those Cherokees in Mexico. Do you think you could lead me to them?"

"I could if I had the time," said Chisholm, "but I'm obligated for a good while yet. I only came out here to see you because Chief Ross and the council asked me to look after you. And because I do care about you, of course. Are you serious about Mexico?"

"Yes."

"I could draw you a map. I think I know where those Cherokees have gone."

Sequoyah reached for his pad and pencil and turned the pad to a fresh page. He handed them to Chisholm, who set to work making a detailed map showing a route from the Cherokee Nation, through Texas and into northern Mexico. He handed the pad and pencil back to Sequoyah, who studied it for a moment.

"Thank you," he said. "This looks good. Now I have one other thing to ask of you."

"Anything," said Chisholm.

"Don't tell anyone about this—about where I might be going. You know, I might change my mind."

"Sequoyah, when I leave here, I might even forget that I came to see you today."

———————

"The killings have started again, Sally," Sequoyah said. "I'm going to take a long trip."

"Where will you go?"

"Somewhere away from here."

"Where it's safe?"

"Safer than here. I don't want you to worry about me. I may be gone for a long time."

"I won't worry," she said. "At least, no more than I've been worrying here. Will you go alone?"

"I'm going to ask our son to go with me," he said, "and young Ujiya. Maybe some more young men."

"That's good," said Sally. "The young men can hunt, and fight if necessary. They can look after you."

Sally helped Sequoyah pack the things he would need for a long trip. He set aside his long rifle and his notepad and pencil. He still had his history to work on. Soon everything was ready, but it was late in the afternoon. He would not leave until morning. Something told Sally that she would never see him again once he rode away from the house.

Sequoyah found Ujiya at home at his cabin near Tahlequah. He told the young man that he needed a place to sleep for the night, and Ujiya provided him with one. In the morning, they had breakfast and coffee. When they were done, Sequoyah said, "I'm going on a long trip. I want you to go with me. I want to leave in three days. Teesee will go with us."

"Of course, I'll go," said Ujiya. "But where are we going?"

"Just trust me about that," Sequoyah said.

"I'll have to get my gunlock fixed before we can leave."

"Never mind about that. I'll get you a gun. Bring your horse, saddle, bridle and other things you'll need for traveling."

"All right. Bring them where?"

"To Teesee's house. In three days."

Sequoyah rode to the store of Andrew Ross, the chief's brother, in Park Hill, where he purchased a new rifle and other necessities for the long trip. He also bought himself a few extra pads of paper and pencils. He had no intention of abandoning his history. From there he rode to Teesee's house, where he told his son what he intended. Teesee agreed without hesitation to ride along. He thought that he could find some other young men who were hungry for adventure to join them.

On the appointed morning, they gathered at Teesee's house: Sequoyah, Teesee, Ujiya and six others. Each man was mounted, and they had three pack horses. No one in the company knew their destination except Sequoyah himself. The young men all had such respect for Sequoyah, now sixty-four years old, that they never questioned him. It was an honor, they felt, to have been invited along, wherever he might want to go. Ready to begin the ride, Sequoyah looked at the young men.

"Where did you tell your friends and families you were going?" he asked.

One of the young men shrugged. "On a visit," he said.

"Good," said Sequoyah. "Let's ride."

"Which way?" asked Teesee.

"To the Creek Nation," Sequoyah said, "west of Fort Gibson."

Sequoyah did not forget his main reason for the journey, but having gotten started, he began to think of other reasons. He would like to visit other Indian tribes and make their acquaintance. He wondered if his syllabary could possibly be used to write their languages. And, of course, he was very much interested in the location and condition of the Cherokees who, it seemed, had fled to Mexico. A trip that had begun as a necessity was beginning to seem like a wonderful adventure for a man of his age to be undertaking. There were new people to meet and new places to see.

They rode at a leisurely pace, and when they came to the home of some Cherokees they knew, they stopped to visit and to partake of the hospitality of the people who lived there. At one such home, the family was all outside: mother, father and children. Sequoyah was well acquainted with the family, and the little girl, five years old, was particularly fond of him. When she saw him, she ran to meet him, and he leaned over in his saddle to meet her little arms that were reaching for him. He took hold of her and lifted her up to sit in front of him in the saddle.

"Where are you going?" she asked.

"On a long trip," he said.

"You're too old to go on a long trip," the little one said.

Sequoyah began to laugh. Holding the little girl in his arms, he rode around the yard laughing and laughing.

"She says I'm to old to go on a long trip," he said. He laughed some more, and repeated her words over and again. His companions laughed as well, as did the child's family. At last Sequoyah rode to near her father and handed her down to him. "We have to be on our way," he said.

"Have a good journey," the father said.

Sequoyah had put a good face on, but even so, he secretly felt a sense of relief when they finally rode out of the Cherokee Nation and into the Creek Nation. When they camped that night, some of the young men went out hunting, and that evening they feasted on fresh venison, bread made from the cornmeal they had packed and coffee. Sequoyah slept the night well.

The next morning, he was a little stiff. It had been some time since he had slept on the ground. They ate more venison and corn bread and drank more coffee, then broke their camp and packed things up. They cleaned up the camp site and mounted their horses. The young men all looked toward Sequoyah for guidance. Sequoyah, in turn, looked at Ujiya.

"I want to visit the tribes living on the Red River," he said. "You lead the way."

Ujiya turned his mount south, and the party moved on. They rode on for several days, crossing the Arkansas River and then the Canadian, and they stopped at the trading post of a man named James Edwards. Edwards was the father-in-law of Jesse Chisholm, and Chisholm's home was not far away. Sequoyah inquired about Chisholm, thinking as he did that Chisholm was the only man alive who knew his destination.

"He's guiding a party west," Edwards said. "When I see him next, I'll tell him you asked about him."

That information fit with what Chisholm had told Sequoyah regarding a previous commitment. The nine travelers stayed the night with Edwards, and Edwards fed them and hosted them well. The next morning, Sequoyah visited a small settlement of Creeks, recently removed from their old country. They told him of a village of Shawnees not far away along the banks of the Canadian River.

"They were in Texas," one of the Creeks said, "and the Texans kicked them out."

When the party was ready to ride again, Sequoyah said, "Let's go see those Shawnees."

The Shawnees welcomed them and fed them.

"The Creeks over there told me that you were in Texas," Sequoyah said.

"Yes, we were, but the Texans chased us out."

"There were some Cherokees in Texas too," Sequoyah said. "Some of them came home to the new Cherokee Nation north of here, but others went other places. Some said they went to Mexico."

"I believe they went to Mexico," the Shawnee said. "We were part of that same group. We were with Chief Bowles. We were only trying to get out of Texas when the Texans attacked us. They killed Bowles and many others that day. We fought them all day long. Those of us who survived the fight ran in all directions. We came up here. Others went who knows where, but I heard some of them talk about going south—to Mexico. There were Cherokees with them too."

They continued south toward the Red River, and when they stopped at night to camp, Sequoyah took out his notebook and wrote. He was continuing his history of the Cherokee people. He wrote about the Spaniards and the trail of devastation they left in the old country when they rode out of Florida looking for gold. Of course, this had all happened long before he was born, but he had heard the old tales told many times over. As he wrote, he could tell that the young men were all curious, but he said nothing about what he was writing. *Let them all wait,* he thought. *Let them wait until it's all done.*

At last they reached the Red River, and Sequoyah saw that it was well named. It was indeed red. They rode along the northern bank until they found a suitable place to cross. In Texas, they camped.

Sequoyah was tired. He was not feeling well. The young men went hunting again, and they returned to the camp with fresh meat. They cooked a meal and ate. They slept the night in their camp, and in the morning they ate again. Sequoyah showed no signs of getting ready to leave.

"Ujiya," he said, "where are the nearest Indians living from here?"

"West, I think," Ujiya said. "Some distance."

"I want you and two others to ride out and find them," Sequoyah said. "The rest will stay here in the camp with me. When you find any Indian villages, find out if there are any Cherokees living with them. We'll wait for you here."

As Ujiya and two of the other young men rode west, Teesee looked at his father. The old man must not be feeling well, he thought, to send them off like that and stay here to rest. He hoped that Sequoyah was just tired from all the riding. After all, he was getting old. The trip had to be much harder on him than on the younger men. He watched as Sequoyah stretched himself out on the ground again with a moan. The old man said nothing more. He rested. Sometimes he slept, but fitfully.

He was awake again around the middle of the day, and he ate a little. Again, Teesee worried. His father did not seem to have much appetite. He did not eat as much as usual. "Is there anything you want?" he asked.

"No," Sequoyah said. "I'll just rest."

Four days went by like that. Now and then, Sequoyah sat up and wrote a little in his notebook, but mostly, he rested. He ate less each meal. On the fifth day, he did not eat at all.

"Nothing tastes good," he said. "Don't worry. Just let me rest."

But Teesee did worry. He worried more each day. The next day, Sequoyah did not eat again. When Teesee offered him food, his answer was always the same. "It doesn't taste good to me just now." And he slept more of the day away with each passing day. Teesee was beginning to wonder if something bad had happened to Ujiya and the others. He wondered if he would ever see them again. And he was worried that his father might just lay there on the ground until he died. Some of the young men brought fresh game home every other day, but none of it appealed to Sequoyah's taste.

"You'll starve yourself to death, Father," Teesee said.

"No," Sequoyah answered. "I'll be all right."

After twelve days had passed, Ujiya and the other two returned. Sequoyah sat up as anxiously as he could. He was weak, and his chest was hurting.

"He hasn't eaten for eight days," Teesee said.

"We have fresh venison and honey," Ujiya said.

"No," said Sequoyah. "That doesn't taste good to me. I'd like to have some bread."

Ujiya looked at Teesee, and Teesee shrugged. "We don't have any, and we have nothing left with which to make bread."

Ujiya's eyes brightened up with a sudden thought. "We found some wild plums," he said. "We have those."

"I'll try some," Sequoyah said.

Ujiya brought a bundle of plums in a scarf and laid them out for the old man. Sequoyah leaned up on an elbow and took one. He ate it all, and then he took another. "These are good," he said. Soon he had eaten several and seemed to feel much better as a result. Teesee felt some relief.

"I'll go back to the nearest village," Ujiya said, "and get you some bread."

"What is the nearest village?" Sequoyah asked.

"A Wichita village," said Ujiya. "They treated us well. I'm sure I can get some bread from them."

"Good," Sequoyah said. "You go on. If I feel better, we'll mount up and ride after you. We'll meet you somewhere along the way."

20

Sequoyah, Teesee and the others rode slowly along the trail. One of the young men who had gone with Ujiya before rode with Sequoyah. That way they knew for certain, without relying on their tracking abilities, that they were following Ujiya's trail. They rode slowly because Sequoyah was not feeling well, and the movements of the horse underneath him jolted his insides uncomfortably. They paused often to rest. Toward evening of the eighth day along the trail, they stopped to camp for the night, and just as they had gotten their small fire going, Ujiya and the others came along. Sequoyah was happy to see them, especially when he found that Ujiya had brought bread, honey and hominy.

Sequoyah, who had been writing, put away his writing materials and sat up to eat. Ujiya, Teesee and the others were delighted to see him eat so heartily. At last Sequoyah was satisfied, and he took out his pipe and tobacco for a smoke.

"Are you feeling better, Father?" Teesee asked.

Sequoyah smiled, a little weakly, and said, "Yes. I am."

Ujiya sat beside Sequoyah. "I'm glad to find you feeling better," he said.

"Thank you," Sequoyah said between puffs. "Where did you get the good food?"

"From some Wichitas," Ujiya answered.

"They have good cooks," said Sequoyah. He finished his pipe and put it away. "I want to lie down now for a while and stretch my weary limbs and rest."

"What is it that's been bothering you, Sequoyah?"

"I've had pains in my chest, and they shoot throughout my body.

But I feel much better now that I've had some good food. Maybe we should rest a few days before we go on. In the morning, let's find a nice stream and camp there."

"Our horses are worn out," Teesee said. "We need to buy some fresh ones."

"After we rest a few days," Sequoyah said, "we'll ride on to the Wichita village. Maybe we can buy some horses there. I don't want to stay long with the Wichitas, though. I want us to go into the woods and hunt."

It was seven days later when they at last arrived at a village of the Kichais where the chief's name was The Man Who Has a Feather in His Head. Ujiya had visited there before, and the chief smiled a welcome when he saw him returning. Sequoyah had not handled the ride well, and once again, he was feeling poorly. The Kichai chief noticed at once, and he looked at Ujiya and spoke. Ujiya answered the man in his own Kichai language.

Teesee said, "How fortunate we are that Ujiya can speak to these people."

"He learned well from Jesse Chisholm on their long sick trip," Sequoyah said, his voice weak. "I knew that when I asked him to come along."

Ujiya looked at Sequoyah. "The Man Who Has a Feather in His Head says that he is sorry to see you so sick. He invites you into his lodge where he can have you properly cared for."

"Thank him for me," Sequoyah said, "and conduct me there."

They followed the chief to his lodge, a large, dome-shaped grass house, and Ujiya and Teesee helped Sequoyah down off his horse and into the lodge. The chief, through Ujiya, gave instructions as to where to place Sequoyah. He made sure that Sequoyah was comfortable, and he had his wives prepare some food. Sequoyah managed to eat some food. Then he stretched out again.

"Let him rest," said the chief. He shooed everyone out of the lodge and followed them. Outside, Teesee, Ujiya and the others were well fed by the Kichais, and the chief visited with Ujiya.

"I'm really sorry to see the old man in such a condition," the chief said. "Where are you going with him?"

Ujiya shrugged. "We don't know," he said. "He just told us that he wanted to go on a long trip. He asked us to go with him. Once we got started, he said that he wanted to visit the tribes along the Red River, so here we are."

"It's not an easy trip for him," the chief said. "It was good of you and the others to ride with him, though."

Ujiya nodded toward Teesee. "That one is his son," he said, "but the old man is Sequoyah. He's a very honored man among our people. When he asked us to ride along with him, we felt honored."

"Sequoyah," said the chief, musing as if trying to place the name. "I think maybe I've heard of him."

"He gave us the Cherokee writing," Ujiya said.

"Ah, yes. That's why I've heard of him. I've heard talk about your writing. I didn't know whether to believe it or not. So it's really true? You can read and write your language just as the white man reads and writes his?"

"Yes. It's true."

"Sequoyah. It's an honor to have him in my lodge. I hope he'll be feeling better soon."

Sequoyah slept well, and he slept late the next morning. He had only been awake a short while when he heard that a man had come from the nearby Wichita village. Ujiya came into the chief's lodge to tell him that the Wichita had invited them to come and eat with them.

"I'm not feeling well enough to go just yet," Sequoyah said. "You and the others go. I'll rest here a while longer."

Ujiya went out of the lodge, and in a short while he returned. "Teesee and I will stay here with you," he said. "The others have gone to eat with the Wichitas."

The wives of The Man Who Has a Feather in His Head brought more food in for Sequoyah, and he ate well. It was around midday, and he was sitting up. "Ujiya," he said, "tell the chief that I'm better. I'd like to visit with him."

Ujiya left and came back with the chief. They sat, and the chief smiled. "I'm pleased that you're doing better," he said. Ujiya translated.

"Thank you. Your wives have been taking good care of me. The food is good."

"I'm very glad to have you here in my lodge," the chief said. "I'm friendly with all the tribes north of here. It wasn't always so, but we've made treaties with them now. We're all friends, and we'll be friends forever."

"Yes," Sequoyah said. "It's not like when the white man makes a treaty. The white man's 'forever' is but a short time."

The chief laughed, and so did Sequoyah, but the laughing made him weak again. "I feel like I need to rest again," he said.

"Yes," said the chief. "You rest. We'll get out of here."

Just as the chief was about to go out his door, a man stuck his head inside. "A Texan came," the man said. "He wants us to come to a council on the Brazos River, near the Waco village."

The chief turned to Ujiya. "Tell your old man," he said, "that I'll talk with him more in the morning. Right now, I'll go see this Texan." Ujiya explained to Sequoyah, and Sequoyah closed his eyes.

Ujiya stayed in the lodge watching over Sequoyah. Having slept most of the day away, Sequoyah opened his eyes in the early evening and sat up. "Ujiya," he said, "I've been thinking."

"Yes?"

"Don't you think that we should send the young men home? I mean all but you and Teesee. They might get sick too if they stay here."

"I think they're getting restless," Ujiya said. "I think that's a good idea."

"In the morning," Sequoyah said, "bring them to me."

Sequoyah was coughing when the eight young men gathered around him the following morning. Clearing his lungs, at least for a moment, he began to speak. "My friends," he said, "it was good of you to come with me on this trip, but I think it's time for you to go home. You've already come a long way. I don't want you to get sick this far away from home. We wouldn't be able to care for you very well. Ujiya and Teesee will stay with me."

The six young men agreed so readily that it made Sequoyah smile. Ujiya had been right about them. They were restless, and they were homesick. They were anxious to turn back, and obviously they were grateful that Sequoyah had made the suggestion. They were packed and riding away in a short time.

"Ujiya," Sequoyah said, "it's time for us to leave here too. Tell Teesee to pack our things, and bring the chief to see me."

Soon Sequoyah, Teesee and Ujiya were once again on the trail. They rode back along the same trail they had taken into the Kichai village. Moving slowly as before, it took them six days to return to their previous campsite. Settled in for the night, Sequoyah told the two young men, "We'll rest here a few days." Then he had to pause because of a coughing fit. "I want to bathe in the cool waters here, and I want you to hunt and to gather more honey. I'm doing better, but I still have pains, and this coughing makes me weak."

For the next four days, Teesee and Ujiya hunted for meat and for honey. Sequoyah enjoyed the clear waters of the nearby stream. He rested, and he wrote. His history was coming along well. He was pleased with its progress. Let the white men write all the lies they wanted to about the Cherokees. He would write the truth, and it would always be there for Cherokees to read. It would not be forgotten. It would not be lost.

"Ujiya, Teesee," Sequoyah said, "come to me." It was the morning of the fifth day. The two young men stepped over close and sat down, attentive. "I don't want you to lose patience with me out here in the wilderness. I want to go to Mexico."

He reached inside his jacket and pulled out a folded paper which he handed to Ujiya. It was the map Jesse Chisholm had drawn for him.

"That shows the way," he said. "Jesse Chisholm made it. You can follow it. Lead the way."

They packed up and headed south, Ujiya riding in the lead, Sequoyah and Teesee following. They rode a lonely trail, seeing no human beings for five days and nights. They camped the nights along the way, and their supply of food was getting dangerously low. Sequoyah's cough continued.

"I hope you won't get tired of a sick old man," Sequoyah said. "If I die along the way, do what you think best, but while I'm still alive, be ruled by me."

They rode on, talking seldom, hunting a little on the way, for ten more days. Then one evening, they came upon a clear running stream, and Sequoyah wanted to stop.

"We'll rest here a while," Sequoyah said. The young men went out hunting. Sequoyah stretched out on the ground with a moan. His body was wracked with pain, and he could not stop coughing. He wondered if he would ever see Mexico. He had no real idea how many more days they would have to ride to get there. And if they should make it, he wondered, would they really be able to find any Cherokees down there? Ujiya and Teesee returned before dark with fresh meat. They ate, and they slept. They stayed at the camp for four days, and then they rode south again, Ujiya studying Jesse Chisholm's map frequently. In a few more days, they came to a river. They stopped again to camp.

They were sitting around their campfire when they heard gunshots, not too distant. "Let's go find out who that is," Sequoyah said. They packed up quickly, mounted their horses and rode alongside the river. "Go ahead and see," Sequoyah called out to Ujiya. Ujiya kicked his horse into a gallop and disappeared. Sequoyah and Teesee rode on after him more slowly. Not far ahead, they found him waiting for them. He pointed ahead to a road.

"Look," he said. "Someone rode this way recently."

"Let's follow them," Sequoyah said.

They moved on together, but not too quickly. The tracks in the road were indeed fresh. It must be the same ones who had fired the shots. Ujiya was cautious. He knew from the map that they were in the country of the Comanches. He had never met a Comanche, but he had heard that they were fierce warriors. There were tales of the Comanches raiding as far north as the Choctaw Nation south of the Cherokee Nation to steal horses. He kept his thoughts to himself, not wanting to alarm his two companions unnecessarily. Soon he held up a hand. He stopped, and Sequoyah and Teesee rode up beside him.

"There they are," he said.

Half a dozen men were gathered around a small fire. They were dressed almost like white men, but there was something about them, their flat-brimmed hats with feathers in the bands maybe, that made Sequoyah comfortable with their looks. Saying nothing, he urged his horse forward. The two young men followed. They had not gone far when the men at the campfire noticed them. They stood straight and stared at them, waiting for them to come close. Getting nearer, Sequoyah and the two young men could tell that the six campers were Indians. They stopped their horses at a polite distance.

"Who are you?" one of the men called out in English.

"Cherokees," Ujiya answered.

"Cherokees," the other repeated, speaking in Cherokee. "Come on in. We're Shawnee. I can speak your language."

Sequoyah's spirits lifted at the sound of Cherokee spoken by the strangers, and he knew Shawnee people. He was glad to run across someone so familiar this far away from home. They rode on into the Shawnee camp and dismounted, and the Shawnees fed them fresh venison, hard bread and coffee.

"We're on a hunting trip," the English-and-Cherokee-speaking Shawnee said. "What are you doing so far from home?"

"I'm very anxious to visit Mexico," Sequoyah said. "I've heard there are some Cherokees down there."

"Yes," the Shawnee said. "I've heard about them too."

"Do you know where they are?"

"No. Just Mexico."

"Well, then," Sequoyah said, "we'll just continue the way we were and hope to find them."

"If you do find them," said the Shawnee, "or anything else interesting, stop and tell us on your way back."

"Yes," Sequoyah said. "We will." But he wondered if he would be able to make the trip back. He wondered if he would want to, even if he were able. He thought about the violence he had left behind in the Cherokee Nation, and he remembered that he could very well be on someone's list of people to kill. "From where we are now," he said, "what's the direction to the nearest Mexican village?"

As they continued on their way, Sequoyah said to Ujiya, "The Shawnees agreed with the way you've been leading us."

"They agreed with Jesse Chisholm's map," Ujiya said. "I know we're going the right way."

They rode on for six days, Ujiya and Teesee wanting to stop now and then to hunt, but Sequoyah kept urging them on. "I don't like this spot," he would say. At last they came to a bubbling spring. "Here's a good place to camp and rest," he said. So they dismounted and made their camp. Right away, Sequoyah noticed a number of honeybees near the water.

"Well," he said, "we're not in such a hurry. We can stop here and look for honey."

Teesee started walking around, looking up in the trees, while Ujiya busied himself with the camp. Sequoyah sat down to rest. "Ujiya, bring me a drink of water."

Ujiya took a canteen to the stream and dipped it in for some fresh water. He walked over to Sequoyah and handed it to him, and Sequoyah drank.

"How are you feeling?" Ujiya asked.

"I'm all right. I'll make it to Mexico. We're getting close now."

"Yes," Ujiya said. "We'll make it soon now."

Teesee returned with honey, and Sequoyah ate some.

"We'll stay here for a few days," he said. "Everything we need is here, and I need a rest."

Sequoyah's cough seemed to improve. He rested well, slept well at night and ate enough each day. He said that he was not quite as sore all over as he had been. "Another day or so," he said. "I'll be ready to go."

The second night at the camp, they were sleeping. Sequoyah heard a snort. He opened his eyes but did not move. He rolled his eyes toward the horses and saw some movement. Slowly he realized what was happening. He sat up quickly.

"Teesee," he called. "Ujiya."

The two young men were up instantly, grabbing for their rifles. In the darkness, they could see the Indians, mounted, with lead ropes tied to the Cherokee horses. When the horse thieves realized they had been discovered, they whooped and kicked their horses into a run, pulling the stolen ones along behind.

"Hey," Teesee shouted. He fired a shot, but it was wasted.

"Come on," called Ujiya.

The two young men ran after the horses and horse thieves as fast as they could run. Sequoyah stood and watched them. He knew that two men on foot would not be able to catch the horses.

They would run until they could run no more, but the horses and thieves would be far ahead of them, long gone. He wondered what they would do now. Of course, the young men would look to him for words of wisdom. He had none for this occasion. They could follow the horse thieves on foot and hope that they would find them somewhere ahead. They could go on their way on foot and hope to come to a town or village where they could buy some horses. They could hope . . .

21

Teesee and Ujiya returned on foot and empty-handed. Sequoyah had expected no more.

"We might have caught up with them," said Teesee, "but we were afraid to leave you alone for so long."

"Well, let's sleep," Sequoyah said. "We'll worry about it in the morning."

The first thing after sunup, Sequoyah told the two young men to follow the horse thieves and try to get back their horses.

"I think they were Tawakonis," Ujiya said. "I heard a few words as they were escaping."

"Then you can follow them to their village," Sequoyah said. "If you talk to their chief, maybe you can get our horses back."

The young men prepared to leave, and Sequoyah thought over what he had told them. He remembered that a few years earlier, Tawakonis had killed two Cherokee hunters, and in retaliation, Dutch and his followers had wiped out an entire Tawakoni village. If these they were pursuing found out that the two young men were Cherokees, and if they remembered what Dutch had done, then they might kill Teesee and Ujiya. Perhaps it was not such a good idea to send them to the village of the thieves. He knew, though, that he would not get far on foot.

"Ujiya," he said. "Forget about our lost horses for now. We might get a chance to get them back later. Instead of following those men, find me a safe hiding place. Tie our things high in the trees for safety. Then you two go on to Mexico. Find the nearest

Mexican village. Maybe you can buy us some horses there. Then you can come back for me."

"But will you be all right?"

"Leave me enough food for a few days," Sequoyah said. "I'll be all right."

So they did as Sequoyah said, and soon they were off, searching on foot for some village in Mexico. Sequoyah nestled down in the wooded nook they had found for him. He had his notepad and his pencil, and he wrote. At last he grew tired, and he lay back to sleep. It was a long time until night, but he had patience. He knew that this was going to be a long wait.

Teesee and Ujiya walked for maybe four miles down the road, and then they came to a wide river. There was no way to cross, but to continue south, they would have to cross it. They turned west and walked along the riverbank, searching for a suitable spot to wade across or to swim, but they found none. Before they knew it, they had walked away the day. They camped for the night. In the morning, they studied the river again.

"We'll have to make a raft," Ujiya said.

They set about cutting trees and trimming them until they had enough logs for a small raft. Then they bound the logs together with deer sinew. They cut some long poles, and at last they were ready to try it. By the time they had crossed the river, most of the day was gone. They walked on for a little longer, moving into some mountains, then camped again for the night. In the morning they began their long walk again. Around noon, they stopped to eat some dried meat. They did not make a fire. While they were eating, they heard the sound of gunfire ahead.

"Gunshots," said Teesee.

"Let's go see what's going on," Ujiya said.

Stuffing what was left of their dried meat into their mouths, they jumped up and trotted ahead. In a little while, they came back down out of the mountains onto a prairie. Ujiya stopped and pointed at the ground.

"Look," he said. "Wagon tracks."

They walked around some, studying the ground, and they found more tracks, all moving in the same direction.

"What do you think, Ujiya?"

"I think there's a town not far ahead."

"Well?"

"Let's wait a little. Let's go in after dark."

"Come on," Teesee said. "We'll go slow."

They walked on, and at last they could see the town about a hundred yards ahead, a cluster of low, squat, adobe houses, and a slightly imposing town square beyond. As they moved closer, they could hear the noises of the town, including voices. They moved in closer, but no one in the town had yet spotted them, or if they had, did not pay any attention to them. The voices coming from the town became clearer.

"What are they talking?" Teesee asked.

"They're talking Spanish," said Ujiya. "Let's sleep out here and go in tomorrow morning."

They spread themselves out on the ground, but they did not sleep well, for gunfire continued throughout the night.

"What is all that shooting, Ujiya?" Teesee asked.

"Just general rowdiness," Ujiya said. "The men shooting are probably drunk. It should be quieter in the morning."

"Can you talk to them?"

"Yes. Thanks to all the time I spent with Jesse Chisholm."

Arising early, Ujiya and Teesee found that the town was indeed much quieter. They walked on in, and they were initially surprised that no one paid them much attention. They walked farther into the town. Then they noticed two soldiers ahead of them, walking in their direction. As they came closer to the soldiers, they could see that they did not intend to walk around them. They came straight at them. Ujiya and Teesee stopped. The soldiers stopped, smiled and extended their hands. Ujiya and Teesee shook hands with them.

"You are strangers here in San Antonio," one soldier said in Spanish.

"Yes," Ujiya answered.

"Welcome. Come with me. I'll show you around."

They walked around the town a bit, until the soldiers saw an officer and called out to him. The officer joined them, and he and the two soldiers spoke together in low tones. Then the officer stepped over to the two Cherokees.

"You talk English?" he asked.

"Yes," Ujiya said.

"Good. Follow me. I'm taking you to see the commanding officer."

Teesee looked questioningly at Ujiya, who just shrugged and said, "Let's go with him. I don't think we have any other choice."

Soon they were inside a small adobe structure, seated in chairs that were lined up against a wall. The officer and the other two soldiers who had conducted them there stood along the wall to either side of them. The commanding officer came out from behind a desk on the opposite wall and paced the floor, looking now and then at Teesee and Ujiya. At last he spoke.

"You're not Mexicans?" he said.

"No," said Ujiya.

"Indians?"

"Yes."

"What tribe?"

"We're Cherokee," Ujiya said.

"I have no use for Cherokees. The Cherokees were fighting against us a few years ago, helping the Mexicans."

Ujiya thought that was not the way he had heard the tale, but he felt it wise to keep those thoughts to himself.

"We're not part of that group," he said instead. "Our home is in Arkansas, in the United States." That was not quite true either, but it seemed the best response he could give. "We're traveling, and a few days past, some Tawakonis came on our camp and stole our horses. We came here to see if we could borrow some horses."

The officer rubbed his chin. "Do you have passports?"

"No," Ujiya said.

"You have to have passports to travel in Texas."

"We were not aware of that," Ujiya said. "We travel often in the white towns in Arkansas, and they never ask us for passports."

"Well, this isn't Arkansas, and it isn't the United States. It's the Republic of Texas, and we demand passports. You'd likely have been shot on sight for wild Indians if you hadn't been wearing those hats."

"Well," Ujiya said, "I'm glad we had our hats on."

The officer laughed a little at that, and Ujiya and Teesee relaxed some. They smiled and nodded.

"So you're down from Arkansas? When were your horses stolen?"

"Four . . . five days ago."

"Well, I'll give you passports and let you go on your way," said the officer, moving back to his desk. He began to write. "But I'd advise you to be on your guard. There are wild Indians out there—all round."

"We'll watch carefully," Ujiya said. "Thank you."

"I don't trust these Texans," Teesee said, as they walked out of the building and onto the crowded street. "Did you believe him?"

"Be quiet," said Ujiya. "Walk slow. Act like nothing is wrong."

They strolled back to the edge of the town where they had come in.

"Where are we going?" Teesee asked.

"Let's just walk out a little farther," Ujiya said. They continued at their apparent leisurely pace, and then Ujiya said, "Come on," and broke into a run. They did not look back until they were well away from San Antonio, and even then, they did not slow their pace very much.

"Let's hurry back to your father," Ujiya said.

"I heard them talking Spanish," Ujiya told Sequoyah, "and I thought that we'd found a Mexican village, but it was not. It was still in Texas. We got out of there as fast as we could. We couldn't get any horses."

"We didn't trust those Texans," said Teesee.

"All right," Sequoyah said. "Rest a while. Then take some time to hunt. Get me enough venison and honey to last me for twenty days and then go again. Stay away from that Texas town. Find a Mexican town. Get horses there and come back for me."

"Father," said Teesee, "are you feeling better? You look well."

"I'm getting stronger," Sequoyah said, "but I'm almost out of food, and I'm hungry. And for a longer stay here by myself, I want a better spot. Someplace safer. While you're hunting, look for another place for me."

Teesee killed a turkey that day, and they built a small fire and cooked it. They sat around the fire and enjoyed the fresh turkey meat and talked. Teesee took some of the longest and prettiest turkey feathers and put them on the three hats of the travelers. He put his own hat back on his head and smiled.

"How's that?" he said.

Sequoyah smiled back at his son and put on his own hat. "It looks good," he said. He looked over at Ujiya. "Yes. It looks good."

"We found a cave, Sequoyah," Ujiya said. "It's just about three miles from here. It's near the bank of the river, but it's high up and safe from flooding. It looks like a good place."

"Can you walk that far?" Teesee asked.

"I'm old, but I'm still alive," Sequoyah said. "Of course I can walk that far. Let's pack everything up and go there. I think I have enough food now."

They walked slowly because of Sequoyah's lame leg and because of his general weakness, and the young men carried all the supplies. Sequoyah leaned on his walking stick and moved along behind them. At last they came to the cave. Teesee and Ujiya helped Sequoyah climb up to its mouth. They moved inside. It was clean and dry. They helped Sequoyah get comfortably situated and placed the supplies within easy reach.

"This is good," Sequoyah said. "You can leave again in the morning."

Ujiya and Teesee walked for two days, swinging wide to the west of San Antonio. They had no desire to meet up with more Texans and meant to do their best to avoid them. It was the middle of their third day out, and they were walking past a cedar thicket when Ujiya heard a noise behind them. He turned to look, and there were three riders coming fast at them. "Look out," he cried to Teesee, and the two of them ducked into the thicket. The riders raced by, slowed and turned their horses. Ujiya got a good look at them.

"I think they're Comanches," he said. He stepped to the edge of the thicket and called out in the Comanche language. "Are you friends?"

The Comanches had stopped their horses by this time. They looked at Ujiya. Then they looked at one another. They slid down off their horses and laid down their weapons.

"Yes," said one. "We're friends. Let's sit down together and have a pipe."

Ujiya walked toward them, and Teesee came out of the thicket. They met the Comanches and shook hands all around. Then they sat, and one of the Comanches produced a pipe. Soon they were passing it around.

"When we first saw you," one of the Comanches said, "we thought you were Texans because of your hats. We were going to kill you. But when we got closer, we saw the feathers in your hats, and we thought you were Shawnees or Delawares."

Ujiya and Teesee laughed at that. "We're Cherokees," Ujiya said. "We live up north in the Cherokee Nation near Arkansas."

"Ah," the Comanche said. "You're the ones who fought the Osages for so long. That's good. But what are you doing way down here?"

"We want to visit Mexico. We heard that some Cherokees were living down there, and we want to see if we can find them."

"I don't know about any Cherokees down there, but we can show you the best way to the Mexican towns. It's a rough and mountainous way, though. We'll ride along with you for a while."

One of the Comanches left them to go back to their own camp and get their women. When he returned some time later with the Comanche women, the entire group headed south. Ujiya told the Comanches about his and Teesee's blunder into San Antonio, and the Comanche laughed. When he stopped laughing, his expression grew serious, and he talked about how mean the Texans were, and he said, "You're lucky they didn't kill you." Ujiya then told him how hard they had run leaving the town, and the Comanche laughed again.

After three days, the Comanches pointed the way, gave some directions and mentioned some landmarks, then went on their way. The two young Cherokee men stood for a moment staring at the rugged terrain ahead of them. Ujiya took out the now battered map that Jesse Chisholm had drawn and studied it.

"Can you find the way?" Teesee asked him.

"Yes," Ujiya said. "I got us lost when we went into San Antonio, but now I think I know where to go. What the Comanche said matches this map pretty well. I think we'll find the way all right."

It was slow going with much climbing, and they had to stop and hunt along the way. The trip was taking longer than any of them had anticipated, Sequoyah included. After fourteen days, they arrived at the edge of a wide river. They stopped and stared across at the other side.

"That's Mexico over there, I think," Ujiya said.

"It's a wide river," said Teesee. "And I don't see any towns. How many days is it now since we left my father?"

"I think we've almost used up our twenty days," Ujiya said. "He'll be running out of food soon."

"What should we do?"

"We can only do what he told us to do," Ujiya said. "We have to cross into Mexico and find a village. Then we'll get some horses and go back for him. We'll go as fast as we can."

"How will we get across this?"

"I guess we'll have to build another raft. It's too late in the day now, though. Let's make a camp for the night."

They were sleeping when the sound of a drum woke them up. They sat up and looked at one another. "There's someone nearby," said Teesee.

"It's across the river, I think," Ujiya said. "We must be close to a Mexican town. We'll build our raft and get across in the morning."

After that, they tried to sleep, but they could not. They lay awake listening to the drum and anticipating the river crossing into Mexico.

Sequoyah huddled in his cave as the rains poured down outside. He had a small fire, but outside was pitch dark except for frequent flashes of brilliant lightning followed by tremendous claps of thunder. He was glad that the cave was high above the water. He thought about trying to sleep, but the noise of the thunder and the flashes of light were too much. He was awake all night. In the morning, he crept to the mouth of the cave. The torrential rains had slowed to a drizzle, but the storm had moved north. He could see the dark sky off in that direction. Then he looked down. The river was roaring by just a few feet beneath him. It was rising fast, and if the rains continued to the north, the river would continue to rise. Soon it would be inside the cave with him.

22

He looked around desperately. Just outside the cavern's entrance was a log propped up toward the top of the rim above. He should be able to climb out by using that log. He looked around inside the cave at all his supplies. He tried to think of a way he could bundle them up and carry them along. He felt the water soaking his moccasins. There was no time for thinking. He stuffed a notepad inside his jacket, flint, steel, spunk and few other small articles into his pockets, wrapped two blankets around himself, picked up his walking stick and hurried to the log. He tried to use the log for handholds and the side of the embankment for footing, but the embankment was too soaked from the rain, and when he placed his foot on a rock, the rock loosened, and the side of the embankment crumbled. He dropped his stick and had to hug the log and shinny upwards. Reaching the top at last, he struggled over onto the level ground. He lay there for a minute or so catching his breath, recovering from the exertion of the climb. Then he sat up and looked at the river, not so far below him now. He could see the last of his things being washed away by the flood waters.

Ujiya and Teesee were up early. They meant to set to work on a raft, but Teesee saw a turkey not too far away. He raised his rifle to his shoulder. He had to make a good shot, for he had only one. It had to count. He eased back the hammer on the long rifle, sighted carefully and squeezed the trigger. The long gun bucked and roared, rocking Teesee back. He looked through the cloud of smoke to see the turkey on the ground.

"I got him," he said.

"Let's fix it and eat," said Ujiya.

Thoughts of raft building did not leave their heads, but they were hungry. It had been a while since their last good meal. They rationalized that they would work faster and better with meat in their stomachs. Teesee prepared the fresh-killed bird while Ujiya built a fire, and in short time, they had nothing left but bones and feathers. They felt well satisfied. They were about to set to work when they saw a rider on the opposite side of the river. He saw them at about the same time and called out a greeting in Spanish. Ujiya answered him.

"Is that Mexico?" Ujiya asked.

"Yes," the man said. "What are you doing?"

"We're trying to build a raft to cross the river."

The man waved an arm toward the west. "Go down that way," he said. "There's a ferry. It's not far."

Sequoyah rested a while from his ordeal. He was wet from the light rain, and his feet were soaked from the rising water in the cave. Luckily the cough and the chest pains that had been bothering him before seemed to have left him. He was hungry, and his food supply was gone. He had no way of hunting, even if he had been physically up to the chore, for he had not brought a rifle along with him. He had relied on the young men to do the hunting. He had no idea where Teesee and Ujiya were, whether they were still on their way to Mexico or on their way back to him. They could be nearby, or they could be still several days away. Already they had been gone longer than any of them had expected. He decided that he could not wait there.

Looking around, he found a tree branch that would serve, and he cut it and shaped himself a new walking stick. It was not as good as his lost one, but it would do. It took a while, but he managed to gather some sticks that were dry enough, and he built a fire. He took off his clothes and dried them at the fire, warming himself at the same time. Dressed again in dry clothing, he took out his pad and pencil and wrote. Tearing out the page he had written on, he searched out a fallen log, lifted it up to lean it against a tree trunk, and fastened the page to the log. He went back to the edge of the embankment for one last hopeful look down at the cave, but it was still entirely under water. There was no longer any reason to delay, so he set out walking. His leg bothered him, so the going was slow and somewhat painful. He leaned heavily on the stick.

Teesee and Ujiya reached the ferry just in time for a crossing. It was already loaded with people, but there was room for two more. They paid for their fare and were soon in Mexico, where an officer met them and asked their purpose. Ujiya talked with the man.

"We came for a visit," he said. "In Texas some Tawakonis stole our horses. We left an old man alone while we look for more horses. We're looking for a Mexican village."

"There's one about six miles from here," the officer said. "I'll take you there."

The people in the small town of adobe huts flocked around the two Cherokees and the officer conducting them said, "Don't be alarmed. They're just curious to see strangers. Follow me."

He led them to a small house, not distinguishable from the rest, and took them inside to meet the headman of the town.

"Who are you," the man asked, "and where do you come from?"

"We're Cherokees," said Ujiya. "We come from the Cherokee Nation near Arkansas."

"What's the purpose of your visit?"

"We brought an old and honored man with us," Ujiya said. "His name is Sequoyah. He wants to visit the Cherokees who are living in this country."

"Where is this old and honored man?"

"We had to leave him behind, because our horses were stolen in Texas. We're looking for more horses, so we can go back to get him."

"So you came through Texas," the headman said. "What did you hear from the Texans? You know, we had a fight with them recently and captured three hundred."

"We went into San Antonio," said Ujiya, "and the Texas officer we talked with said he did not like Cherokees. We ran away from there as fast as we could go."

The headman laughed. "Well," he said, "the people you're look-ing for are about thirty miles from us. There's no time for you to get over there today. Stay the night with us." He made a gesture toward the officer who had brought the Cherokees to him. "This man will show you where you can stay. In the morning, before you leave, come to see me again. I'll make you some passports."

For the rest of that day, the two Cherokees were shown around the town, feasted and treated to a display of military might. The town, being so close to the border, was fortified in case of invasion from Texas. After midnight, they went back to the house assigned them and slept.

Sequoyah moved slowly along the swollen riverbank. He contem-plated all his lost supplies, but the greatest loss, in his mind, was the notepads with his history in them. He had managed to save only one, the one in which he had been writing most recently. Then something caught his eye, stuck in the current against some rocks near the bank. He made his way over there, and he was overjoyed to see that he had spied his own saddlebags. He quickly retrieved them, opened the pouches to check the contents, and found his precious notepads, amazingly, not even badly soaked. Closing the flaps again and tossing the saddlebags over his shoul-der, he straightened up and looked up and down the bank of the swollen river. Perhaps something else had survived. Moving on slowly, he found a tent and three blankets. It was already getting toward the end of the day, so he made himself a camp and stopped to rest for the night.

Teesee and Ujiya received their passports the next morning, but they spent the rest of that day and another night in the village. They were constantly worried about Sequoyah, but no one was willing to lead them to the next town until their second morning there. At last, one of the Mexicans took them the thirty miles to a place called San Cranto. It was much like the other town, except for the lack of a strong military presence.

"Where are the Cherokees?" Ujiya asked.

"There are two of them here," said his guide. "We'll try to find them for you."

When Ujiya translated for Teesee, Teesee's face showed his disappointment. Another day was gone. They had not yet located the Cherokee village.

"Maybe these two can tell us something," Ujiya said.

At last, the Mexicans came with two men, and one of them spoke to Teesee and Ujiya in the Cherokee language. The weary travelers' spirits lifted immediately.

"You're Cherokees?"

"Yes. I'm called Standing Rock, and this is Standing Bowles."

"Bowles?" said Teesee.

"My father was Chief Bowles. When the Texans killed him, some of us ran down this way."

"But where have you come from?" asked Standing Rock.

"We came down from the Cherokee Nation near Arkansas," Ujiya said. "We brought Sequoyah. He wanted to find you. This is Sequoyah's son with me."

"Ah, and where is Sequoyah now?" Bowles asked.

"We had to leave him in Texas after our horses were stolen," Ujiya said. "We need to get some more horses and go back for him. But where are the rest of your people? Are there just the two of you?"

"No, our village is about ten miles farther. We'll take you there."

Sequoyah's progress was slow. The morning after his first night on the trail, he had found a brass kettle that had washed out of his cave, and he retrieved that, so in addition to his general physical condition, he was now heavily burdened with the tent, the saddlebags, the two extra blankets and the kettle. He stopped often to rest.

The Cherokees were delighted with their two visitors from the Cherokee Nation. They fed them well and asked many questions. There were questions about friends and relatives back up north. They were especially interested when they discovered that Teesee was the son of the great man Sequoyah and that Sequoyah was not far away, waiting to be rescued and brought on down to see them. Word of Sequoyah's great invention had reached even these in Mexico. They were anxious to see him and eager to help.

"We need some horses," Teesee said.

"Ah, we have none," Standing Rock said. "We lost all of ours coming into Mexico. Those that survived the trip died shortly after. Some of us will go with you, though, and we'll go back through San Cranto and borrow horses from the Mexican soldiers there."

Teesee, Ujiya, Standing Rock and Standing Bowles came out of the officer's quarters in San Cranto, accompanied by a soldier. Five other Cherokees stood waiting. Teesee walked over to them while Ujiya, Standing Rock and Bowles walked on with the officer.

"He can only spare us one horse," Teesee said. "He said he had to send all his extras to another post. But he's giving us some other supplies: coffee, meat, bread, salt, sugar. Ujiya and those others are going with him to get all that stuff."

The horse became a pack horse, for nine men and one horse move no more quickly than nine men without a horse. They moved as quickly as they could, though, for Teesee and Ujiya told them how they had left Sequoyah.

"We're worried about his health," Ujiya said.

"Even his life," Teesee added.

Sequoyah stopped at the edge of a river. He knew that he had to get across, but it was too deep to wade and too wide to swim. He looked toward a nearby grove of trees and considered the work and time involved in building a raft. There seemed to be no other solution. He looked to the west of the trees at a small hill, and he wondered what he might see if he climbed up to the top. Perhaps he would see something that would give him another idea. He walked toward the hill. Reaching the base of the hill, he sat down to rest, breathing heavily. His leg was hurting. He caught his breath as quickly as he could, stood up and started up the hill. At the top, he stopped suddenly, surprised.

Three men were there almost upon him. They stopped too, as startled as was he. "We're Delawares," one said. Sequoyah understood enough of their language to know what the man had said.

"I'm a Cherokee."

"Ah," said one Delaware. "I know your language."

"Camp with us tonight," said another.

Sequoyah was grateful for the offer. He had not eaten a good meal for some time. At the Delaware camp, he was well fed. He slept the night well, glad to have some company. In the morning, the Delawares offered to take him to their village.

"I can't go with you," Sequoyah said. "I have two young men I sent to Mexico. They'll be coming back looking for me. Instead, you can go with me to look for them."

The Delaware looked at the ground and shook his head. "No," he said. "We can't do that. We've had good hunting though. We'll give you some meat, and we'll give you a horse to ride."

Ujiya dropped down on one knee and studied some moccasin tracks on the ground.

"Wild Indians are around," he said. "Not far. Comanches, maybe Tawakonis. We'll have to be careful."

Teesee gave him a look, and each man knew what the other was thinking. Sequoyah was alone, old, crippled, sick perhaps— and unarmed. He would not be able to defend himself against an attack.

"We're moving too slowly," Teesee said. "Let me and two others hurry ahead to the cave where we left my father. They rest of you can follow and meet us there. We'll take along enough food to make him a good meal."

Ujiya agreed, so Teesee and two of the Cherokees from Mexico ran on ahead. The rest continued at their slower pace.

When Teesee and the other two at last arrived at the cave, Teesee could see that the river had risen. Anxious, he dropped over the edge of the embankment down to the ledge at the mouth of the cave. He could see at once that the cave had recently been flooded. There was no sign of Sequoyah or of his provisions. Teesee felt a panic set in. He climbed back up to the top, using the same log that Sequoyah had used.

"There's no sign of him," he told the others. "The cave was flooded. Everything is gone."

Teesee sat down on the ground and put his head in his hands. "I knew we were gone too long," he almost wailed.

"Maybe he got out in time," said one of the others. "Maybe he's all right. You said there's no sign. So it could mean anything."

But Teesee would not be comforted. He sat alone and dejected until Ujiya and the rest finally arrived. One of the Cherokees with Teesee told Ujiya what had happened there.

"Let's look around some," Ujiya said.

"What's the use?" moaned Teesee.

"What's that?" one asked, pointing to a fallen log.

Ujiya walked over to look and saw the sheet of paper attached to the log. He took it loose, unrolled it and recognized the Cherokee writing of Sequoyah.

"Teesee," he called out. "Come here. Quickly."

Jumping up, Teesee ran to stand beside Ujiya. Together they read the writing.

"My friends," it said, "after you left the river rose into the cave. I was driven out and lost almost everything. I decided that I had better move along on my journey. If you're not gone too long, you should be able to find me. As I go along, I'll burn some grass behind me. You may see some smoke or you can follow the burned grass." And it was signed, "Sequoyah," with his characteristic redundant symbol for the hissing sound in front of the symbol for the first syllable of his name.

"He's all right," Teesee exclaimed.

"At least," said Ujiya, "he was all right when he wrote this note and left it for us. He has no food, and he has no rifle."

"We should be able to catch up with him easily," Teesee said.

"Let's get going then."

They found Sequoyah's trail without much difficulty and followed it as quickly as they could. They came across the places where he had stopped to rest, and they located the spots where he had camped for the night. At last, they came to a campsite where they found animal bones and the prints of a horse. They were sure that the footprints, and the mark of a walking stick, were those of Sequoyah.

"He has food and a horse," said Teesee. "He is all right."

"Where could he have gotten those things?" one of the others asked.

"He must have come across someone along the way," Ujiya said. "Someone friendly who gave him meat and the horse."

"Who could it have been?"

"Certainly not Texans," said Teesee.

"Let's hurry on."

They raced ahead to the next camping ground, and there they found again the prints of the horse, Sequoyah's footprints and animal bones. They hurried ahead, but the borrowed horse was beginning to tire and it was getting late in the day. Ujiya thought it had been so much trouble to get the horse, he did not want to take a chance on losing it by wearing it out. They would have to slow down. They would have to stop and rest.

"Two of you go on," he said. "The rest of us will make a camp here."

"I'll go," said Teesee.

"And I," said Standing Rock.

Standing Rock and Teesee ran ahead, leaving the others behind to settle into the camp. They slowed down only to read the signs along the way, to examine footprints and camp sites. They ran past the blackened spots of burned grass. They ran until the sun went down. At last they stopped.

"What should we do now?" Teesee asked.

"Let's keep going as long as we can," said Standing Rock. "If he stopped to camp somewhere around here, we might see his fire in the darkness."

They ran a while longer, until they came to the edge of a river. There they stopped. "We can't cross this in the dark," Teesee said. "We'll have to go back now."

"Wait," said Standing Rock.

"What is it?"

"Be quiet."

They stood still side by side in silence for what seemed like a long moment, and then Teesee heard what had caught the attention of Standing Rock. It was unmistakably the sound of a horse neighing from somewhere not too far away in the darkness.

23

I t's either someone out there with a horse, or a horse all by itself," Teesee said. "Let's go find out."

"I think it came from that direction," Standing Rock said. "Come on."

They moved cautiously up to the top of a slight rise. As they moved closer to the top of the knoll, they dropped down on all fours and crept along. It could be Comanches or Tawakonis over there, even worse, white Texans. From their position on top, they saw a small campfire gleaming on the other side of the hill. Teesee put a cautioning hand on the other's shoulder.

"I see one man," said Standing Rock. "One horse."

"It's my father," Teesee said in a harsh, excited whisper.

"Maybe. Let's get closer and be sure before we give ourselves away."

They eased themselves toward the bottom of the hill, still on all fours, and about halfway down, Teesee sprang to his feet and ran toward the fire.

"Father," he called out.

The lone figure at the campfire stood up unsteadily with the use of a stick and looked out toward the hill.

"Teesee? Is that you?"

Standing Rock stood up then and hurried along to catch up with Teesee. In another moment, the three Cherokees were standing close together near the fire, father and son embracing.

"I didn't know if I would ever see you again," Teesee said.

"I knew you'd come back," Sequoyah said, "but I was getting hungry there for a while. I'm all right now, though." They laughed together, and then Sequoyah said, "Who is this that you have with you?"

"This is Standing Rock," said Teesee. "He's from the Cherokee village in Mexico."

"Ah," said Sequoyah, his eyes brightening in the gleam of the campfire, "then you found them."

"Yes," said Teesee. "Of course."

"I've been wanting to meet you and the others for a long time," Sequoyah said, taking Standing Rock by the hand.

"And I'm honored to meet you," Standing Rock said. "Word of your great accomplishments has reached even us in Mexico."

"So where is Ujiya?"

"He's on our back trail," said Teesee, "with some more of Standing Rock's people. We'll meet up with them tomorrow morning, I expect."

"Oh, that's good. Well, now, I have some fresh meat. Let's sit down together and eat. And I have coffee."

As they sat, Teesee asked, "But how did you get fresh meat? And a horse?"

"And coffee," said Sequoyah. "I met some friendly Delawares along the way. They gave me these things."

"We have one horse," said Teesee. "And we had a tough time getting that."

"How many men are with Ujiya?"

"Uh, six more. One of them is the son of Chief Bowles."

"Ten men and two horses," Sequoyah said. "Well, we'll make out just fine. So, tell me about your travels. What took you so long?"

"It's farther than we thought," Teesee said, "and we had to stop along the way in a Mexican town. We also had several rivers to cross. We had to build a raft. And, of course, we were walking."

"Yes, of course."

"But tell me about you. We saw that your cave was flooded. So what did you do then?"

"I had to climb out of there," Sequoyah said, "as I'm sure you guessed. I had lost almost everything, even my stick. I had to make a new walking stick. Then I started walking." He went on to detail for his son and Standing Rock all of his own adventures since the waters rose to the cave. It was very late that night before they slept.

The next morning, Ujiya and the others arrived at Sequoyah's camp. Everyone was happy. The long ordeal seemed to have at last come to an end, for Sequoyah as well as for the others. They ate and drank coffee and visited for most of the morning. At last, they relaxed and smoked their pipes.

"This is a good spot," Sequoyah said. "I think we should stay here for a few days and get ourselves well provisioned before we start out again. I think you can find deer and turkey and even some good honey."

They all agreed, and so they rested and hunted for five days, before heading back for Mexico. Sequoyah rode one of the horses all the way. The others walked, the second horse being used as a pack animal. Sequoyah felt tremendous relief to be riding again. He was tired, and his leg had been bothering him considerably. The trip took several days, but they made it to the Mexican Cherokee village without incident. The Cherokees there welcomed them joyously. They were all delighted to meet Sequoyah, and Sequoyah was just as anxious to get acquainted with them and to teach them to write with his syllabary. That way, they could become connected once again with their friends and relatives in the Cherokee Nation, at least by correspondence. Teesee met and became enamored of Standing Bowles's sister, Rebecca. When Ujiya asked how long they would stay, Sequoyah was evasive. It occurred to Ujiya that the old man suddenly seemed very content in the Cherokee village in Mexico, and Teesee was certainly not anxious to leave.

The Cherokee Nation, *1845*

As Jesse Chisholm trotted his horse through the main gate of the John Ross home at Park Hill, the armed guards who were gathered there scattered to both sides to get out of his way. They knew Chisholm, and they were not about to question his business with the chief. Chisholm rode down the long drive to the front porch, where he was met by a Black slave dressed in fine livery who took the reins of his horse.

"Mr. Chisholm?" the slave asked.

"That's right."

"Mr. Ross is expecting you, sir. Please come with me."

The slave tied the reins to a hitching post and led the way up the steps to the large front porch and over to the door. Opening it, he stepped aside. Chisholm, taking the hat off his head, walked into the house and looked around at the opulence. John Ross had done quite well for himself following the Trail of Tears. The slave closed the door, stepped around Chisholm and headed for another room.

"Mr. Ross will be right with you, sir," he said. "Please make yourself at home."

Chisholm paced the floor. A moment later, Ross appeared with a broad smile on his face and his right hand extended. Chisholm took the hand.

"Jesse, my friend," said Ross, "thank you for coming."

"You knew I would," Chisholm said.

"Of course. Please, let me offer you some refreshment."

"Coffee would be fine," said Chisholm.

Ross issued orders and the slave vanished into the back of the house. Moments later a female slave brought coffee into the room on a silver serving tray. Chisholm mixed some cream and sugar into the coffee in his cup. Ross waited for the slave to finish serving and leave the room before he spoke again.

"Jesse," he said, "I have a serious problem, and you're the only man I can trust with it."

"I'll do anything I can," said Chisholm.

"You know," the chief said, "we've started publishing our newspaper again. In Cherokee as well as in English, as before. The reappearance of the Cherokee language in print has put the inventor of the system much in the minds of the people again. 'Where is George Guess?' they're asking. 'What has become of Sequoyah?' And we have no answer for them. Jesse, Sequoyah is one of our greatest citizens. He is certainly our best known. We cannot appear to be unconcerned. All we can find out is that he left his home a few years ago on some kind of visit. He told no one where he was going. Some young men have been found who traveled with him for a distance, but they say he sent them home and went on with only his son and another man, called the Worm. Find him, Jesse. Find him, alive or dead, as soon as possible. And bring back word to us here. If you find him alive, bring him home. Tell him he's needed."

"I'll do my best, sir," said Chisholm.

"The sooner the better, Jesse."

"I'll get started right away."

As Chisholm mounted his horse to leave Ross's mansion, he thought about the map he had drawn for Sequoyah, and he recalled how Sequoyah had sworn him to secrecy. He told everyone else only that he was going on a trip. Other than the ones who went along on the trip, Jesse Chisholm was the only person who knew where Sequoyah had gone. It was interesting, he thought, that he was also the first person the principal chief of the Cherokee Nation called on to search for the lost Sequoyah. Chief Ross had no idea how right he had been to call on Jesse Chisholm.

Chisholm rounded up some good and trusted friends, both Cherokees and Delawares, outfitted them for a long frontier journey, and headed for Mexico. He had a pretty good idea where to look for the Mexican village, and he was fairly certain that if Sequoyah was still alive, that was where to find him.

Chisholm and his companions were all seasoned frontiersmen, and they knew the country over which they would travel. They knew that the trip would be a long one, that the country was often wild and rugged and so were many of the men they would encounter, white and Indian alike. The major advantage they had on their side was that Jesse Chisholm was well acquainted with all of the Indian tribes in the area. They were more worried about the Texans than the Indian tribes, but Chisholm, knowing that his old friend Sam Houston was back in power in Texas, was not too concerned with even that.

They were well provisioned, and they took their time, yet they did not waste any time. They met few people along the way, and when they did meet someone, they stopped to converse only briefly. The trip was not one to tell tales about. Even so, after they had been on the trail for two months, word reached Tahlequah that they had encountered some Comanches along the way, and they had all been killed. The word was false. The party, ignorant of the rumor, was still moving steadily toward Mexico.

If Sequoyah's party had encountered trouble along their way to Mexico, the Chisholm party had none. They were dusty and a little trail weary, but that was all. They arrived at the Cherokee village in Mexico in early September and were made welcome by Standing Rock, the acknowledged chief of the town.

"This is the second time recently we've had visitors from the Cherokee Nation," Standing Rock said. "We're very glad to see you. Anything we have is yours."

"Thank you," said Chisholm. "We've come for a specific reason. We've been sent here by the principal chief to find Sequoyah. Is he here with you?"

"He was here with us," said Standing Rock. "I regret to tell you that the old man has died."

"I was afraid of that," Chisholm said. He took off his hat and bowed his head. Sequoyah was an old and dear friend, and even though Chisholm had expected the worst, he was saddened to actually hear the report.

"Would you like to talk with his son and the other one who came with him?" Standing Rock asked.

"Yes. Thank you. I would."

Standing Rock called out to someone to bring Teesee and Ujiya around to meet Jesse Chisholm, and soon they were there. They wore long faces as they shook hands. "It's good to see you," Ujiya said to Chisholm.

"Standing Rock told me about Sequoyah," Chisholm said. "I'm sorry to hear it."

"You came all this way looking for him?" asked Teesee.

"We were sent by John Ross," Chisholm said. "Your father is a very important man in the Cherokee Nation. People were wondering and worrying about him. Can you show me his grave?"

Something about the way in which Teesee and Ujiya looked at one another, almost furtively, bothered Chisholm, but he did not mention it.

"Yes. Of course," said Teesee. "Just let me go and get something.

I'll be right back." He glanced at Ujiya and said, "Wait here."

As Teesee walked away, Chisholm turned to Ujiya. "Is the grave far from here?" he asked.

"Not far," Ujiya said. "Teesee will be back soon."

Chisholm could not help but feel that something was wrong. Something about the way the young men had looked at each other, something about the way Ujiya did not look at him at all. Even though he had not seen these two young men for quite some time, they were both friends of his. Ujiya, especially, had spent considerable time with Chisholm on the trail, visiting with plains Indian tribes and learning their languages. They had grown close. Something was amiss. He could tell.

"I understand you had some trouble on your way down here," he said, carefully avoiding the issue.

"Oh, yes. We did have some trouble. We had to run from the Texans in San Antonio. Tawakonis stole our horses in Texas, and we had to leave Sequoyah alone for a long time, more than twenty days. Much of the time, he was not well, and he ran out of food before we could get back to him."

"He was not well enough to undertake such a trip in the first place," Chisholm said. "Especially not at his age."

He stopped talking when he saw Teesee returning. Teesee walked up close and said in solemn tones, "Follow me." Chisholm fell in step behind him, and Ujiya joined them. They walked past several small huts, and when they came to another, a one-room adobe with a low, thatched roof, Teesee opened the door and stepped aside. He looked at Chisholm. Chisholm gave him a curious look back.

"Is the grave in a house then?" he asked.

"Go on inside," said Teesee.

Chisholm ducked his head to walk through the low doorway. It was dark inside the hut except for a burning tallow, and in the quivering firelight, Jesse Chisholm was astonished to see the smiling face of Sequoyah.

"Welcome to Mexico, my friend," Sequoyah said. "Do you think you're seeing a ghost?"

"What is this, Sequoyah?" Chisholm asked. "I don't believe in ghosts, but they told me you were dead."

"Only because I told them to say that. You have some others with you here. Some of them I don't even know. I don't want anyone outside of this village to know that I'm still alive. I mean to stay here with these people in Mexico for the rest of my days. If you go back home and tell them there that I'm alive, more of them will come looking for me. I don't want to be bothered with any of that anymore."

"Then why didn't you just let me go on believing that you were dead?"

"You're my friend, Jesse. We've always told the truth to one another."

"You want me to return to the Cherokee Nation and say that you are dead and buried in Mexico? Is that right?"

"That's what I want, and my friend, and it's the last secret I'll ask you to keep for me. It's almost true anyway. You'll never see me alive again."

"Sequoyah, you're a very important man in the Cherokee Nation. I don't know if you fully realize your own importance."

"Major Ridge, his son and Elias Boudinot were important men, were they not?" Sequoyah asked.

"Yes," said Chisholm, "well, but it was the chief himself who sent me on this trip to look for you. Or for your grave."

"Then tell him that you found my grave."

Jesse Chisholm heaved a long and heavy sigh. "If that's what you want, of course that's what I'll say, but what about all your friends? What about Sally?"

"You ask about my friends. What about my enemies? It was you yourself who warned me about them. As for Sally, well, she's young enough yet. She can find another husband, if she wants one. I learned at a very early age that Cherokee husbands and fathers are not all that important. She'll be all right. She might even be better off without me."

"All right," Chisholm said.

"There are no white people here either," Sequoyah said. "Oh yes. If they ask you how to find my grave, just make up something. It won't matter, as long as they don't find me. Now, before you go, let's smoke a pipe together."

———

On their way back home, Chisholm's party met up with another party of Cherokees on their way to Mexico. The leader of this group was called Unole. He and the others with him were both pleased and surprised to see Jesse Chisholm alive and well.

"We were told that you had been killed by Comanches," Unole said. "They even put the story in our newspaper. I'm glad to see that it's not true. But when we heard that false report, the chief and the council sent us in search of Sequoyah."

"But not in search of me," said Chisholm.

"Oh, well—"

"That's all right, Unole. Let's camp together for the night. In the morning, you can start the ride back home with us."

"But we're supposed to—"

"Find Sequoyah?" said Chisholm. "We found him. He's dead and buried in Mexico. We saw Ujiya and Sequoyah's son who made the trip with him, and we talked with Standing Rock and Standing Bowles who live in the Cherokee village in Mexico. They were with him when he died, and they saw him buried. We have letters signed by all of those I just mentioned, and we saw the grave."

"Well then," Unole said, "there is no further reason to pursue our mission. We can turn around and go home. We'll do as you say and camp with you and ride back with you. I'm glad that we found you."

"Well," Chisholm said, "I can't tell you how pleased I am that the report you had of my demise was false."

He felt just a little guilty then, thinking of the false report he had just given concerning the demise of Sequoyah.

Jesse Chisholm thought about Sequoyah as he settled in the camp for the night. The old man had a great many people worrying about him and chasing after him. Who would ever have believed it back in the old days? Chisholm had known Sequoyah all his life, and he had always liked him, but there had been times, he recalled, when, like others, he had thought him the most worthless Cherokee he had ever known: lazy and shiftless, crazy even. He had never believed the stories of witchcraft, though. Just that Sequoyah would never amount to anything. He, like others, had pitied poor Sally. Poor Sally. But Chisholm knew that the Cherokee Nation's council had voted a pension for Sequoyah for the rest of his life, and in the event of his death, the pension would be paid to Sally. She would be all right.

And now Sequoyah had become the most famous of Cherokees. Even white people back east knew his name and heralded his accomplishments. He had been written about in eastern newspapers, and white scholars had presented lectures on his "genius." And there had been times when Sequoyah had relished all that attention, but those times had been short-lived. The public acclaim had been fun for a while, probably because of the way in which he had been ridiculed and shunned before. But at last, he had discovered that he much preferred the simple life of a private citizen, and Chisholm thought that he understood Sequoyah's seemingly peculiar decision to stay in Mexico and be reported dead. Well, Jesse Chisholm had made him a promise, and he would keep that promise. Sequoyah's last secret would go to the grave with Jesse Chisholm.

In his hut in the village in Mexico, Sequoyah contemplated his situation. At first, he had thought to visit the Cherokees in Mexico for a time, perhaps teaching them to read and write, and then return home. But there was something about the place that made him change his mind. Or maybe it was something about being away from home. Maybe both. Smiling to himself in the darkness of his room, he lay back contented. He would no longer have to worry about being caught up in the squabbles of political factions at home. He would not have to wonder if some disgruntled Cherokee would slip up behind him and stab him in the back because of something he had said or some piece of paper he had signed his name to. It was peaceful in this small village of Cherokees far away from home. His life had been long, and it had been eventful, but all that was behind him. He had experienced one last grand adventure and survived it. Now it was time for a well deserved rest.

He smiled, thinking about his final fling. It had been a good one, he thought. And now he would not be subjected to any more nagging by his wife, nor the carping of the Christian missionaries.

He would no longer be paraded around for the benefit of special political purposes, and he would most likely not see another white person for the rest of his life. There would be no more interviews with the same insipid questions coming at him: How did you, an illiterate savage, come up with such a grand scheme? Do you mean to say that you speak no English? Do not even understand it? How could you even begin to understand the concept of reading and writing? What are your politics? Your religion? Have you more than one wife, as I understand is the savage custom? Well, no more of that.

Yes, the village in Mexico was a refuge. And there were plenty of beautiful, young Cherokee girls in this village. He was too old to do anything about it, of course, but it was pleasant to have them around. Yes, indeed, he was quite content with his choice. He even felt a bit smug about it. For once, he had put something over on them all. He lifted a bottle of tequila up from the floor beside the bed and took a long and satisfying drink. Now, if they ever want to see me again, he said to himself, let them look for my grave.

Author's Note

When I first embarked on this incredible journey with Sequoyah, I discovered that no two historians or biographers agree on much of anything about his life. He was born in 1760 or 1780, or any number of years in between. His name means "Pig Place," "Pig's Foot," "The Lame One," or nothing at all and is not even a Cherokee word. His father was Nathaniel Gist, an Englishman, or George Gist, a German, or an unnamed full-blood Cherokee. Or his grandfather was a white man. He was lame from birth, or crippled in a hunting accident at an early age or wounded in the Battle of Horseshoe Bend. He had one wife or five, two children or twenty. He left for Mexico either in 1840 or 1842. His grave has been "positively" identified in at least three different sites in Mexico and one in southern Oklahoma, and there are persistent rumors that he is buried somewhere near Tahlequah. Sequoyah is at once the best known and the least known Cherokee.

Even the very thing on which his fame rests, the invention of the syllabary, is controversial. Most historians and biographers agree that Sequoyah, in choosing symbols for the Cherokee sounds, copied many out of a newspaper or a book that had come into his hands, but a document in his own handwriting in the Gilcrease Museum in Tulsa, Oklahoma, disproves that. It shows the old syllabary and the new one. The "copied" symbols are in the new syllabary only, and the old symbols bear no resemblance to the new.

Several writers have expressed the belief that Cherokees could read and write in the Cherokee language long before Sequoyah. In his controversial book, *Tell Them They Lie: The Sequoyah Myth*

(Westernlore, 1971), Traveller Bird maintains that the United States government knew of the Cherokee writing and undertook a major conspiracy to suppress it and any knowledge that it had ever existed. Unfortunately, Bird presented his case in a way that is very difficult to accept. The hero of William O. Turner's novel, *Thief Hunt* (Doubleday, 1973) is in search of a deerskin robe which was stolen from the Cherokee Nation and proves that the syllabary predated Sequoyah. My own novels of the Real People, particularly *The Way of the Priests, The Dark Way* and *The White Path*, (Doubleday, 1992, 1993 and 1993), involve Cherokee priests who are scribes around the year 1500. Of course, all of these can be easily discounted as fiction. They prove only that there are writers, some of them Cherokee, who believe that Cherokees were writing their language long before Sequoyah came around. More unsettling, perhaps, to traditionalists and those who are comfortable with pat answers, is a story quoted in Russell Thornton's *The Cherokees: A Population History*, (University of Nebraska Press, 1990), recorded originally in 1717 by North Carolina trader Alexander Long, wherein an unidentified Cherokee man is telling a migration story and says, "in those days, our priests could read and write."

In puzzling over these and many other questions involved in the story of Sequoyah, I read everything I could find that even mentioned his name. Probably the best single source is Stan Hoig's recent and very thorough biography, *Sequoyah: The Cherokee Genius* (Oklahoma Historical Society, 1995). Grant Foreman's *Sequoyah* (University of Oklahoma Press, 1938) is standard and still useful. Other more or less useful accounts of the life of Sequoyah include *Sequoyah's Gift: A Portrait of the Cherokee Leader* by Janet Klausner (HarperCollins, 1993), "The Life and Work of Sequoyah" by John B. Davis (*The Chronicles of Oklahoma*, June 1930), *Sequoyah of Earth and Intellect* by Jack F. Kilpatrick (Encino Press, 1965), and the "young adult" books, *Sequoyah: Young Cherokee Guide* by Dorothea J. Snow (Bobbs Merrill, 1960), *Captured Words* by Frances Williams Browin (Aladdin Books, 1954) and *Sequoyah: Leader of the Cherokees* by Alice Marriott (Random House, 1956). *Sequoyah: Prophet Without Honor* by Peggy Jo Hall is an interesting, unpublished but produced play. Finally, nearly all of the standard Cherokee histories include at least some discussion of Sequoyah and his work.

In addition to academic research, I spent much valuable time talking about Sequoyah with knowledgeable friends, Cherokee and others, including Tom Belt, David Scott, Ed Jumper, Murv Jacob, Pat Moss, Peggy Hall, Talmadge Davis, Perry Blankenship, Hastings Shade (the current deputy principal chief of the Cherokee Nation and a descendant of Sequoyah), my wife Evelyn (Snell) Conley, and others. I am also grateful to Delores Sumner and the very helpful staff of the Special Collections Room, John Vaughn Library, Northeastern State University in Tahlequah.

While all of these fine people have helped me tremendously, none of them are in any way to blame for anything in my novel that any reader might find offensive, foolish, insulting, erroneous or misleading. I share the blame for that sort of thing with no one.

Robert J. Conley
Tahlequah

DATE DUE

#47-0108 Peel Off Pressure Sensitive